Windsor a

9580000

D1577183

BEFORE
— THE —
DAWN

BEFORE
— THE —
DAWN

EMMA PASS

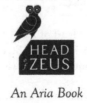

An Aria Book

First published in the UK in 2022 by Head of Zeus Ltd,
part of Bloomsbury Publishing Plc

9 7 5 3 1 2 4 6 8

A CIP catalogue record for this book is available from the
British Library.

ISBN (HB): 9781803282930
ISBN (E): 9781801105521

Typeset by Siliconchips Services Ltd UK

Printed and bound in Great Britain by
CPI Group (UK) Ltd, Croydon CR0 4YY

Head of Zeus
5–8 Hardwick Street
London EC1R 4RG

WWW.HEADOFZEUS.COM

For Graham

"Hope" is the thing with feathers –
That perches in the soul –
And sings the tune without the words –
And never stops – at all –

—EMILY DICKINSON
"Hope" is the thing with feathers
c. 1862

PROLOGUE

RUBY

Bartonford, Devon, 1939

It was a sunny morning at the beginning of September when Alfie Blythe came tearing through the dunes to tell me war had finally been declared.

The sky was brushed with feathers of cloud, the sea silver-calm, the breeze fluttering my hair around my face as I meandered up the path from Bartonford beach with Toffee, Mrs-Baxter-down-the-lane's fox terrier, zigzagging in front of me and cocking his leg on clumps of marram grass. I was daydreaming about starting my new job as office girl at the *Bartonford Herald* tomorrow, and making a mental checklist of chores I needed to do when I got back to the little cottage Father and I shared in the grounds of Barton Hall hospital: prepare lunch, polish my shoes, press my skirt and blouse.

I'd heard all the talk of war, of course. Father, one of the head psychiatric doctors at the hospital, was forever making worried predictions from behind his newspaper at breakfast, and every evening we turned on the wireless to listen to news reports about the imminent horror in Europe. I'd overheard conversations in the butcher's and the greengrocer's about the possibilities of food rationing, gas attacks and bombs. And there was the blackout, which had begun a few days ago. But I was only fourteen; to me, war seemed like something out of a Hollywood film, not something that could happen in the sleepy little Devon town of Bartonford. It certainly wasn't something that could happen to *me*.

'Ruby!'

I turned and saw Alfie running towards me, cheeks pink and chest heaving, his little sister Annie close behind. The Blythes lived next door to Mrs Baxter, just down the road from the hospital; Alfie's mother was cook and housekeeper at Barton Hall, and came in twice a week to clean for Father. Alfie and I had been friends ever since we started school.

'Have you heard?' he wheezed when he and Annie reached me. 'We're going to war! Chamberlain has just announced it on the wireless!'

I stared at him. 'Gosh.' It came out sounding rather flat, not because I didn't care but because I was thinking, *I must get home. I must see if Father's all right.* Even Alfie's breathing – small and slight for his age, he suffered from asthma – didn't worry me like it usually would.

'Ma says there's gunna be no jam in the shops. And marg on our bread 'nstead of butter!' Annie piped up.

'Oh, shush, Annie.' Alfie had recovered a bit now, although his breath still whistled in his throat. 'Pa says it'll all be over in six months. But I saw you coming up here earlier and I thought you'd want to know.'

'Th – thank you.' I bent to clip Toffee's lead to his collar. 'I must go. Goodbye, Alfie.'

I ran all the way home.

'Oh, isn't it terrible?' Mrs-Baxter-down-the-lane said when I called in to return Toffee. 'I can't believe this country is going to war again, and so soon after the last one! If Edward was here…'

Edward Baxter had served in the Devonshire Regiment with Father. One night, in a trench at Ypres, their unit had been waiting to go over the top when they were gassed. Father had been one of the lucky ones; Mrs Baxter never saw Edward again. She wrung her hands, knotting her swollen, arthritic fingers together. 'Our poor boys. You mark my words, Ruby, it will be a terrible time for us all.'

When I entered the cottage the house was silent, not the quiet of an empty house but the hush of a storm about to break. Father was sitting in the parlour, the wireless still hissing. He turned to me, white-faced, the scar on his cheek livid as a brand.

'Father, is it true?' I said. 'Are we at war?'

He nodded. 'Oh dear,' he said. 'Oh dear, oh dear.'

A spasm of coughing shuddered up from deep inside him and he fumbled his handkerchief from his pocket, pressing it to his mouth. I hurried to the kitchen for a glass of water and his tablets. The gas attack that killed Edward Baxter had not only left the marks on Father's face and hands but also caused permanent damage to his lungs, which flared up whenever he was ill or distressed.

I gave him the water and tablets and sat down in the other armchair, waiting for his coughing fit to pass. The parlour was gloomy – the cottage was overshadowed by the high wall that separated the hospital grounds from the road outside – and the air smelled faintly of last night's cabbage, and furniture polish. Like the rest of the cottage, it was neat but shabby. It had Anaglypta wallpaper painted a curious shade of green, an ancient sofa and chairs, a bookcase and a threadbare rug, all of which belonged to the hospital. The only piece of furniture that was our own was the piano, which no one ever played; on the top stood my mother's photograph, in a silver-gilt frame. Looking round at it all I was assaulted by a sudden pang of longing to be back on the beach, surrounded by the sea and the sky and the bright calls of the gulls; to be back in that moment before Alfie came running up to me and war was still something people were just talking about in the grocer's, the butcher's and the post office.

Father ignored the tablets, sipping the water until his coughing subsided. He had a glassy, faraway look on his face, the one he got when he shouted himself awake at night and I had to run to his room and grab his flailing arms to stop him sending the jug on the washstand smashing to the floor, or when he trembled at the sound of Alfie's father's motorcycle backfiring out in the road. I knew he was back in that muddy trench in Belgium in 1915, cowering with the rest of his regiment as the shells screamed overhead.

'We'll be all right, Father,' I said, in the cheerful tone I always used when he was like this. 'I doubt old Hitler'll bother with a place like Bartonford.'

He frowned at Mother's photograph, working his hands together. Gradually, his gaze cleared. He looked so forlorn that I got up, went over to his chair and crouched down beside him, patting his hand as if he were the child and I the adult.

'I couldn't bear it if anything happened to you, Ruby,' he said. 'You're all I've got.'

'I know, Father. And I'm not going anywhere. We'll be safe enough here, you'll see.'

He gave me a smile, although his eyes were still full of worry. 'You're a good girl. I don't know how I'd manage without you, I really don't.'

'Let's have a cup of tea,' I said, still in that bright voice. 'We'll both feel better then.'

He nodded slowly. I stood and went through to the kitchen to put the water on to boil.

Many years have passed since then, but that day still stands out as clearly in my mind as if it was yesterday. Remembering it, I can't help wondering why the moments that change your life – the ones that really, truly change it forever – can feel so insignificant at the time. When Alfie came to find me, I felt certain it would be the declaration of war that would tip my world on its head. Now I realise it wasn't until that German plane fell from the sky, four years later, that the wheels were set in motion for everything else that followed. It makes me wonder: if we could see our fate bearing down on us like a juggernaut, would we do things differently? Would we try to step out of its way?

Would I have loved you, even though it made me reconsider almost everything about what I thought mattered to me, and what family really meant?

Yes. Of course I would. There's nothing I'd have done differently – nothing at all.

Because to not know you? To not love you?

To not have Ellen, who, for so long, was the only person who could bring a smile back to your face?

That would have been far worse.

PART ONE

1943

I

RUBY

July

Hidden amongst the dunes above Bartonford beach, I threw my head back and yelled. The wind snatched my voice away and Toffee looked at me with his head tilted sideways, one ear pricked. I bent and rubbed the top of his head. In front of me, through a gap in the dunes, I could see all the way past the beach defences to the sea where steely waves tumbled fiercely over one another, capped with brownish foam. A summer storm had blown in last night and the wind was still charging across the bay like an express train.

It was just past seven o'clock in the morning, and I was the only person here. Just as well, really – if anyone heard me screaming like this, they'd think I'd gone quite dotty. But mornings like these, when I had the bay to myself, were the only time I truly felt like *me*. At eighteen, my life was one of strict routine: unless I'd been on duty the night before I rose at half past six, washed and dressed, and walked Toffee for Mrs-Baxter-down-the-lane who was so hampered now by her rheumatism that she couldn't manage it anymore. Then I returned home, fetched Father's paper from the main house and laid the table for breakfast.

After we'd eaten, Father walked over to the psychiatric unit and I made my sandwiches and did the dishes, unless it was Mrs Blythe's day to come in. Then I cycled to the *Herald* offices. After work I came straight home. Usually the rest of the *Herald* staff went for a drink at the Bartonford Arms Hotel; Vera was always pestering me to come too, but I already spent several evenings a week out on duty, and the thought of leaving Father with only the wireless for company every night of the week made me feel unbearably guilty. Anyway, he often needed me to help him type up his notes.

When I was on shift, though, I'd change into my Air Raid Precautions uniform – a smart blue serge tunic – straight after supper and cycle back into town to the sector post, my helmet with its white 'W' painted on the front looped over the handlebars and my gas mask in the basket, unable to help the spark of rebellious joy deep down inside me at the break from routine it afforded, however small. I would have loved to have done something practical – work in a factory or as a land girl – but because leaving Father was out of the question I'd become a warden instead, signing up to the Women's Voluntary Service the day after my sixteenth birthday.

Toffee pulled stubbornly on his lead, desperate for a good run. 'Sorry, boy,' I told him. 'I can't let you off. Not here. I'd never forgive myself if you got tangled up in all that wire.' I shivered as the wind cut through my thin coat with its too-short sleeves; I didn't have enough coupons for a new one yet. I was about to turn for home when something caught my eye: a group of three men at the other end of the beach, one digging around the bottom of one of the posts, the others looping a heavy length of chain around it. The end of the chain was attached to a bulldozer. Panic spiked through me. Had the Germans invaded at last?

I crouched behind a hummock of marram grass, trying to see through the stalks as they tossed in the wind and wondering if I was brave enough to challenge the men. I imagined the headline in the *Herald*: *PLUCKY REPORTER DEFEATS ENEMY INVASION!* The more sensible part of me reminded me that I could hardly be called a *reporter*, and that if they *were* Germans, they'd have guns. But I wanted to get my facts straight before I fetched the constable. *Check, double-check and check again for luck* – that's what Vera always said.

Then I looked again and let out a relieved laugh. The men were wearing Home Guard uniforms; I *knew* them. Barnaby Sykes, who was blind in one eye – another casualty of the last war – was doing the digging and helping him were old Tom Bidley and Alfie Blythe. I stood, brushing sand off my skirt and coat, picked Toffee up and made my way down there, squeezing past the enormous cubes of concrete placed to prevent enemy tanks from being able to drive up into the dunes, and stepping carefully through the rolls of barbed wire. Several posts had already been taken out and lay scattered across the sand like tree trunks uprooted by a playful giant.

'Hullo, Alfie,' I said as I reached them. Alfie jumped. He was trying to tighten the chain while Barnaby carried on digging around the base of the post with a shovel, Tom watching with one hand resting on the bulldozer.

Toffee was wriggling; I put him down and he strained forwards on his lead, wagging his tail. Alfie ignored him. 'Ruby! What are you doing here?' he said.

I raised my eyebrows. 'I might ask you the same thing. I thought you were Jerry, digging up the defences so you could invade the town!'

Alfie, Barnaby and Tom looked at one another, and Alfie pressed his lips together primly. 'I can't tell you anything, I'm afraid.'

'Might as well,' Tom interjected in his thick Devon burr. 'Whole town's gon' know soon 'nough.'

Alfie and Barnaby exchanged another glance. Then Alfie said: 'It's for the Americans.'

'The Americans?' I asked.

'The American troops. They're coming here. They're going to be training on the beach. We have to clear it for them.'

'Buildin' some girt big huts up on them dunes, they will be, too, and a dance 'all too if the lil' bird that told me about it is right.' Tom grinned at me from underneath his bushy white moustache, showing the gaps in his teeth. 'That'll liven things up for you and that friend o'yours at the newspaper, eh, missy?'

My heart skipped a beat at the thought of whirling around to the sounds of an upbeat dance band in the arms of a handsome American soldier or airman.

Alfie saw my smile and sniffed. 'I do hope everyone's not going to go completely silly about them.'

I sighed inwardly. Alfie had shot up suddenly last year, his arms and legs filling out with sinewy muscle. Because of his asthma he couldn't sign up, or go to his father's engineering works, so he'd taken a job at the post office, delivering letters, which meant he called in at the *Herald* nearly every day. I caught him looking at me like this sometimes, as if he was sizing me up for something and finding me lacking, and I wasn't sure I liked it. I missed the wiry, cheerful boy in baggy shorts I'd gone to school with, and the easy closeness we'd once had, more than I cared to admit. But perhaps it was inevitable – we were both growing up, after all.

'I shouldn't think so,' I said. 'The Americans'll be on the lookout for something far more exotic than a lot of country bumpkins from Bartonford. Anyway, I'll leave you to it. See you later if there's any letters, Alfie.'

'Don't say anything to anyone!' Alfie warned as I walked away.

'Don't worry, I won't!' I called over my shoulder, and smiled, wondering exactly how he proposed to hide the fact that the beach defences were being torn up.

'You're in a good mood,' Father said from behind his newspaper as I poured the tea and made the toast.

I realised I was humming to myself. 'Oh, yes, I suppose I am.'

He smiled. 'I'm glad. I've been worried about you lately, Ruby. You look worn out.'

'I'm OK,' I said. I *was* tired – I didn't seem to have a minute to myself these days – but I didn't want him to start pestering me to give up my ARP post. When I had my uniform on, I felt as if I was doing something useful; something *real*.

I wondered whether to tell him about the Americans, then decided not to; I wanted to break the news to Vera first. As Tom had said, everyone would know soon enough anyway. I wondered what Father would make of the news, or if he'd even care. When Barton Hall was requisitioned by the government as an Emergency Medical Service hospital, a few months after the war began, it looked as if we would have to move too, but

Father was asked to stay on to treat the psychiatric cases. As a result, his workload had doubled. Sometimes I even caught him muttering about his patients during our Saturday night games of Monopoly.

I ate my toast and marg as fast as I could. Annie Blythe had been right about the jam; you couldn't get it anywhere these days, not even the stuff with sawdust pips in. When I'd eaten I made my escape, grabbing my gas mask in its cardboard case – Father insisted I carry it everywhere with me, and became terribly anxious if I forgot – and fetching my bicycle from where it was propped up beside the Anderson. I freewheeled down the hill into town as if Hitler himself was after me, rehearsing what I was going to say to Vera in my head: *You'll never guess what I've found out!*

'Have you heard about the Americans?' she said when I burst into the little office we shared on the first floor of the *Herald* building.

I stared at her. 'How did you know?'

I didn't know why I was surprised; there was a good reason everyone said Vera Spencer was the best reporter in our little corner of Devon. She was twenty-five, and what I wouldn't have given for her glossy dark curls and her figure with its curves in all the right places – she could have made a piece of blackout curtain look stylish. I'd turn nineteen in October, but I was still all elbows and knees, and my hair never stayed neat no matter how many pins I stuck in it. People sometimes told me I looked like my mother, Ellen, but I couldn't see the resemblance. A successful theatre actress, she hadn't just been pretty but beautiful, whilst my features could at best – and if you were feeling especially kind – be described as *agreeable*.

Vera blew a stream of cigarette smoke into the air with that mysterious half-smile of hers, the one that made her look like Lauren Bacall. 'A little bird told me.'

'Well, a little bird told me, too,' I said. 'I saw Barnaby Sykes, Alfie Blythe and old Tom on the beach earlier, pulling up the defences. Tom says they're going to be building huts up in the dunes. And a dance hall!'

'A dance hall?' Vera's face lit up. 'Oh, darling, how simply splendid!'

I sat down at my desk, smiling too. She didn't have the scoop on everything after all!

Vera finished her cigarette and stood, gathering up her notebook and Brownie box camera. 'I've got to pop over to Ilfracombe this morning – Howler wants a story about the evacuees from Bristol and Exeter at the school there. Will you be all right here on your own? We'll go down to the Red Cross canteen for a cup of coffee when I get back.'

In front of me were three stacks of envelopes I hadn't had time to finish looking at on Saturday because Mrs Dobbs had got it into her head that someone needed to tidy up the archive, and that someone had, of course, been me. The envelopes contained small ads offering positions and places to live, birth and marriage announcements, and obituaries. These days, the third pile was always the largest. It was one of my many jobs to open them, check the content was suitable and type them up before passing everything to Dobbsy, who had the final say in what made it into the paper. 'I'll be fine,' I said breezily. 'Plenty to do! And a cup of coffee later would be lovely.'

Deep down, though, I couldn't help feeling a tiny spark of envy. It was my dearest wish that Howler would let me write a real story for the paper – one of my most enduring daydreams was of being a war reporter, travelling overseas and interviewing servicemen in the thick of the action. But there was no use in dwelling on it; I knew it would never happen. I'd probably spend the rest of my life right here in Bartonford.

As Vera looped her satchel over her shoulder there was a knock on the door. Vera made a face. 'I bet that's Dobbsy.' But it was Alfie. He'd changed out of his Home Guard uniform into his post office uniform, and looked very smart. 'Good morning, Vera. Hullo again, Ruby. I've brought the post.' As he put a fresh bundle of envelopes down on my desk, I noticed he was holding a small, battered biscuit tin. 'Oh, and, er, Ruby, my dad asked me to give you these. His hens are laying like billy-o at the moment.'

I prised off the lid to see four eggs inside, nestled in a bed of straw. 'Alfie, you shouldn't have!'

He coughed, shuffling his feet. 'Oh, it's nothing. We've more than we need.'

'That's very kind.' I smiled at him. 'Do tell him thank you. Father will be pleased.' I put the lid back on the tin and set it down carefully on my desk before feeding a sheet of paper into my typewriter, a monstrous Underwood that was at least twenty years old with stiff keys that hurt my fingers if I used it for too long. I looked at the piles of envelopes and squared my shoulders resolutely.

'He's sweet on you, you know,' Vera said when Alfie had gone.

Startled, I turned in my chair. 'What? No – I don't think so.'

Shrugging her coat over her shoulders, she raised her perfectly plucked eyebrows. 'Oh, *don't* tell me you haven't noticed. That's the second time he's brought you eggs this month. He never brings *me* any.'

My face grew hot. 'He's just being kind, that's all.' Years of caring for Father had made me something of an expert on bad chests, and when we were younger, I'd walk to school with Alfie and sit with him in the playground so he didn't feel left out while the other boys tore round with their footballs and cricket bats, making sure he kept the big, green woollen scarf his mother insisted he wore at all times tucked snugly around his neck. He had always been like a brother to me; I'd never thought of him in any other way and it certainly hadn't occurred to me that *he* might think of me as more than a friend.

Vera raised her eyebrows again. 'Well, see you later. If I finish early I might wander down to the beach and see if I can get us an exclusive about the Americans!'

Then she was gone too.

As I turned back to my envelopes, I couldn't help suppressing a sigh. Before the war, the *Herald* had had a full staff, but, bit by bit, they'd volunteered or been called up. Now there were only six of us. Mr Howlett – Howler – was the editor, and an acquaintance of my old headmistress, which was how I'd ended up with this job in the first place. He spent all day shut away in his office on the second floor, only emerging for two reasons: to go to the pub or to shout about something. You could hear him bellowing before he'd even reached the top of the stairs, which was why Vera and I had nicknamed him Howler. I'd been scared of him to start with, but it hadn't taken long to discover his bark was worse than his bite, even if his yells did, on occasion, make me wonder if the office windows, covered in diagonal lengths of scrim to prevent glass flying everywhere if we got bombed, would stand up to the strain.

Next door to us was Mrs Dobbs' office. Dobbsy, as Vera and I called her, was Howler's sister, a formidable widow who wore lumpy knitted cardigans and had an enormous wart above one eyebrow. As well as being in charge of what went in the paper, she answered readers' letters, transcribed recipes for carrot fudge and prune pudding, and – to anyone who was unlucky enough to be in earshot – bemoaned the paper rationing which had cut the *Herald* down to a shadow of its former self, both in size and content. Meanwhile, down in the basement, Charlie Hopkins and Robert Towle, both of them the same age as old Tom Bidley and with even fewer teeth between them, manned the press, a fearsome, clanking beast. Then, of course, there was Vera.

I'd started out as the office girl, answering the telephone, making the tea, changing typewriter ribbons and doing all the other little jobs no one else wanted to do, but now, like everyone else, I had to fill in for the people who were no longer here. That meant checking copy, typing the small ads and obits, and occasionally – excitingly – going out on a story with Vera. Between us, we all kept the paper running, although it was often a scramble to get everything ready in time for it to go to print on Wednesdays.

Unable to face the obituaries just yet, I picked the first envelope up off the small ads pile. As I opened it carefully – we kept envelopes to be reused, and woe betide anyone who tore one – I allowed myself to daydream about the Americans. My soldier would be called Dirk, I decided. He'd look like Cary Grant but he'd sound like Clark Gable, and after a whirlwind romance we'd elope, leaving dreary, war-smashed England behind for the glamour and bright lights of America...

That was where my imaginings ended, washed away by

reality. Father was the only family I had. He was ill – he needed me – how could I even think about leaving him? Anyway, I couldn't see myself with an American soldier. I'd read enough stories in Father's *Times* to know what they were like. *Not for me, thank you.*

Resolutely, I slammed a mental door on the imaginary Dirk and began to type.

2

SAM

Coltonsburg, Virginia, USA, July

'See you tomorrow, Sam,' Mr Addison said as I propped my broom in the corner and untied my apron, hanging it on the hook beside the door connecting the store to the Addisons' house. He smiled at me from underneath his moustache. 'You've done a great job today, as always.'

I smiled too, although my back was hurting and I was exhausted just thinking about the walk home. 'Thanks, Mr Addison.'

'Wait a moment.' He went behind the counter and filled a little striped paper bag with hard butterscotch candies – Meggie's favourite. 'Here. You take these home for that sister of yours.'

No use wishing it was something that could feed all of us, like a bag of oatmeal or a packet of bacon; I'd never told Mr Addison how bad things really were at home and I wasn't about to start now. He'd only look at me like my teacher used to when I'd turn up at school in the winter with no coat and holes in the bottoms of my shoes, all sad and sorry, like I was a stray puppy. I thanked him again, dropping the candies into my pocket.

As I turned to leave, the door to the street burst open, setting the bell above it to jangling. Mr Addison's five-year-old granddaughters, Elsie and Lou, ran in. They were twins, cute as buttons. 'Grandpa! Grandpa!' Elsie yelled, flinging herself into her grandfather's arms. He lifted her in a bear hug and twirled her around, making her braids fly out behind her. Behind them, their mom, Catherine, entered the store at a more sedate pace. She and the girls had come to live here last year after Carl, Mr Addison's son, was killed fighting in Algeria. She smiled at the sight of Elsie laughing, but her eyes had their usual sad, haunted look, as if part of her had died right along with her husband. It was a look I'd gotten used to seeing around Coltonsburg the last eighteen months or so, since Pearl Harbor got bombed and America entered the war.

Mr Addison reached out a hand. 'Catherine, you look tired. Go in the house and sit down. I'll mind the kids for a while until Jean gets back.' Jean was his wife, a snow-haired woman of sixty-eight who ran several committees in town with ruthless efficiency, including Coltonsburg's American Red Cross, the soup kitchen and the local branch of the Women's Bureau.

I slipped outside. As the door closed behind me, the bell jangling again, I felt a pang of sadness. Why couldn't I have a family like the Addisons? Even with Carl gone they were a tight unit, always looking out for one another. Not for the first time, I found myself wondering what, exactly, decided the hand you got in life. Fate? The universe? God? Who knew. Anyway, I'd stopped believing in God a long time ago.

I walked the two miles back to Kirk's farm slowly, trying to enjoy the evening sun on my face. It was no good; the closer I got, the tighter my stomach tied itself in knots. *If I'm lucky,* I told myself, *he'll have already left for town. If I'm really lucky, he'll get so drunk he won't come home until tomorrow. And if I'm really, really lucky, the stupid sonofabitch'll stay away for a couple of days – maybe even get locked up in jail.* He did that every now and then, for just long enough for me to start hoping he wasn't coming back at all.

I walked into the yard, dragging my feet, a familiar sense of gloom settling over me as I looked at the collection of ramshackle sheds, the long-empty chicken coops and pieces of rusted machinery with weeds growing up through them. Even the house looked as if it was on the verge of giving up: the roof sagged in the middle, the porch had collapsed at one end, the windows were filthy and the screen door hung off its top hinge where Kirk had punched it one day. If you turned up uninvited, you'd be forgiven for thinking no one lived here at all – until Kirk started shooting at you, that was.

Everything was quiet. I began to feel hopeful again. Then the peace was shattered by a high-pitched scream.

I crossed the rest of the yard in about three strides, bursting into the kitchen to find Ma cowering in a corner with Meggie cradled in her arms. Kirk was standing over them both with his fists raised, and Ma's left eye was swelling shut, blood trickling from the corner of her mouth. A blackened saucepan lay in the middle of the floor, soup splashed up the wall.

'There!' Kirk spat at Ma. 'See what you made me do, Dolores! You stupid, no-good *whore*!'

'You leave her the fuck alone, you bastard!' The words burst out of me before I could stop them, my voice coming out cracked and high-pitched like it still did sometimes, even though I'd turned seventeen in January.

Kirk turned, his lips curving in a mocking sneer. His overalls were so stiff with dirt they could've stood up by themselves – he liked to pretend he was a farmer, even if all he could grow was pigweed and crabgrass – and a hank of greasy hair flopped over one eye. Ma once told me he was handsome when he was younger, but I'd never been able to see it. He looked like what he was: dumb as a sack of rocks, and mean as cottonmouth. The ugliness in him ran right to the bone.

'Oh yeah? And what're you gonna do, Sammy boy?' he said.

When I didn't answer, he stepped towards me. It took everything I had not to flinch away – the reaction was automatic, even though I was taller than him now. 'Your ma burned the dinner, *again*,' he drawled, the half-smoked cigarette dangling from his lower lip bobbing as he spoke – no matter how little food there was on the table, he could always find money for whisky and smokes. 'I was *educatin'* her so she don't do it again, that's all.'

He always called it *educatin'*, like he was doing you a favour when he gave you a black eye for closing a door too loud while he slept off a bender, or a punch in the kidneys for looking at him the wrong way. Hell, he'd go after you for *breathing* wrong if he was in the mood to. He glanced down and his eyes narrowed. I realised I was clenching my hands into fists, my fingernails digging into my palms. Kirk smiled. 'Come on then, Sammy boy.' He was almost purring, like a cat. 'Let's see you stand up for yerself for once.'

Not for the first time, I wished I had the guts to grab a kitchen knife and drive it through his neck. I'd thought about it many times, what it would feel like to push the blade in, how I'd stand over him and laugh as I watched him writhing at my feet as the blood pumped out of him and his eyes glazed over…

Kirk took another step towards me, his mouth twisting again.

'Y'all should be grateful to me.' His voice was real soft now, like he was sharing a secret with me. 'I feed y'all, I put a roof over y'alls' heads. And this is the thanks I get?'

His hand whipped out and he grabbed me by the chin, his fingers digging into my jaw as he pushed me back against the table. As always, his wiry strength took me by surprise. 'Always got somethin' smart to say, ain't you, Sammy boy? You're nothin' but a dumb kid. That big mouth of yours is gonna get you in trouble someday. *Big* trouble.'

He was so close I could smell his rotten breath and the stale booze seeping out of his pores. I wondered what he'd do if I threw up over him, but it was hours since I last had anything to eat. My stomach clenched and I gagged, but there was nothing to come up.

'Kirk! Leave him!' Ma gasped. 'Please!'

'Shut it, you dumb bitch,' Kirk growled. He held me there a moment longer, staring into my eyes. *You fucking creep*, I yelled at him inside my head, half scared, half hoping that if I thought it hard enough, he'd be able to hear me. *I wish Ma had never met you. I wish you were dead.*

I looked away first, like I always did, and Kirk let me go with a hard shove that sent me staggering back, knocking over a chair and sprawling on the floor. As I scrambled to my feet, Ma thrust Meggie at me. 'Go, Sam! Get her out of here!'

I hustled Meggie out of the house and headed for the old

barn on the other side of the pasture, far enough away from the house that Meggie wouldn't be able to hear Ma screaming when Kirk started *educatin'* her again.

'I – is Ma going to be OK?' Meggie sobbed, clinging to my neck as I sat down with her on the edge of an old plough that had been left in the barn to rust.

'Yeah, she'll be fine.' The lie rolled automatically off my tongue. 'Don't worry about her.' I rocked my little sister back and forth. Then I remembered the candies in my pocket. 'Here.'

Her face lit up. 'Are those for me?'

'They sure are,' I said with a cheerfulness I couldn't have been further from feeling. Meggie was seven, and even though she was only my half-sister I'd have died for her if you'd asked me to. I'd never been able to figure out how it was possible for her to be related to someone like Kirk.

'Would you like one, Sammy?' She offered me the bag.

I shook my head. 'I'm OK, honey. They're all for you.'

Meggie slid off my knee to sit cross-legged in the dirt, sucking on a candy, her tears forgotten. 'Will you draw me a picture, Sam?'

I took out the pencil and the little blank book I kept in my back pocket. Last year, Mr Addison had caught me drawing on the backs of some old letter bills when the store was quiet one afternoon. I was worried he'd be mad at me, but he said, 'You need something to keep all your drawings in, son, so's you don't lose them. I've got just the thing,' and gave me the book. It had a red leather cover, gold edges to the pages, and heavy, cream-coloured paper. It was so nice that at first, I'd been scared to use it.

I sketched a page of fantastical scenes and creatures for

Meggie – pictures straight out of a storybook. Then I drew her as a giant, a hundred feet tall, stamping and raging amongst the skyscrapers of New York like King Kong. She giggled, her tears all dried up.

I couldn't put the scene inside the house out of my head so easily. I kept seeing Kirk's fists landing on Ma's face, her stomach, her legs, and the bruises they'd leave behind – or maybe something more serious. She'd be laid up for a few days and then, when she'd recovered enough to leave the house, she'd go round telling anyone who'd listen that she walked into a door or fell downstairs, or had an accident in the yard. It made me furious, the way she covered for him. Furious with myself, too, because there I was, angry with Ma for letting Kirk use her as a punching bag and doing nothing to stop him. Why couldn't *I* stand up to him? Why did *I* let him push us around? In my head, it was easy to fight him, but whenever he threatened me, I ran away and hid, just like I was doing now.

Kirk was right. I was nothing but a dumb kid, and there wasn't one damn thing I could do about it.

3

SAM

The bell over the door jangled as someone came into the store, making me jump. I was stacking cans, so deep in thought about how to get Ma and Meggie away from Kirk that I'd forgotten where I was, and daydreaming about finding fifty dollars tucked away behind the Campbell's soup. No use asking me how the money got there or who'd left it – I hadn't figured that out yet. All I knew was that fifty bucks would get the three of us a bus to Washington, some food, maybe even a room somewhere. Then I could get a job, and after that go back to school and study drawing like I'd always wanted to. And I wouldn't have to look at Ma walking round with her eye swelled shut and her lower lip split open or see the dinner still splashed up the kitchen wall from three days ago that Kirk wouldn't let anyone clean up. *Leave that be,* he'd growled at me when I'd tried to scrape it off. *It'll remind your dumb bitch of a mother to keep her mind on what she's doing.*

I often wondered what my life would have been like if my pa was still around. He and Ma both grew up in London,

England. They met at a jazz club when he was twenty-one and she was nineteen; she was a waitress and he was a clarinet player. Her parents disapproved of him so they decided to elope, running away to America to find fame and fortune. But in the cramped third-class cabins of the *Queen Beatrice*, typhoid found them first. Pa didn't even make it across the Atlantic, and Ma, already pregnant with me before they left, became so weak that the both of us almost died too.

I used to have a photo of Pa – it was him I inherited my crooked smile and sandy hair from – but a few years ago Kirk found it and burnt it. The only thing Kirk hadn't managed to beat out of Ma was her English accent, which she'd half passed on to me. Even though the other kids at school used to tease me for it, I clung onto it because I knew it pissed Kirk off that I didn't sound like him. I didn't want anyone mistaking me for his son, not even for a second.

Someone coughed politely. I looked round and saw a tall, dark-haired guy standing just inside the door. He wore a khaki shirt and trousers and a peaked cap, his boots so shiny you could practically see your face in them. My head swam; for one crazy moment, I thought it was Carl Addison, come back from the dead.

Mrs Addison, who was behind the counter today, looked as startled as I felt. 'Can I help you, soldier?' she said.

The man held out a hand. 'Mrs Addison? Ma'am? My name's Private Tomlinson. I served with your son. He was a fine man and talked a lot about his ma and pa and the little store they had back home. I'm stationed over in England now, but I'm on leave and passing through the area, so I thought I'd call by and see it for myself.'

A smile broke across Mrs Addison's face. She clasped

Private Tomlinson's hand, tears springing into her eyes. 'Oh, Private, that's wonderful. You're most welcome here.'

Private Tomlinson smiled too, showing two rows of shining white teeth. 'Please, call me Bobby.'

'Bobby, will you come through to the back and meet my husband? He'd be very pleased to make your acquaintance, I'm sure.'

Bobby smiled again. 'I'd love to, ma'am, if it's no trouble.'

'No trouble at all. And please, call me Jean.' Mrs Addison turned to me. 'Sam here can mind the store for a little while, can't you, Sam?'

'S – sure,' I stammered, as Bobby turned his brilliant smile on me.

'Is this another one of the family?' he asked Mrs Addison.

Mrs Addison laughed. 'Oh, no, Sam's a local boy – he works here.'

'You not letting him join up, then?'

'I'm only seventeen,' I said quickly. The last thing I wanted was Private Tomlinson thinking I was a coward.

'Pity. The army could use more strong young men. You get a regular paycheck – thirty dollars a week – and three square meals a day.' He winked at me. 'And the girls just love a man in uniform!'

'Now, you leave him alone.' Mrs Addison swatted him on the arm, steering him towards the door that led through to the house. 'We need Sam right here.'

I stared after them, Private Tomlinson's words echoing through my head: ...*a regular paycheck... thirty dollars a week...*

Thirty dollars a week. *Thirty.*

I got paid to work at the store, of course, but it wasn't

much, not once Kirk got his hands on it. He made me give him half to pay for *living on my property*, as he put it, and the rest, which I kept in a coffee tin in the kitchen so Ma could use it for bills and food, usually disappeared into his pocket too. I'd tried keeping some back once, telling Kirk I'd had a pay cut, but he marched up to the store and demanded to know why Mr Addison was ripping his son off. It was the only time I could ever recall him claiming we were related.

I spent the rest of the afternoon and all that night looking for reasons not to go through with the plan that had started to form in my head. There were plenty of them, but when Kirk came crashing in at midnight, thumping up the stairs to the bedroom he shared with Ma, and I had to put my pillow over my head to block the sounds coming through the paper-thin wall, none of them seemed real important anymore. By the time Kirk had gone back downstairs to get another drink, leaving Ma sobbing softly, my mind was made up.

Usually, I went straight back to the farm after I finished at the store, but the next day, after I'd hung up my apron, propped up my broom and said goodbye to Mr Addison, I headed downtown to the National Guard recruiting office. I often passed it when Mr Addison sent me on deliveries, and there were always men queuing outside, waiting to sign up.

This evening, instead of walking past the line, I joined it, my heart thumping. Before I left the store I'd ducked into the storeroom to change my overalls for slacks and a shirt, and slicked back my hair. Mr Addison had grinned at me. 'Got a girl, eh, Sam?'

I'd tried to grin back. 'Something like that, sir.'

'You can't fool me. Ah, to be young again. Well, whoever she is, you treat her right, you hear?'

He was still grinning, but his words made my stomach twist. Was that a warning? Did he think I was like Kirk? I'd made my excuses and got out of there as fast as I could.

I looked at the other men standing in the queue, relieved to see that I wasn't the shortest one there. The guy in front of me barely came up to my shoulder. As I shuffled into place at the back of the line, he turned. His eyes widened. 'Sam?'

'Jimmy Maplin! What are you doing here?'

'Shhh.' Jimmy frowned, indicating the other men with a sidewards glance. He was my age and had been in the grade below me at school – we'd become friends after we'd joined the baseball team. I hadn't seen him for months.

'How's your ma? You still living with her?' I said more quietly.

A shadow passed across his face. 'Yeah. It ain't good. She hardly leaves the house these days. The doctor gives her pills but they don't do anything. How about you? You still living on your stepdaddy's farm?'

Before I could answer, the line began to move; a guy wearing sergeant's stripes was ushering us in through the doors.

Inside, we had to sit down at rows of desks like we were back at school. I noticed a guy to my left staring hard at me and Jimmy. He was big and square-shouldered, with a blond buzz cut and small, mean-looking eyes squashed up in the middle of his face like a couple of raisins pushed into a ball of dough. When he saw me watching him he held my gaze for a moment. 'They letting kids in the army now?' he said to his pal next to him, loudly.

'Looks like it, Freddie,' the other guy said, and they laughed. I stared at the top of my desk, trying to work out if I knew them. Could they be Kirk's friends? I didn't think so;

Kirk only hung around with other bums. This guy was too well fed, and his clothes looked expensive. No, I didn't know the guy, and he didn't know me. Thank God.

The sergeant handed out a bunch of forms. After chewing it over for a moment, I wrote my birthdate down as May 1923. When we'd finished, the forms were collected back in and we were sent through to another room for a medical. Two years of hefting sacks of beans and flour and cornmeal at the store had left me with fairly decent muscles – the doctor barely looked at me before waving me through to the next room, where a dentist was waiting to check our teeth. 'How old are you, sonny?' he said, after he'd frowned into my mouth a while.

'Twenty.' My heart was beating so hard now it felt as if it was about to burst clean out of my chest. *You idiot – that's too old – shoulda said you were eighteen...*

'Hmmm,' he said, but he let me get out of the chair. Jimmy was next. He shot me a worried look, but after a couple of questions, the dentist let him go too.

After that, those of us who'd passed the medical were sent back to the main hall. Eventually, the sergeant marched in and stood at the front of the room, his back ramrod-straight. 'Welcome to the United States Army,' he said. Someone whooped, and he added, real dry, 'You won't be cheering for long, son. This ain't the Boy Scouts. Talking of which—'

He paused. Me and Jimmy, who were sitting next to each other, exchanged quick glances. I noticed Freddie staring at us again, a small smile playing on his lips.

'Some of you don't appear to have birth certificates,' the sergeant said. 'I want all those who don't to stay behind.

The rest of you, report back here at oh-six-hundred hours tomorrow morning for swearing in.'

Fuck. My birth certificate was back at the farm, in the tin box where Ma kept all her documents. If I had to fetch it they'd see I was only seventeen. So much for my grand plan.

Freddie shot me a triumphant grin as he left the room with the others. *Game's up, buddy*. There were five of us left, including me and Jimmy. The sergeant stalked around the room, brandishing more pieces of paper. 'These are age verification forms,' he told us. 'You need to take them home to your parents, get them to sign it in front of a notary, and return with it at oh-six-hundred hours tomorrow, signed *and* notarised. Is that clear?'

One kid scraped his chair back and walked straight out the door, his face red. I took a deep breath and held out my hand for my form. So did Jimmy. Once we were a safe distance away from the office, I let out a whistle. 'Shit. What are we gonna do?'

Jimmy glanced behind us as if he thought someone might be listening. 'I know a guy. He helped a pal of mine to get into the navy, and he was only fifteen. But—'

'But what?' If I couldn't come back tomorrow with my form signed and notarised, there was no way I'd earn enough to get Ma or Meggie away from Kirk. Not now, not ever. I needed that thirty dollars a week more than I'd ever needed anything my whole life.

Jimmy chewed his lip. 'He'll want money. A *lot* of money.'

'How much?'

He told me, and my heart sank. We stood there for a moment. I scuffed my toe against the sidewalk, thinking about what life would be like if I stayed here in this shitty little town and let Kirk carry on beating Ma whenever he felt like it.

Thinking about what he might start doing to Meggie as she got older.

'You really wanna do this?' I said.

Jimmy nodded, looking hard at me. 'Yeah, I do. I – I gotta get outta here, Sam. My mom – she's driving me crazy.'

I'd never met Jimmy's ma, but I'd heard people talking about her when we were in school – how she had some sort of sickness in her head that made her crazy religious, and mean with it. It was why his pa had upped and left, and Jimmy often came to school with weals across the palms of his hands where she'd gone at him with a switch. 'She was tryin' to beat the devil outta me,' he'd told me once.

'Yeah, I gotta get away from here too.' Suddenly, an idea popped into my head. I tried to push it away at first – it was as rotten as an old tooth – but deep down, I knew it was the only option I had. 'I reckon I can get half the money, if you can get the rest.'

'I can do that. Meet me back here in two hours?'

I nodded.

I didn't go back to the farm. There wasn't a cent in the house – Kirk had taken it all last night when he went drinking. Instead, I headed to the store. It was closed, but the storeroom window round the back had a loose catch that could be opened from the outside if you knew how; Mr Addison kept saying he'd get round to fixing it but he never did. And I happened to know the Addisons were out of town this evening, visiting Mr Addison's sister.

The window was just big enough for me to wriggle through. I landed on a pile of flour sacks, sending up a cloud of white dust. I stuffed my fists into my mouth, terrified someone would walk past and hear me choking and sneezing.

When I'd gotten myself together, I stood up, brushing flour off my clothes, and crept into the store. The huge till, covered in ornate black and gold scrollwork, sat on the counter. Mr Addison kept the key on a little hook underneath. At first, I couldn't find it. When my fingers finally closed around it the cold metal burned against my skin like a brand.

Taking a deep breath, I opened the till. The drawer sprang out with a *ding!*, revealing the week's takings inside. I reached in, then snatched my hand back, feeling sick. I couldn't do this. The Addisons were like family to me.

Then I remembered the way Mrs Addison had laughed as she told that soldier yesterday, *Oh, no, Sam's just a local boy.* I'd thought she'd meant it kindly, but perhaps she hadn't. Perhaps what she'd really been saying was: *Thank goodness, because you should see the excuse of a man who calls himself his father.* And I thought about Ma's face – those purple-brown bruises she'd wear for weeks – her sobs coming through the bedroom wall last night.

I counted out what I needed, taking a little extra for Ma; I'd leave it somewhere Kirk wouldn't be able to find it. Slamming the till shut, I stuffed the bills in my pocket. I stole back through the store like a ghost, wriggled out the storeroom window and ran all the way back downtown to the street corner where I'd said I'd meet Jimmy, brushing the last of the flour off my clothes as I went.

4

RUBY

September

The air raid siren started to wail just as I was returning to the sector post to sign off for the night.

'*Drat*,' I muttered under my breath. It was almost eleven-thirty p.m. I'd been working all day, with barely half an hour to run home and grab a bite to eat before I'd had to rush back out to report for duty. After several hours walking the streets, checking no one had any lights showing, my feet ached and all I wanted to do was go home and have a cup of cocoa with Father – who'd be waiting up for me; he always did – before falling into bed.

'Ah, Ruby, there you are,' Mr Jones, the head warden, said when I put my head around the office door. 'Can you go up to the shelter near the school, please, and see people in?'

I nodded, putting my helmet back on. *This bloody war*, I heard Vera's voice groan inside my head as I trudged wearily back up the street. She said it all the time; it had become a sort of mantra between us.

Ten minutes later, just as I reached the shelter, I heard the rumbling drone of the German planes going over. I didn't know what sort of planes they were – I had no idea about that sort of thing, although if Alfie was here I expect he could've told me – but it sounded as if there were a lot of them. I craned my neck but couldn't see anything except the searchlights sending thin pencils of light into the sky above the town. The noise sent shivers down my spine. It was so sinister, like a swarm of giant, deadly hornets. The guns began firing along the coast, a dull *BOOM... BOOM* that made the very air shake.

'I do hope they aren't planning on dropping anything on us tonight, miss,' a woman said as she hurried her family into the shelter. I didn't know what to say, so I gave her a smile I hoped was reassuring instead, even though it was so dark she probably couldn't see it. Once everyone was inside I hurried in after them, standing near the door. I listened to the planes go over, adrenaline surging through me and washing away my tiredness. I was thinking of poor Exeter last year, when the Germans smashed it to bits, and the awful pictures in Father's newspaper. Was it Bartonford's turn tonight?

But the planes must have been heading for Exeter again, or Taunton, because eventually the sound of the engines faded away and at last came the single, sustained note of the siren sounding the all-clear.

As I ushered everyone out of the shelter again, my exhaustion returned, crashing over me in a wave. I looked at my watch. Half past twelve. *Gosh*. I'd be glad to get home tonight.

'What's that noise?' someone said.

'What's what?' someone else asked.

'Sounds like a plane.'

'Can't be – siren's not sounded.'

'It is – I'm telling you! Listen!'

I strained my ears as more voices erupted around me. Then I heard it: the stuttering drone of a single engine, gradually coming closer.

'Gotta be one of ours, ain't it?'

'Sounds like it's been hit.'

The sound of the engine got louder, a choppy roar. Whoever it was, they were flying much too low and much too fast – and they were coming this way. 'Get back in the shelter!' I shouted, blowing my whistle. '*Back in the shelter! Now!*'

Everyone did as I asked. As I reached for the door to pull it closed the plane's engine cut out. There was a moment of silence; all I could hear was the blood rushing in my ears, then a terrible whining sound that grew and grew until it was the only sound in the world as the plane tumbled out of the sky. It felt as if it went on forever, although it could only have been a few seconds.

There was an earth-shattering crunch, and silence again.

'They've hit the school!' someone cried.

Everyone rushed for the door. I was helpless to stop them; all I could do was follow, running after them up the hill to Bartonford Junior School where a shuddering orange glow filled the night sky. Thankfully, the building itself was unscathed; the plane had come down in the field beside it and the fuselage was burning fiercely. Even though the black and white crosses on the wingtips were clearly visible, my stomach still turned at the thought of what it must have been like to be trapped inside. Surely no one could have survived?

Before long, it seemed half the town had arrived to stare

at the spectacle. People tried to approach the plane but were beaten back by the flames. Even from where I was standing I could feel their fierce heat on my face and hands. I was relieved when the constable arrived. He ordered the crowd to step back. 'Are you all right, miss?' he asked me. I nodded.

'Fire engine's on its way,' he said. 'Not that there's much that they can do. Can you keep an eye on things here until they arrive, make sure no one tries any funny business?'

I looked round at the crowd watching the plane burn. 'Er, I—'

But he'd already gone. Inevitably, people began to trickle back, children among them, trying to get as close to the plane as they could. The flames leapt into the air, becoming more ferocious than ever, and there was an eye-watering stench of burning fuel. 'Please, keep back!' I shouted, but no one was listening. Their excitement was like an electric current running through the air.

'Ma'am, can we help? We were in town and saw the plane come over – we got here as fast as we could.'

I turned to see two soldiers in American uniforms standing behind me, one dark-haired, the other one – the one who'd spoken – with hair that was somewhere between brown and blond. Neither of them appeared to be much older than me, their uniforms new and crisp.

'Oh, yes, thank you,' I stammered. 'I need to get people away from the plane – it isn't safe.'

The two soldiers ran across the grass and began ordering the onlookers back. Everyone obeyed immediately; the American army had finally arrived in Bartonford last week, pouring into the camp overlooking Bartonford Bay, and they'd been causing quite a stir. That evening, Father had called me into the parlour. 'You must be careful, Ruby,' he'd said. 'I don't want you associating with the Americans. These men... I've heard all sorts of things about them – the things they do – taking advantage – only after one thing—'

Fat chance of that, a devilish little voice in my head had spoken up. I'd squashed it back down. 'Don't worry, Father, I'm not the least bit interested in the Americans. I'm far too busy for all that!' I'd reassured him.

'Oh, good, good.' He'd patted my hand. 'I don't mean to lecture you – I know you're a sensible girl. But—' He'd begun to cough. I'd fetched him a glass of water and escaped to my bedroom, where I threw myself down on my bed with a resigned sigh. I loved Father dearly, but sometimes I suspected he thought I was still twelve years old, a silly child in pigtails who was going to have her head turned by the mere sight of a man in uniform.

As the two soldiers shepherded the last person to what I hoped was a safer distance, there was a flash of light and another tremendous, ground-shaking roar. I was flung off my feet; people screamed, and I felt earth, clods of grass and shrapnel raining down on top of me.

When the commotion had ceased, I struggled to my feet, my ears ringing. Where the plane had been was an enormous, smoking crater, flames still leaping into the air. *The plane must have still been carrying its bombs*, I thought dazedly.

Someone touched my arm.

I cried out, startled, and whirled around. It was one of the soldiers, the one with the sandy hair. My ears were still ringing, but as they cleared I was able to make out what he was saying. 'Sorry, ma'am. I didn't mean to scare you. I was speaking, but you didn't seem to hear me.'

I was absurdly relieved to see that he wasn't injured. His friend was helping people up. 'Is anyone hurt?' I asked the first soldier, trying to cover up my embarrassment by fumbling in my satchel for my first aid kit. The smoke caught in my throat, making me cough; my eyes were watering.

'There's someone here with a cut on their leg,' the second soldier called. I hurried over to tend to the woman, who'd been caught by a piece of metal flying from the plane and had a bloody gash across her shin. As I bandaged her up, two more wardens arrived with the constable and the fire engine, and the firemen got to work fighting the flames.

By the time everyone was tended to – thankfully, the only injuries were minor cuts and scrapes – it was almost a quarter to two. 'Thank you for your help,' I said to the soldiers as we left the playing field. 'I'm ever so grateful.'

'You're welcome, ma'am. Glad we could be of assistance,' the one with the sandy hair said. In a daze, I returned to the air raid shelter, where I'd left my bicycle. When I got back to Barton Hall I left it leaning up against the Anderson and let myself into the cottage. It was in darkness. 'Father?' I called.

There was no answer. Taking my torch, which had tissue paper pasted over the beam, I went out into the garden to check the Anderson. That was empty, too.

I went back into the cottage and shone my torch into the cupboard under the stairs. Father was huddled amongst the coats and tins of shoe polish and furniture wax, white-faced, rocking, his arms clasped around his knees. 'Gas, gas, *bloody gas!*' he said in a high, broken voice, staring wildly at nothing, when I gently touched his arm. I tried not to think about how long he must have been in there; what he'd been imagining as the plane crashed and its bombs detonated. It took me almost fifteen minutes to gently talk him back to reality and get him into the parlour, another twenty to get him to drink a cup of tea, sweetened with a precious teaspoon of sugar, and fifteen minutes more to coax him up to bed. By that time, I felt as if I was wading through treacle. The sight of the burning German plane was imprinted on my mind – I knew I'd remember the moment of the explosion as long as I lived. Thank goodness those American soldiers had been there. If they hadn't, and people had still been standing near the plane...

It wasn't until I was almost asleep that something occurred to me: I'd never thought to ask them their names.

5

RUBY

'Gosh, you look all in,' Vera said as she came into the office, making me lift my head up off my desk with a guilty start. 'Did you hear about the plane crash last night up at the school?'

'Yes, I was there,' I said.

Her eyes widened. '*What?*'

As briefly as I could, I told her what had happened, and about the two American soldiers helping me get everyone to safety moments before the plane's bombs had detonated.

'Bloody hell.' She lit a cigarette, took a little paper packet of Benzedrine tablets from her handbag and offered me one. I shook my head. Last time I'd tried that stuff, after a night of heavy air raids, it had woken me up but made me feel horribly nervy, too, as if I was teetering on the brink of some shadowy, looming disaster.

'What you need is some fresh air and a cup of coffee at the WVS canteen if they have any,' Vera said, pushing back her chair and standing up. 'I've got to go out and about this morning interviewing people about the crash. Why don't you join me? You can tell me all the gruesome details.'

I looked up at her. 'Won't Howler mind?'

Vera shrugged. 'Probably.'

'And what about my adverts?' Listlessly, I indicated the pile of envelopes next to my typewriter, the remains of yesterday's work I hadn't quite managed to finish.

'They'll still be there after lunch, won't they?'

'Oh, all right, then.' I fetched my handbag and my coat.

'I'm off – taking Ruby with me!' Vera called to no one in particular as we made for the stairs. I doubt anyone even heard her. From behind Mrs Dobbs' door came the steady *rat-a-tat-a-tat* of her typewriter ('Seventy-six words a minute, Miss Mottram!' she'd told me proudly when I first started working here). Howler was, as usual, ensconced in his office upstairs.

Once we were outside, I began to feel better. A fresh breeze whipped against my face, and I could see patches of blue sky starting to show over the sea. Vera tucked her hand into the crook of my elbow. 'Let's go down to the High Street. I expect they'll have plenty to say there.'

Before long Vera had enough notes for her story ten times over; the crash was all people wanted to talk about. 'En't it turrible?' Mr Short, the fishmonger – who was over six feet tall and thin as a racing greyhound – exclaimed as he wrapped a piece of haddock up for Mrs Clayton. 'Blame Jerry, missus, not me,' he added when she grumbled about the price. 'And just be thankful it 'ent rationed like everythin' else.' He turned back to us. 'Coulda flattened the school *and* the houses all around it if it had landed a few seconds sooner, they say. And just think how much worse it would'a bin if it'ud been daytime and the kiddies there.'

Mrs Clayton left, still grumbling about the cost of the fish. We followed.

'Watch out!' Vera said as we started to cross the road. She grabbed my arm, pulling me back as a vehicle roared around the corner.

It was an American jeep, dark olive green with a white star in a circle painted on the bonnet. Three GIs hung out of it, laughing. 'Sorry, doll!' the driver called to Vera as the jeep tore past in a rush of air and fumes, and Vera clamped her hat onto her head to keep it from blowing away. I caught sight of a handsome, tanned face with a wide grin, and dark curls under a cap balanced at a rakish angle.

'Well I *never*,' Mrs Clayton, who was standing beside us, said in shocked tones. 'Those Americans – you wouldn't believe some of the things I've heard about them!'

Vera, taking her notebook from her pocket, tried to steer her onto the subject of the plane crash, but Mrs Clayton was like a dog with a bone and it was almost ten minutes before she'd finished telling us all the stories she'd heard about the Americans – stories that would have had Father nodding along in grim, worried agreement: how they ate strange food, listened to dreadful ('some might say wicked!') music, and, of course, when they came into town, they were only after one thing, and didn't all the local girls know it...

You wouldn't be saying any of this if you'd seen them last night! I wanted to cry. *Those two soldiers saved people's lives!*

'Silly old gossip,' Vera muttered once we'd got rid of her, and were out of earshot. I rolled my eyes in agreement.

We went up to the crash site so Vera could snap a few photographs. It looked even worse in daylight: the hole in the field, with the charred, twisted skeleton of the aeroplane still sticking out of it, was enormous. I didn't go too close to the edge of the crater; I was scared the remains of whoever had been inside might still be there.

At lunchtime, we dropped into the Red Cross canteen for a potted meat sandwich and a cup of ersatz coffee. 'What I wouldn't give for some *proper* coffee instead of this old muck!' Vera sighed quietly as we dutifully swallowed it down. After that we returned to the office, where I spent the rest of the day trying not to fall asleep at my desk as I typed up *Positions Vacant* and *Positions Wanted*, the events of last night still running through my head on a loop. After work I cycled wearily back to Barton Hall. 'Ruby!' I heard a voice call as I pedalled up the lane, and saw Mrs Baxter waving at me from her doorstep. I hadn't seen her for over a week; she'd been visiting her sister near Bournemouth.

'Did you have a nice holiday?' I asked her as Toffee pushed through her legs to greet me.

'Yes thank you,' she said. 'Although this weather didn't do my rheumatism any good – it's terribly cold for September, isn't it?' Although she was smiling her face was pinched with pain; I could tell that even standing was an effort for her today.

Toffee gave an impatient little yap as if to say, *What about me?* 'Would you like me to take him for a walk?' I asked. My tiredness had morphed into a doomy restlessness, as if I'd taken one of Vera's Benzedrine after all, and the thought of sitting in our stuffy little cottage, waiting for Father to come home with the smell of the hospital clinging to his clothes – a pungent mix of Jeyes Fluid and the patients' meals – felt unbearable all of a sudden.

Mrs Baxter's face brightened. 'Oh, would you? I hate to ask...'

'I don't mind at all. Let me take my bike home and I'll be right back.'

'You can leave it here if you like,' she said, so I wheeled it up the side passage while she fetched Toffee's lead. 'He needs a new one, really,' she said as I took it from her and clipped it to the dog's collar. 'It's getting terribly frayed! But we have to make do, don't we?'

I frowned at it. It *was* getting rather tatty, and Toffee did pull so. I wondered if I should tie a knot in it.

Keeping an ear out for jeeps, I walked back down the lane to the dunes, a slow amble with Toffee stopping to sniff each lamppost we passed. Every step felt like an effort. When we reached the top of the dunes, Toffee gave an excited little yap.

'I'm sorry, boy, we can't go down there,' I told him. 'The beach is still out of bounds, remember?'

Although the dunes obscured my view of the beach, there was a cloud of oily black smoke rolling into the air, a dark stain against the sky, and I could hear yelling and engines revving. What were the Americans doing down there?

There was a sudden dull *boom*. I jumped and gave a little scream, and a startled seagull that had been hidden in the dunes nearby flapped into the air, squawking indignantly. Toffee barked and lunged after it, giving a hard yank on the lead, which snapped in two. As he rocketed away through the dunes like a ginger-coloured torpedo, I stared stupidly at the frayed piece of rope still hanging from my fingers. It took my weary brain a moment or two to catch up.

Oh *no*.

'Toffee! *Toffee!*' I ran after him, reaching the other side of the dunes just in time to see him racing towards a group of soldiers marching along the water's edge. The seagull – which was long gone – had been completely forgotten; Toffee's tail windmilled as he made a beeline for the sergeant bellowing orders at the line of men hurrying along the wet sand. They were laden with guns and heavy-looking packs.

Toffee, overjoyed at what he must have thought was a tremendous game, made a leap for the sergeant. Even though he was only a small dog, he caught the man by surprise, knocking him off balance. Arms flailing, the sergeant staggered and fell just as a particularly large wave came crashing into shore. It drenched him from head to toe.

'Oh, gosh, I'm so sorry!' I gasped as I ran to the men and tried to grab Toffee, who danced just out of my reach, barking, thinking I was playing too. The sergeant was still on the sand, flailing and spluttering as another wave broke over him. The rest of the soldiers were trying to hide their laughter, but they weren't making a very good job of it. My cheeks burned.

'Hey, Rover!' One of the soldiers dropped to his knees and made a soft, kissing sound. Toffee ran to him, tail going faster than ever. As soon as he was close enough the soldier grabbed him.

'I think he's gonna need a new leash,' he said, carrying Toffee over to me as the dog wriggled and twisted in his arms, trying to lick his face. Then he said, 'Oh. Hello again.'

With a jolt, I realised he was one of the young soldiers from last night, his mop of sandy hair peeking out from underneath his cap. In the daylight I could see he had grey eyes and a sprinkling of freckles across his nose. I noticed his accent, too; it had a distinctly British twang to it, which hadn't registered last night. As he handed Toffee to me our gazes met and this time, the heat in my face was nothing to do with my embarrassment.

'Um, th – thank you,' I stammered. Toffee struggled, desperate to give the boy's face one last good wash – for he really *was* no more than a boy. As I attempted to tie the broken ends of the lead together with one hand there was another one of those explosions. I jumped, dropping the lead again. For the first time, I realised just how *busy* the beach was: there were soldiers everywhere, marching, scrambling under lines of barbed wire stretched across the sand, and packed into jeeps and armoured vehicles racing along the waterline. Shouts echoed from all sides as orders were given and obeyed and, a little further down the beach, something was burning fiercely behind a low concrete wall – the source of the oily smoke and, I assumed, the bangs. A group of soldiers crawled towards it on their stomachs, guns cocked. I stared at them, amazed at the transformation of sleepy little Bartonford Bay.

'Here, let me help you,' the boy said, bringing me back to reality. While I hung on to Toffee, he knotted the lead back together. 'That should hold him.'

He smiled at me and I felt something inside me burst into life, like a flame being touched to a lantern wick.

Just as I was about to smile back, the sergeant, dripping and purple-faced, thrust himself between us. 'Get that goddamn dog off this goddamn beach!' he shouted, spittle flying from his lips. 'This is a military training ground – civilians ain't supposed to be down here! And you, English, get back in goddamned line!' he roared at the boy. I suppose he called him that because of his accent. The boy made a face at me when the sergeant wasn't watching – a conspiratorial sort of look, his eyes widening slightly and another smile playing at the corners of his mouth – and stepped back to join the other soldiers.

I swallowed, hard. 'Y – yes, sir. I'm sorry.'

'What's your damn name?' the sergeant bawled.

'R – Ruby Mottram, sir.'

'And what goddamn school do you go to?'

'I – I don't go to school, sir. I work at the *B – Bartonford Herald.*'

'Then I'll make sure whoever's in charge there hears all about this! Now – *scram*!'

With Toffee still jammed under my arm, I fled. The sergeant's yells followed me all the way back up into the dunes: '*Suppose you bunch of pansies thought that was funny... I want a hundred press-ups from all of you, NOW...*'

I didn't stop running until I was halfway back to Barton Hall, and too out of breath to carry on.

6

SAM

'God*damn*.' Jimmy Maplin collapsed onto the bunk next to mine with a deep groan. The sergeant – who the guys had nicknamed Hardass – had worked us until we were falling over. You'd think what had happened with that dog was *our* fault.

Someone switched the wireless on. 'Hey, turn it over!' everyone yelled as opera blared through the loudspeaker. There was a rush for the set, which was mounted on the wall at one end of the hut I and twenty other guys called home. Stanley Novak, a lean forty-something with a sardonic smile who'd previously worked as a journalist at the *Washington Post*, got there first. There was a blast of static and the opera changed to the Andrews Sisters.

I rolled my shoulders, trying to work out the knots in them, and returned to the letter I was writing to Ma, chewing on the end of my pencil and frowning. I'd never been quite as good at words as I was with pictures.

Dear Ma,
 *I hope you and Meggie are all right and that Mr Addison
is giving you my letters and checks...*

Sometimes, I still couldn't believe I was here. Everything seemed to have happened so fast. I'd run back to meet Jimmy on the street corner as fast as I could, the cash from the Addisons' till burning a guilty hole in my back pocket, and gone to get our forms signed by a seedy-looking guy at the edge of town. Then I'd returned to the farm to pack the few possessions I had – a change of clothes, and my notebook. Kirk was in town, doing the rounds of the bars as usual, but I'd chickened out of saying goodbye to Ma and Meggie and left them a note instead, slipping out before dawn the following morning to return to the recruiting office. I knew if they found out what I was doing, they'd try and change my mind.

Boot camp had been a hellhole of a place built out on the swamps with the worst accommodation reserved for the black troops, who weren't permitted to mix with us at all. 'You ain't individuals anymore, boys,' the sergeant had drawled as we shuffled into line for our first drill. 'You're a unit. A team. Don't you forget that.' We'd practised the same basic skills over and over, day and night, with a hundred guys like Hardass screaming at us the whole time. Even the smallest screw-up meant getting punished, sometimes your whole unit. And with Freddie Gardner around, screw-ups had happened all the time. I hadn't seen him since the recruiting office, but on my first day at camp, as Jimmy and I lined up on the parade ground, I'd spotted him in the next line. He'd seen me at the same time, and scowled. 'So they let you in, huh?' he'd said later, when we were queuing up in the mess hall. 'How'd you manage that, then, kid? What are you, like, twelve?'

Jimmy had kept me going, reminding me constantly why I was there. 'What'll your ma and your sister do if you give up now?' he'd say. And gradually, it became – well, not easier, but I got used to it.

Right from the start, I'd laid my wages aside, only spending what I had to and sending the rest back home. I couldn't send anything to the farm in case Kirk got his hands on it, so I posted checks to Mr Addison to pass on to Ma. I'd paid back what I'd taken from the till, too, writing a long letter to explain and ask for his help. Mr Addison had sent a curt reply, making it clear how much trouble I'd caused for him and his family – which I deserved, I guess – and I hadn't heard anything since. But he'd said he'd pass the rest of the money on.

After boot camp we'd left for England, sailing on a converted cruise ship. We'd been tossed around on the Atlantic like sardines in a bucket, and what the locals must've thought when thousands of us disembarked at Liverpool, grey-faced and stinking of vomit, I have no idea; I'd felt so sick I was past caring. The weather was cool and rainy, just like we'd been told it would be, and as we passed through the city I'd stared at the bombed-out buildings. I knew the Germans had been hitting England hard, but *damn*. How could anyone survive this?

Once we'd got to Devon, though, and I'd had a couple of nights' sleep and some food, I'd felt more like myself again. Despite the tape criss-crossed over the windows and the stern notices in the shops reminding people about rationing, Bartonford was a swell little place. Even the cabbages growing in the park had a certain charm. Thanks to his pa, Freddie had wangled a post with the military police, so he was in separate quarters from me and Jimmy, and as for the beach, I'd never seen anything like it – even on a stormy day, it was beautiful. It made me wonder what possessed my parents to leave England in the first place, and why Ma decided to stay in America after Pa died, never mind marry Kirk. The only reason I could come up with was, like me coming here, she'd felt she had no choice.

I hope you are not worrying about me, I wrote now. *I am fine and the army is still treating me well. The people where we are posted are real friendly and seem glad to have us here...*

My thoughts drifted again, this time to the girl I'd met last night, then seen on the beach this afternoon, Ruby Mottram. Was she one of the locals? She must be; she'd said she worked for the *Bartonford Herald*. Stanley Novak had been reading a copy at breakfast this morning.

I hoped Sergeant Hardass hadn't meant it when he said he was going to march down there and get the girl into trouble. What had happened was an accident – anyone with half a brain could see that. But Sergeant Hardass wasn't the forgiving type; he probably thought Ruby let the dog jump up at him on purpose to make him look a fool, and he was likely on his way down there already. No, scratch that – by now, he'd've gone and come back.

Another idea suddenly popped into my head. What if *I* went down there and explained what had really happened? Me and Jimmy were due a rest day tomorrow and we were planning to walk into town anyway. We could ask around, find out where the newspaper office was. Maybe I'd even get to see Ruby again.

I put my letter away and turned to Jimmy. 'Hey. Wanna help me out with something?'

'The *Bartonford Herald*?' the woman in the brown cardigan said. 'Just down there.'

'*Finally*,' I muttered. Jimmy and I had been in town an hour, and everyone we'd spoken to had been friendly, apologetic, and maddeningly tight-lipped. Even a kid – who couldn't have been more than nine, with grazed knees poking out of his short pants – said, 'I'm not allowed to tell you because Mummy says there's a war on and anyone I don't know might be a spy.' Then he'd had the cheek to grin at us and say, 'Got any gum, chum?'

Finally, when we stopped to ask the woman, I'd drawn myself up, squared my shoulders, produced my papers from my inside pocket and, in a heavy drawl, added, 'It's important army business, ma'am. The colonel himself sent us and if we don't get there by noon we're gonna be in a whole world of trouble.' I'd been praying she wouldn't ask who the colonel was – I'd seen him around the camp, from a distance, but I couldn't for the life of me remember the guy's name.

We walked down to the newspaper office, a narrow, white-painted building with a green front door, its windows taped up just like everywhere else. There was nothing to indicate what the building was for, but there was a slightly cleaner square on the wall near the door where it looked as if a brass plate had been taken down – in case of invasion, maybe. As I rang the bell, an army jeep roared past, scattering pedestrians who glared at me and Jimmy as if it was all our fault. I squared my shoulders again, trying to look important and hoping no one had been watching out of the windows just now.

The door was answered by a young woman. My heart lifted for a second, then dropped again. It wasn't Ruby; she was older, more sophisticated-looking, wearing a neat olive green skirt and jacket.

'Yes?' she said in a cut-glass accent, utterly unlike anyone else's round here.

'Hi.' I brandished my papers again, just in case. 'Can you please take me to see your, er, the guy in charge?' The correct word – *editor* – came to me a few seconds too late.

The woman raised her carefully plucked eyebrows. 'Mr Howlett? He's not in.'

'Oh, er, in that case, is, er, Ruby here?'

'Ruby? What do you want with her?'

'I, er, have something for her.' From my pocket, I took out the leather dog leash I'd managed to find in a dusty corner of the ironmonger's on our way here. It had cost me, as the Brits liked to say, an arm and a leg.

The woman frowned. Jimmy was grinning. I felt my face heating up.

'You'd better come in.' The woman ushered us into a narrow hall with a wooden hat stand, peeling walls and a black-and-white tiled floor, and a rickety-looking flight of stairs going up the right-hand side. 'But stay down here. I could do without Dobbsy asking awkward questions, and so could Ruby.'

Before I could ask who 'Dobbsy' was or why she'd be asking awkward questions, the woman had gone, hurrying up the stairs. She came back down a few minutes later, followed by Ruby.

My stomach did a sort of somersault. She was even prettier than I remembered, her wavy, reddish hair held back from her face in two tortoiseshell combs. When she saw me, her eyes widened and she went bright pink.

'Hi,' I said.

'Aren't you going to introduce me?' the woman who'd let us in asked Ruby drily, and I remembered that Ruby – who was still staring at me – didn't even know my name.

'I'm Sam,' I said quickly. 'And this is Jimmy. We're both in the 116th Infantry Regiment. From Virginia. We're at the camp above the beach.' I coughed. *Where else would you be, idiot?* 'Um, I hope you didn't get in any trouble for what happened yesterday.'

The woman looked from me to Ruby and back again. Ruby still hadn't spoken a word.

I held out the leash. 'I, er, bought this for you. I thought it might help stop your dog, you know, escaping again.'

Ruby all but snatched the leash from me. 'Er, thank you. I – I'd better get back to work,' she stammered. She turned and ran back up the stairs. I stared after her. What had I said?

'*Well,*' the woman said, her eyebrows arching higher than ever. 'I can't wait to find out what all *that* was about.'

Just then, the front door opened and a portly man with great bushy side-whiskers and little wire-framed glasses balanced crookedly across the bridge of his nose bustled in. 'Ah, Vera,' he boomed. 'Glad you're here – got a job for you.' Then he noticed me and Jimmy. 'Good day, gentlemen. Can I help you?'

'We were just leaving, sir,' I said. 'Thank you.' Leaving Vera to explain, we got out of there as fast as we could.

'I guess your girl wasn't too happy to see you, huh?' Jimmy chuckled as we walked back up the sloping street in the bright autumn sunshine and I resisted the urge to glance behind me.

'She's not *my girl.*' I said, feeling unaccountably flat. But why *should* Ruby have been happy to have seen me? I'd probably imagined that look that passed between us yesterday. No doubt she was embarrassed about what had happened and upset because she'd gotten in trouble for it.

Then it hit me. '*Damn*. I bet that guy with the whiskers was the editor – the one Hardass was going to report Ruby to. I forgot to tell him that the dog getting loose wasn't her fault.'

'Aw, but you gave her the leash.' Jimmy was laughing properly now. 'At least her dog won't be knocking Hardass over again.'

I punched him lightly on the arm. Should I go back? No, I'd made enough of a fool of myself for one day. 'Let's go back to the camp and get some coffee,' I growled.

7

RUBY

October

At the beginning of October, the weather changed. Blustery winds surged down from the north, turning the sea to a sheet of choppy, churning steel, and with them came the approaching anniversary of Mother's death. Father's mood darkened accordingly, his night terrors growing worse, and he developed a hollow, hunted look, his face grey. I should have been used to it by now – it happened every year – but it still took a toll.

To distract myself, I made an effort to keep busy – so busy I barely had time to think about anything, least of all Sam. I wasn't avoiding the possibility of bumping into him when I took Toffee for walks in the gardens in the middle of town instead of up at the dunes; it was just that the weather was bad, and I didn't want Toffee to get loose and run onto the beach again (although there was little chance of that happening, thanks to his splendid new lead). I took the longer route to work, telling myself it was because I needed the fresh air and exercise, not so I could duck into an alleyway if I saw someone in a khaki uniform approaching. Sam was just someone I'd run into once – all right, twice – and would be unlikely to meet again. Much to my relief, his sergeant hadn't carried out his threat to report me to Howler.

One Thursday morning, after a few snatched hours of sleep following a long ARP shift, I woke late to discover Father already at the breakfast table, grim-faced. 'I suppose you've heard about the Pearson girl?' he said.

Still foggy-headed, my mind whirling with everything I needed to do before I got ready for work, I gazed blankly at him. 'The Pearson girl?'

'Jennie Pearson. You went to school with her, didn't you?'

Suddenly, I remembered her. She was my age, a quiet, mousy sort who'd never seemed to be interested in anything much; we'd not been friends then and we weren't now, but we sometimes stopped to chat when we bumped into each other around town. 'What about her?'

'She's got herself in trouble with one of those American soldiers. He's denying he had anything to do with it, of course, but her mother is certain.'

'In trouble? What sort of trouble?' Then the penny dropped. '*Oh.*'

Father peered keenly at me. 'You are doing as I asked, aren't you, Ruby? You are keeping away from those men?'

'Of course I am!' I said. To my horror, I felt my face growing warm. 'I haven't been anywhere near them!'

'Good.' The frown line between his eyebrows smoothed out. 'Oh, forgive me, I know I worry. But I want what's best for you.'

'Of course, Father,' I said. I bolted down some tea and

porridge and rushed back upstairs to clean my teeth. When I went outside, I discovered my bike had a puncture. I didn't have anything to patch the tyre, so I had to run all the way through the rain to work.

By the end of the morning, I had a raging headache. 'Oh, go home,' Vera told me after lunch, when she caught me leaning my elbows on my desk and massaging my temples. I'd taken an aspirin, but it hadn't done much good.

I smiled wanly at her. 'I'm all right.'

'No, you're not.' Her tone brooked no argument. 'There's never much to do on Thursdays anyway, not once we've gone to press. Go on. If Howler asks, I'll tell him you were having female problems. He'll go red and mutter into his moustache and disappear back into his office faster than you can say *air raid*.'

Gratefully, I gathered my things. Before I went, I asked Vera, 'Have you heard about Jennie Pearson?'

She made a face. 'Who *hasn't*? Apparently the soldier who's got her in the family way promised to marry her, but he's changed his mind and won't have anything to do with her now. People are shunning her in the street.'

'Yes, that's what Father said – about the soldier dropping her, I mean. He gave me a talking-to this morning – wanted to make sure I wasn't associating with the Americans in any way.'

Vera rolled her eyes. 'He needs to give you some credit – you've infinitely more sense than Jennie Pearson! Even if you *did* start seeing one of the Americans I'm sure you wouldn't get yourself in a mess like that. I feel sorry for the poor thing, I really do, but that girl was born with cotton wool between her ears where her brains should be. Anyway, what are you still doing here? Shoo!'

I made my way downstairs, looking forward to a quiet house and a few hours to myself before Father returned from work. Perhaps I'd read. I'd borrowed a couple of novels from the library, and I could already hear them calling to me.

My coat pulled close around me against the rain, I ducked into Ropewalk Alley at the side of the *Herald* offices. It was an unpleasant little cut-through, narrow and dark, the slimy cobbles strewn with rubbish that had spilled out of the bins lined up along one side, but as a shortcut, it would save me at least ten minutes.

As I edged past the rubbish bins, I heard voices – American voices – and footsteps turning into the alley behind me. My heart leapt into my throat, but I stuck my chin out and kept walking; there wasn't exactly anywhere else I could go.

Behind me, someone whistled. 'Whoo–*ee*. Looking fine, lil' lady!'

If I was Vera, I might have turned round and winked at him – perhaps flipped my hair over my shoulders – but there was something in his tone that made my stomach clench, my hands curl into loose fists. I kept walking, staring straight ahead.

'Hey, where you goin'? We just wanna talk to you!' the voice called. The footsteps behind me sped up; moments later I found myself flanked by two burly soldiers wearing the white helmets of the military police. "Snowdrops" everyone called them, although I couldn't have come up with a less appropriate name for this pair if I'd tried.

The taller of the two leered at me, leaning against the wall in front of me. To a passer-by, it might have looked casual, but he was blocking my way with his arm. He had blond hair, and a wide, white-toothed grin that didn't reach his eyes; they were like a snake's, small and cold in the middle of his fleshy face. Fleetingly, I found myself wondering if one of these two was the soldier who'd got Jennie Pearson in trouble.

'So, honey, what's your name?' he said. 'I'm Freddie. This is Gene.'

I glanced round at the other soldier, who was standing behind me. He was thinner than Freddie, dark-haired with a humourless expression. 'Hey,' he said.

'Excuse me,' I said, making to step forwards. 'I must go.'

Freddie moved his arm down a little. 'Hey, why the hurry? It's dinner time, isn't it? Oh, sorry, *lunch*time.' He said the last two words in a mock-English accent. 'Why don't you come up to the club with us and get something to eat?'

'I'm quite all right, thank you.' My heart was pounding.

'Aw, that's not very polite, is it, Gene?' Freddie said over my head. 'I thought these British girls were supposed to be so *nice*.'

He moved closer. I tried to step back, but I was sandwiched between him and Gene. My stomach twisted.

'What's wrong? You already spoken for?' Freddie drawled. 'Or ain't I good enough for you?'

'Oh!' I said, pretending to stare at something over his shoulder. 'There's my father – the constable. Father!' I waved. Freddie jerked his head round, and I ducked under his arm and ran.

'Hey!' I heard him shout after me. I didn't slow down until I was several streets away and certain he and Gene weren't following me.

As I hurried home, I swore I would have nothing more to do with the Americans, even if they *begged* me. Father was right; I was best keeping well away from them – all of them, even Sam.

But fate had other ideas.

'No buts, no ifs, and no *I can'ts*,' Vera said the following morning, flinging a rectangle of paper down on my desk. 'You're coming with me, and that's that, even if I have to tie you up and drag you there. I'm fed up of seeing you moping around with a face like a month of wet Sundays.'

I gazed at the piece of paper. It was a printed invitation from the Americans to a dance at the camp at seven o'clock this Saturday evening – the night before my nineteenth birthday. Vera's name was written in a looping scrawl at the top, with *bring a friend!* scribbled at the bottom in the same hand.

'Where on earth did you get this?' I asked.

Vera waved a hand in the air. 'Oh, there's this soldier – George or John or something. He's rather sweet on me, I think.'

'Are you seeing him?'

Vera snorted. 'Not likely! He's good-looking, but much too sure of himself. I just let him think he might have a chance, is all.'

'Isn't that a bit... awkward?'

'Goodness me, no! It's jolly well worth it if you ask me. He's getting me some stockings next time I see him, and not nylons – silk!' Vera stretched out a shapely leg, eyeing it critically. 'Just as well, too. If these get any more holes in them I'm going to have to start colouring my legs with old tea leaves and painting seams up the backs with gravy browning like Elsie Hammond at the greengrocer's!'

I looked down at my own stockings. They were a mass of darns, sagging at the ankles. 'Oh, I'm sure he can get you some too,' Vera said, lighting a cigarette. 'I'll introduce you at the dance. Or perhaps *your* soldier can get you a few pairs.'

'He's not my soldier,' I said woodenly. 'Stop saying that. I haven't seen him again since that day he came here. And anyway, I can't go – I promised Father I'd have nothing to do with the Americans. And Saturday night is mine and Father's Monopoly night – you know that.'

'You are *not* spending Saturday night playing Monopoly.' Vera sounded positively outraged. 'That father of yours can spare you for one night – you know he can! And you don't have to tell him where you're going!'

Slight panic gripped me at the thought of lying to Father. 'But I don't have anything to wear,' I said. It was true: I didn't possess a single frock suitable for a dance. All my dresses were plain and patched, let down and let out, faded and threadbare.

'Leave that to me,' Vera said. 'You're coming to this dance and *that's that.*'

Just then, there was a knock at the door. Before either of us could say *come in*, it opened and Alfie Blythe stuck his head round. In one smooth movement Vera swept the invitation to the American dance into her bag.

'Oh, hullo, Alfie,' she said. 'Got anything for us?'

He handed over the usual bundle of post, but instead of leaving again, stood in front of my desk, knotting his fingers together.

'Help you, Alfie?' Vera said brightly.

Alfie looked straight at me. 'Er, you see, the thing is—'

My heart sank.

He cleared his throat, his Adam's apple bobbing. 'There's a dance at Dad's works on Saturday night. I, er, I was wondering if you might like to go with me, Ruby.'

He looked so hopeful that I felt like absolutely the worst person in the world as I stammered, 'I – I'm sorry, Alfie, but I can't. I – Vera and I are going to see a film.'

Alfie pressed his lips together and gave a curt little nod. 'I understand.' Before I could say anything else, he left, closing the door softly behind him.

Vera laughed.

I shook my head at her. 'Hush! He'll hear you!' I was still hot and cold all over with guilt.

'I'm sorry. But it's just too funny. The poor boy's *besotted* with you.'

I glared at her. 'He's *not*. Stop saying that! And it's not funny at *all*.'

'Oh, but it is. Don't you see? You'll *have* to come to the American dance now. Alfie only lives just down the lane from you – if he doesn't see you going out on Saturday night he'll think you were fobbing him off.'

I slumped back in my chair with a sigh. 'OK, you win.'

'Jolly good.' Vera gave a triumphant little smile. 'Now, let's work out what you're going to wear.'

That evening, I braced myself to talk to Father. 'Father, there's a dance on Saturday night…' I began as we ate our lamb chops.

'Oh?' he said, not looking up. As usual, he had a notepad on the table beside him and was frowning at it, his fork in his left hand and a mechanical pencil in his right. I remembered the time not so long ago when he'd stabbed the pencil into his potatoes by mistake, and I wondered if he might do it again. I felt slightly hysterical laughter bubbling up in my throat and swallowed hard.

66

'It's at the A – at Alfie's father's works,' I said, the lie tumbling smoothly out of my mouth.

'Well, I suppose you do need to let your hair down every now and then,' he said, scribbling something down. 'It can't be much fun, staying in with your aged father every Saturday night.'

He still didn't look up from his notes. I let out a silent, relieved sigh.

On Saturday evening after work I went back to Vera's to get ready. She rented a room at the top of one of the tall houses on the seafront, where she'd lived ever since coming to Devon from the Home Counties five years ago. When I'd first got to know her and she'd told me about herself, I'd been a little surprised she'd come here instead of going to work on a newspaper in London or another big city, but she'd said she used to visit an aunt and uncle in Devon when she was a child, and had wanted to live here ever since, so when the job at the *Herald* came up, she applied. 'Anyway,' she'd added with a wink, 'I always thought Bartonford could use a bit of glamour.'

Although I would've been nervous about bombing raids if I lived here, I loved to visit. The room was as different from the poky little cottage at Barton Hall as it was possible to get, large and airy, with windows set into the sloping ceiling looking out to the sea on one side and over the roofs of the town on the other. Although the furniture was old and shabby, Vera had draped bright silk scarves over the armchairs and a pretty shawl across the bed. There was a cheerful hooked rug on the floor, photos of Hollywood actors and actresses pinned to the walls, and a bright fire crackled in the grate.

Vera lent me her second-best dress, a dark green silk she'd bought in London just before the war. 'It's a tatty old thing really,' she said dismissively as I put it on, but it was a hundred times nicer than anything I owned: mid-calf length with short sleeves, fitted at the waist with a little belt and flared slightly at the hips. It had shoes to match, which Vera stuffed with newspaper to make them fit.

'No,' I said firmly when she advanced on me with her makeup case.

'But you can't go to a dance without anything on your face!'

'Really, Vera, I mustn't. I told Father I was going to the dance at Blythe's. He'll get suspicious if I—'

'Oh, do stop worrying about your bloody father,' she snorted. 'You can wash it off before you go home. He'll never know. Unless he's psychic?'

It was no use protesting. I closed my eyes and let Vera go to work. 'Where's all this from?' I asked as she expertly flicked a pencil through my brows. 'You can't get makeup *anywhere* these days.'

'A little bird.'

'A little *American* bird?'

I opened my eyes just in time to see one side of her mouth quirk up in a smile. 'Perhaps.'

When she'd finished, I went to look in the mirror, which was standing in the corner with another shawl draped over it.

'Wait!' Vera stepped in front of me, brandishing a bright red Max Factor Hollywood Tru-Color lipstick, which looked brand new as well. 'There,' she said after she'd slicked it onto my lips and shown me how to blot them with a tissue so the colour didn't smudge. She pulled the shawl off the mirror.

I gazed at my reflection, turning this way and that to get

a better look at myself. The green of the dress brought out copper highlights in my hair and lent a creamy tint to my pale skin, and Vera's expertly applied makeup made my eyes look enormous, and turned my mouth into an alluring Cupid's bow. I smiled. The girl in the mirror didn't look like me at all; she was extraordinarily, thrillingly grown up.

Vera smiled again. 'You'll do. And keep the lipstick. Birthday present for tomorrow.'

'Oh, no, I couldn't possibly—'

'You could and you will. No arguments.'

As we walked to the town square to catch the bus laid on by the Americans to take people up to the camp, nerves gripped me. What if Sam was there? What would I say to him? And – my stomach dropped momentarily – what if I bumped into Freddie or Gene? I kept my head down and my coat pulled close around me, not looking at anyone else in the queue. It seemed as if half the town was there. And I tried very hard not to think about Father, all alone back at the cottage, thinking I was at Blythe's Works with Alfie.

We arrived at the camp at half past seven. Until now, I'd only seen it from a distance. As we walked up to the gate, the towering wire fences around the perimeter loomed above us. *Keep out!* they seemed to say. *Keep away!*

'Vera, are you sure—' I began.

'I do hope there's something to eat,' Vera said over her shoulder to me as she handed our invitation to the guard on sentry duty. 'I'm *famished.*'

'Plenty for everyone,' the guard said with a wink, waving us into the camp.

'*Well.*' Vera straightened her jacket, smiling her Lauren Bacall smile.

As we made our way through the rows of huts and canvas tents, I heard music up ahead, bright and jazzy. My heart beat fast, keeping rhythm.

'Where on earth is the dance? In one of the huts?' I'd seen pictures of the insides of the American army's Nissen huts in Father's *Times*; I was trying to imagine the beds pushed back against the curving walls, a gramophone cranking out the latest dance tunes.

'Gosh, no! It's in the recreation hall,' Vera said.

'Recreation hall?' Then I remembered the dance hall old Tom Bidley had told me about the day I found out the Americans were coming to Bartonford.

We turned a corner and I saw another Nissen hut, an enormous one, with rows of windows along the sides – all blacked out, of course – and huge, roll-back steel doors, waves of music and voices escaping into the night every time they opened to admit someone. The inside was even more impressive. There were bright flags and bunting hanging from the ceiling, and a band – a real band! – performing on a stage at the back. The polished wooden dance floor was crowded with bodies, moving in time to the music, and lined up against one wall were tables groaning under the weight of more food than I'd seen all year: whole joints of meat, soft white bread, butter, grapes and oranges, even a pineapple, next to rows of bottles of what looked like dark-coloured, fizzy vinegar with *Coca-Cola* embossed on the sides.

More tables, with chairs pushed under them so people could sit down, had been arranged across the opposite side of the hall. Everything was bursting with colour and noise, as if someone had waved a magic wand over this tiny portion of drab, bomb-scarred Devon and brought it back to life for a night. I stood just inside the door, my nerves forgotten – the *war* forgotten – drinking it all in. I was relieved that Vera's green silk didn't look too shabby in comparison to the dresses the other women were wearing.

Then I spotted Freddie, weaving through the crowd towards us. All at once I felt as if someone had poured ice-cold seawater over me. *It was a mistake to come – a terrible mistake*, I thought desperately. *I should leave at once.* But I was rooted to the spot.

'Hey, gals, care to dance?' he said with a wide, white-toothed grin, staring at me. If he recognised me, he didn't give any indication. His eyes were as cold and expressionless as they had been the first time I met him.

No, don't! I wanted to shout as Vera said, 'Oh, why not,' and offered up an arm for Freddie to take. 'Don't look so downhearted, doll,' he said to me. 'I'll come back for you later.' A shudder went down my spine as he whirled Vera away, leaving me by myself.

I felt like an animal cornered in a cage, startled and staring. All I wanted was to go home – back to Monopoly and cocoa with Father – but the bus back into town wasn't until a quarter to ten, and the night was moonless and cloudy. It would be madness to try and walk home in the dark in these heels, and anyway, all my things were at Vera's. I was stuck here.

I edged through the people thronging the dance floor until I reached the food. A soldier was serving doorstop sandwiches, carving the meat off an enormous joint of hot beef so tender it was falling apart. Despite everything, my stomach growled. I couldn't remember the last time I'd had roast beef, or bread that didn't taste and look like it was made from sawdust and floor sweepings.

'Here you are, ma'am.' Before I knew what was happening the soldier had thrust a plate with a towering sandwich on it into my hand.

'Oh, I wasn't—' I protested, but he'd already moved on to someone else. Pink-cheeked and flustered, I picked up a bottle of Coca-Cola, wondering if it tasted better than it looked, and retreated to an empty table in the corner where I could hide. I had to admit, the sandwich *was* good. So was the Coca-Cola, although it was overpoweringly sweet and the bubbles tickled my nose.

'Er, hi.' Someone slid into the seat beside me.

8

SAM

I couldn't believe it. She was here. I stared at her, wondering what to do. Should I say hello? What if she gave me the brush-off again?

C'mon, Sam. Don't be such a damn coward, I told myself. I went over to her table. The band was so loud, I had to sit down next to her to make myself heard. 'Er, hi,' I said.

She looked up. Her eyes widened. 'Oh, hullo,' she stammered.

Hullo. That was a good start, wasn't it?

'It's Ruby, ain't it?' I cleared my throat. 'I mean, isn't it?' *Way to go, Sam, sounding like a hick.*

She nodded.

'I'm Sam. You might not remember me. I—'

'I do. You bought me that lead for Toffee. It was very kind – thank you. I should have said so at the time, but I was—' She shook her head, her cheeks flushing. 'Oh dear. You must have thought me terribly rude.'

'Aw, no. I thought I'd scared you, is all.'

Finally – *finally* – she smiled. 'No. You *did* startle me, though – I wasn't expecting you and your friend to turn up like that! I was so embarrassed about what happened on the beach.'

'Don't be. Dogs are always doing dumb stuff like that. I had one once called Lou. He was a big idiot, but I loved him.'

I looked down at the table, remembering for a moment. Ma had bought Lou for my seventh birthday, not long after we'd moved to the farm. He'd been brown and white with black spots, a mix of all sorts with long ears and stubby legs. He'd follow me – even to school if I'd let him – and slept on my bed at night. Kirk hated him. 'What use is a dog if it ain't gonna earn its keep?' he'd growl when Lou refused to hunt rats or rabbits. One morning, I woke up and Lou wasn't there. I'd found his body out by the chicken sheds, stiff and cold, his mouth open in an agonised snarl and froth on his lips. 'Musta got into the rat poison,' Kirk had said, but I knew. I *knew*. It was the way he'd been smirking as he said it. I didn't want another dog after that. I was too heartbroken, too scared it would happen again.

'Oh, he's not mine.' Ruby's voice jolted me back to the present. 'He's my neighbour's. She has rheumatism, so I walk him for her. He is a nice little dog, though.' She gave me another of those smiles – warm, kinda shy – and that spark lit up inside me again, just like the first time we met.

Damn.

'Sorry for startling you, then. It was dumb of me to turn up like that.' I was speaking too fast, trying to cover up how flustered I felt.

'Oh, I didn't mind, not really. It's just my father—' She clamped her lips shut, as if to stop herself saying something she shouldn't.

Of course. 'Your pa's in charge of the newspaper?' I asked, remembering the guy with the side-whiskers.

'Oh, goodness, no. That's Mr Howlett – Howler, we call him.' She gave a brittle laugh. 'My father's a doctor – a psychiatrist. He works at Barton Hall, the military hospital up on the hill – we live there, too.'

I frowned. 'So why would he—'

'He's – it's complicated. He worries about me.'

'But he let you come tonight?'

She gave a little shrug and looked down at her plate, picking up crumbs with the end of her finger. 'Not exactly. He thinks I'm somewhere else.'

'Ah,' I said.

We were interrupted by a sudden commotion on the dance floor nearby. A girl's voice – British – cried out sharply, 'I say, do you mind?'

I looked round to see the woman who'd let us in when Jimmy and I turned up at Ruby's office, Vera, glaring at Freddie Gardner. It looked as if they'd been dancing together. Freddie was grinning; I guess he'd been putting his hands somewhere they weren't wanted. He shrugged and said something I couldn't hear over the music. Vera tossed her head back and walked away. Ruby started to get up. 'That's my friend – I should see if she's OK.'

But Vera had already turned to talk to Stanley Novak, laughing and touching his arm. The smile slid off Gardner's face. Ruby sat back down, looking relieved.

Oh, crap. Gardner was approaching our table, grinning again. 'Hey, doll, looks like your friend got tired of me,' he said to Ruby. 'Wanna have that dance now? Or are you gonna run away again?'

'No thank you.' Ruby's voice was stiff; under her makeup, the colour had drained out of her face. What was wrong?

'She's with me,' I said quickly. Gardner's gaze flicked over to me like I was an annoying bug. 'Aw, c'mon,' he said to Ruby. 'You ain't telling me a pretty lil' thing like you can't dance. Maybe I can teach you.'

He sounded so much like Kirk when that bastard tried to turn on the charm it made my guts twist. 'Actually, we were just going out for some fresh air,' I said. 'Weren't we?'

Ruby shot me a grateful look and nodded. We stood and made for a side door near the stage, leaving Gardner to glower after us.

Outside, I fetched an upturned wooden crate and pushed it against the side of the hut, draping my jacket across it so Ruby wouldn't get splinters in her dress. She slumped onto it, letting out her breath in a whoosh. '*Thank* you.'

'No problem.' I peered at her in the darkness. 'You met that guy before or something?'

She gave me a weak smile. 'In a manner of speaking, yes.'

Haltingly, she told me about how she'd left work early a few days ago and was cornered in an alleyway by Gardner and his pal Gene Trubman. 'It was horrible,' she said. 'They seemed to think I was some sort of... of *possession*, or something.'

'Gardner's an idiot,' I said. 'Thinks he's someone 'cause his daddy's a high-up in the army. Don't let him rattle you. Will your friend be OK?'

'Oh, he picked on the wrong one there.' Ruby gave a little chuckle. 'Vera can look after herself.'

'You wanna go back in?'

'Do you mind if we stay out here for a while? It's rather nice.'

She was right; it *was* nice. The night was surprisingly mild, and over the muffled sound of the band inside the hut I could hear the waves crashing against the shore below the camp. There was no moon, but every now and then the clouds parted to give a view of the stars, which were sprayed across the sky like silver paint. The ground was dry so I sat down beside Ruby's crate and crossed my legs, resting my arms on my knees.

'So, Sam, er—' Ruby said. 'Gosh – I don't even know your surname.'

'Sam Archer.' Awkwardly, I held up a hand for her to shake. 'Pleased to meet you, ma'am. And you are…?'

She laughed again. 'Ruby Mottram. Pleased to meet you too, Sam Archer. So what brings you to Devon? I mean – of course, you're in the army, I know that, but what made you decide to join up?'

I wondered how much to tell her. 'I needed the money,' I said at last. 'My ma and I – we don't have much. And I have a little sister, too. I had a job but it didn't make enough.'

'What about your father?' she asked.

'He's dead.'

'Oh, I'm sorry. Trust me to put my foot in it.'

'Naw, it's OK. He died before I was born.'

'So it's just you and your mother and your sister?'

'Yeah.' I turned my face away, scowling into the darkness. 'And my stepfather.'

'Oh.'

I didn't say anything else. Even thinking about Kirk felt like summoning the Devil.

'That makes two of us, I suppose,' she said at last. 'Although in my case it's my mother who's not here anymore – she died when I was a baby.'

'I'm sorry,' I said.

'Oh, it's OK. I don't really remember her.'

I attempted to steer the conversation onto safer ground. 'So how did you end up working at a newspaper? You enjoy it?'

'I suppose so. I don't exactly do any writing, though. That's Vera's job. Mine is mostly checking through the small ads and announcements before I type them up and give them to Dobbsy, I mean, Mrs Dobbs – she's Howler's sister; I suppose you'd call her the subeditor these days – so she can go through it all. I long to be a proper reporter, though. It must be so exciting!'

'Don't you ever get to go out on a story?' I asked.

'I do if Vera wants me to come and help her, but usually I'm stuck in the office. I do all sorts of other jobs there, too – I have to, because most of the staff were called up.'

'Hope they don't work you too hard.'

'Oh, no, it's all right. I mean, I do get awfully tired – I'm an ARP warden too and sometimes when I get to work I could happily curl up under my desk and sleep all day! But I get every Sunday off unless there's some sort of emergency, and the pay's not bad. I'm sure I'll get to do some real writing one day.'

I couldn't remember what we talked about after that, only that we talked about everything, laughing like loons one minute, serious and heartfelt the next. It was as if I'd known Ruby forever, which was crazy, because how was it possible to feel like that about someone you'd only just met properly?

Suddenly, Ruby jumped up. 'Goodness, we must have been sitting out here all night – Vera will be going frantic!'

I got up too. 'Let's go find her.'

But before we went back in the hall, I caught her arm. 'Say, could I see you again?'

'I—' She paused. 'It's difficult for me to get away.'

'I know, your pa. But he lets you leave the house, right?'

'It's not just that. He – he doesn't really approve of the Americans.'

'Doesn't approve of us? Why not?'

'He thinks – oh, it's silly really, but there's been stories in the papers and, well, once he gets an idea in his head…'

'What about when you're walking that dog for Mrs What's-her-face? Couldn't we meet up then?'

Just able to make her out in the starlit darkness, I saw her bite her lip. 'This is a small town – everyone knows each other. If someone saw us, and told him…'

'Isn't there somewhere we could go where no one would see us?'

I realised, too late, how that sounded, and felt my face go hot. 'I mean, just so we can talk and all,' I added quickly. *Please don't say no*, I begged her inside my head.

She bit her lip again.

'Hey, what about that little beach at the foot of the cliffs just out of town?' I said. 'There's a couple of caves there – I found them on a walk a few days ago – you know the place, right?'

'A cave? You must mean Wreckers Cove,' she said. 'That's the only place around here with caves. A long time ago, people used to hide there and shine lights to lure ships onto the rocks.'

'Well, how about it? It's a bit of a scramble to get down there, but it's private.'

She paused; I could tell she was thinking about it.

'Could you make it next Sunday morning?' I asked gently. 'Say, about ten o'clock?'

She hesitated again. Then she said, 'I – I could try.'

A smile broke across my face. 'I'll send you a message.'

She turned to face me. 'All right, but *don't* send it to Barton Hall – Father might see it and want to know who it's from. Send it to the office.'

I nodded, and followed her back into the hall, where she was pounced on almost immediately by Vera. '*There* you are! I've been looking all over for you! We must go – we'll miss the bus!'

When she saw me behind her, she raised one eyebrow slightly. Ruby flushed. It made her look prettier than ever. *We were just talking*, I wanted to say, but at that moment the band struck up again, louder than ever, making anything except yelling at the top of my lungs impossible.

Glancing over her shoulder at me, Ruby followed Vera out of the hall. I watched her go, feeling an absurd sense of loss, as if I was watching her walk away forever.

Eight days until I saw her again. *Eight days*. It felt like a lifetime. I just hoped she didn't change her mind before then.

9

RUBY

'Spill,' Vera said the minute we got off the bus in the middle of town and were walking back to her flat, pointing the meagre beams from our covered torches at the ground so we wouldn't draw the wrath of whoever was on blackout duty tonight. 'Who is he?'

'There's nothing *to* spill,' I said. 'His name's Sam. Sam Archer. We were talking, that's all.'

'*All night.*'

'Yes—'

'What on earth about?'

'I – I don't remember, exactly. This and that. We forgot the time.'

'*This and that*, eh? Are you seeing him again?'

A wave of hot and cold went through me as I remembered how I'd more or less agreed to the clandestine meeting next Sunday. What had I been thinking? I hardly knew him. It was madness – utter madness. If Father so much as got wind of it...

'Well?' Vera nudged me, grinning.

'Yes, but—' Fresh panic gripped me suddenly. 'Oh, he said he'd get a message to me, and I asked him to send it to the office so Father wouldn't see it – but Alfie will!'

'So? How's Alfie going to know who it's from?'

'How many letters arrive at the *Herald* personally addressed to me? And from the American camp? He's sure to put two and two together – I told him I was going out tonight—'

'You worry too much – who cares what Alfie thinks?'

'I don't, but—'

Vera stopped and put her hands on my arms. 'Ruby, you're allowed to have some fun. It's high time you did. And you shouldn't let feeling guilty about that father of yours, or Alfie Blythe, or anyone else for that matter, stop you. For goodness' sake, you're *nineteen* tomorrow.'

I sighed. 'I know.' And I *had* had fun tonight – more fun than I could remember having for an awfully long time.

After I'd changed back into my own clothes and washed my face, Vera walked with me to the edge of town, where I told her I'd be OK to go the rest of the way back to Barton Hall by myself. It was a quiet night; all I could hear was the rustling of small creatures in the hedgerows and the occasional hoot of an owl, hunting over the fields. At the end of my lane, breathing hard from the slog up the hill, I heard footsteps approaching and saw a faint circle of light from another dimmed-out torch moving along the ground. 'Who goes there?' someone called in a stern voice.

'Alfie? Is that you?' I said.

We met just outside his gate. 'Oh, hullo, Ruby,' he said, and snapped off the torch. I could hardly see him, but I could smell the faint odour of hair cream and stale tobacco clinging to him.

'Did you enjoy your dance?' I asked.

'Yes, thank you. It was very entertaining. Did you enjoy your film, then?' I could hear the question in his voice.

'Oh, yes, it was great fun.' I was relieved he couldn't see me blushing.

He gave a slightly hollow laugh. 'To be honest, you didn't miss much, not coming to the dance. Jennie Pearson's brother was there and he got in a terrific fight with one of the other men. The other chap was saying things about Jennie, apparently. Though I can hardly blame people for talking about her,' he added with a prim little sniff.

I felt a flash of irritation. What right did Alfie have to be so judgemental? It wasn't poor Jennie's fault that the soldier she'd been seeing had decided he wanted nothing to do with her. If he'd had even the smallest shred of decency, he'd have married her immediately. I thought back to sitting outside the rec hall with Sam, and felt a wave of heat go through me as I imagined, just for a second, what it would be like if that was me in that position. I couldn't help it.

For goodness' sake, think of something else, Ruby! I told myself sternly. Quickly, I steered the conversation onto safer ground. Alfie and I talked for a little while longer, exchanging chit-chat. It all felt rather forced; I couldn't help comparing this to talking to Sam; with him, the words had simply flowed, and I'd felt as if I could tell him anything. I was tired now, and itching to go to bed, but I couldn't think of a way to get away from Alfie without seeming rude.

'Gosh, I nearly forgot – I have something for you, Ruby,' he said. 'Will you wait here a moment?'

Before I could answer, he'd gone, dashing back to his own house. Rather drearily, I wondered what it was this time –

more eggs? A few moments later, he returned, and thrust a small package, wrapped in brown paper and string, into my hands. 'This is for tomorrow, for your birthday. There's a card from Annie, too.'

I felt a stab of guilt for being so uncharitable. 'Thank you. That's very kind of you.' I slipped the package into my handbag, nestling it next to the lipstick Vera had given me. 'I must go in now – Father will be waiting.'

'OK. Well, happy birthday,' Alfie said gruffly.

Father was in the parlour, reading a book, a fire glowing in the grate to ward off the damp inside the cottage. 'Did you have a nice time?' he said mildly, but the frown lines on his forehead betrayed his anxiety. 'I was starting to wonder where you'd got to.'

'I'm sorry, Father,' I said. 'I was just out in the lane, talking to Alfie.'

'Well, as long as you're all right.' He got up. 'Would you like some cocoa?'

'Yes please.'

We sat by the fire with our mugs and chatted, mostly about Father's work. Normally it would have been cosy in here with the fire crackling, but tonight I felt as if the thick walls of the cottage were pressing in on me. I didn't want chit-chat; I wanted to talk about things that *mattered*, to laugh until my belly hurt and I could hardly breathe again, like I had with Sam.

I didn't remember Alfie's present until I'd changed into my nightgown and was about to get into bed. It was a small wooden box, beautifully carved, its lid painted with a delicate pattern of autumn leaves. He must have done it himself. Remembering Vera's words earlier today – *The poor boy's* besotted *with you* – my stomach clenched. For one awful, heart-stopping moment, I thought there was going to be something inside, like a necklace or a bracelet, but to my relief, it was empty. I slid it into the back of the drawer where I kept my underwear, not wanting to look at it. I put Annie's card – a childish picture of a birthday cake that she'd drawn herself on some brown paper – on my dressing table.

My last thought before I drifted into sleep was *Sam, Sam.*

As always, my birthday passed quietly. Father bought me a new watch, and Mrs-Baxter-down-the-lane surprised me with a skein of wool when I went to collect Toffee for his walk. I took him to Wreckers Cove to look at the caves.

The path down to the cove was narrow and steep, thick with gorse and brambles, which tore at my jumper as I pushed through them. People said the caves were a spooky place, but I'd never thought so. Certainly, they were populated by ghosts, but I'd always quite liked the way the spirits of the past seemed to gather around, as if to say, *I was real, once, like you!* When I could – which wasn't very often – I came here to think, or to read.

I tried to imagine myself here with Sam, wondering when – *if* – he'd send me a message. What if he forgot about me, or started seeing some other girl? What if he was seeing someone else already? I heard Father's voice inside my head: *...only after one thing...* and panic bubbled up inside me. He was wrong – Sam wasn't like that, I *knew* he wasn't – but all the same, I couldn't help thinking of Jennie Pearson. I'm sure she thought that about *her* soldier too, before everything went wrong.

Thankfully, the next few days were so busy that I didn't have time to stew over things. There was the usual rush to go to press on Wednesday – all of us at the *Herald* had to work late, and then I was on duty and there was the inevitable air raid. Luckily, this one turned out to be uneventful and when I got home, Father was sound asleep. On Thursday, I stumbled into the office, yawning. Vera had made us each a strong mug of tea, and there were already two piles of envelopes waiting for me on my desk. I couldn't face the announcements just yet, so I started on the advertisements. 'You'd think people could manage without cooks and maids while there's a war on,' I grumbled as I carefully slit the envelopes.

Vera was scowling at a piece of copy, a pencil stuck in her hair. 'I wish *I* had a maid,' she said, rather savagely. 'She could write this bloody story about the Bartonford harvest festival for me and I could have a couple of hours' kip!'

Making sympathetic noises, I opened the next envelope.

A thin slip of paper fell out. The advertisement was just a couple of lines long, written in a neat, slightly backwards-sloping hand:

> WANTED – *red jewel. Caves Sunday* 10 *o'clock?*
> *(If no emergency!) S*

Frowning, I read the message two times, then a third. Who was this mysterious 'S'? And why on earth did they want a red jewel? Racking my brains, I tried to work it out, but I was too muddled with exhaustion for it to make any sense. Perhaps it had come here by mistake. Perhaps it was a top-secret note from the army that had gone astray, or from the Americans, or...

Oh.

Oh.

Heat flooded my face. I glanced at Vera. She was engrossed, her scowl more ferocious than ever. I thought about showing her the message, but something stopped me. I folded the slip of paper and slid it into my pocket.

Red jewel – that was a ruby. *Ruby.* Me. And 'S', of course, was Sam. He'd sent a message, just as he'd promised.

Back at the cottage that evening, I read the slip of paper several more times before crumpling it up and dropping it into the stove, watching as the flames licked around its edges until it was nothing more than smoke and ash.

I began laying my plans on Saturday, asking Mrs-Baxter-down-the-lane if she'd like me to take Toffee for an extra-long walk the next day. 'Oh, yes please, dear,' she said. 'He ate one of my butter ration coupons this morning! He's always so naughty when he's been cooped up.'

Toffee grinned innocently at me through his ginger whiskers as if to say, *Who, me?*

Sunday morning dawned cold but sunny. It felt as if I'd never get away – there was breakfast to make, the dishes to do, the beds to straighten. And just to make matters worse, there was a story in Father's *Times* about a group of GIs in London getting involved in a brawl. 'Disgraceful!' he spluttered, scowling at the newspaper as he sat in his armchair to read it after breakfast. 'I do hope they won't start any trouble like that here. And if they do, I absolutely forbid you to report on it – you must tell your editor I say so!'

My fingers tightened around the teapot handle as I poured him another cup of tea, but somehow I kept my demeanour calm. 'Of course, Father,' I said.

His scowl disappeared and he flashed me a quick smile, patting my hand. 'I'm glad you're such a sensible girl, Ruby. I must admit, I was terribly worried when these Americans first arrived here, but I can see I had nothing to be concerned about.'

Oh, God, maybe I should just call the whole thing off today, I thought with a surge of panic and guilt. Mentally, I gave myself a little shake. I was going to see Sam again, and nothing was going to stop me. Sam wasn't like those soldiers; he *wasn't*.

Finally, at a quarter to ten, I was able to grab my coat and bag and head down the lane. As I was walking down Mrs Baxter's front path, Toffee pulling at the lead, Alfie's front door opened rather suddenly. 'Ruby! Off out?'

Oh *no*.

'I saw you from, um, upstairs,' he said, his cheeks flushing a little. 'I wondered if you might like some company? Mother has a headache, so we're not going to church this morning.'

I frowned. Had he been watching out for me? 'That's awfully kind of you, Alfie. But I – I'd prefer to be alone today. I'm feeling a bit – you know—'

He frowned too.

Hastily, I added, 'But perhaps we can go for a walk another time?'

'Oh. OK,' he said, looking crestfallen.

Then Annie appeared. Now ten, she looked like a miniature version of Alfie with pigtails and dirty knees sticking out from under her dress. 'Hullo, Ruby!' she said, grinning. 'Do you want to come and see my chickens? I've got three of my own now!'

'Hullo, Annie. A – another time,' I stammered, aware of

Alfie looking keenly at me. I could feel the minutes whizzing past, and every muscle in my body was tensed with wanting to get away. Toffee was busy sniffing something by Mrs-Baxter-down-the-lane's gate. 'I'll see you later, Alfie,' I said firmly, and dragged Toffee away, feeling Alfie's gaze boring into me all the way along the street. *He knows, he knows!* I thought, and had to tell myself not to be so ridiculous.

I hurried up to the path above Bartonford Beach, which led around the headland to the cove. I didn't know what time it was now, but I was going to be late. Would Sam wait for me? Would he even turn up?

By the time I reached Wreckers Cove I was pink-faced and breathless. I let Toffee off his lead and he immediately caught the scent of something. With a sharp little bark, he disappeared into the gorse, leaving me on my own.

The cove was deserted. I sat down on a boulder just inside the entrance of the largest cave – the only one that was big enough to stand upright in – gazing out at the sea. It was completely silent save for the gentle lapping of the waves, the faint roaring of blood pulsing in my ears and a magpie chattering somewhere. The air was still and cool and a silvery veil of mist hung over the water, the autumn sun not quite strong enough to burn it away.

I should have got here sooner, I thought. *He thought I couldn't be bothered – he's given up and gone.* I was startled at how disappointed I felt.

Then I heard a shower of stones clatter down onto the beach. As I jumped to my feet, Sam appeared in the entrance to the cave.

IO

SAM

'Sorry!' I said. 'I couldn't get away.'

'Oh, don't worry, I was late too – I thought you'd been and gone.' Ruby was smiling; I was grinning like a loon, relieved she hadn't given up and gone.

'Well, we're here now, I guess. So you got my message? I was scared you wouldn't understand it, or it'd fall into enemy hands.'

She grinned again. 'That was very clever of you.'

'It's all that army training.'

'Really? Do they teach you things like that?'

'Nah.' I laughed at her serious expression. 'My little sister and I – we went through a phase of writing notes in code when I was younger. Just a dumb game, really – it helped keep her busy when—'

I trailed off, my grin fading as I remembered the elaborate distractions I used to create to keep Meggie out of the way when Kirk was laying into Ma. I'd never been sure who needed them more – her or me. Now, there was no one to distract her.

Don't think about that.

'This place is incredible,' I said, tilting my head back to look up at the roof of the cave, arching high above us. 'You could live in here.'

We went a little further into the cave to get out of the wind, and that little dog – Toffee, wasn't he called? – came running in. He bounded up to me, tail wagging, and I had to fend off a shower of licks. A few seconds later he heard something and was off outside again.

Ruby and I sat down on some rocks that had been worn smooth by the tide. All of a sudden, I was positively tongue-tied. I had no idea why; it had been so easy to talk to her at the dance. Here, we were completely on our own, and it felt different, somehow.

'There's gonna be another dance next weekend,' I said at last. 'D'you think you can come?'

'Oh, I'd love that!' Ruby smiled again. Then her face fell a little. 'That's if I can get away, of course.'

'Your pa being difficult?'

She gazed at her feet. 'He's not difficult, exactly. It's just – oh, I don't know. I didn't exactly tell him where I was last Saturday. I pretended I was somewhere else. I don't know why I lied to him. No, of course I do. It's because he's got such a – a *grudge* against anything and anybody American and he'd go absolutely mad if he knew I was here with you. But I'm not sure he'll believe me if I say the same thing again.'

I let out a low whistle. 'That sounds hard. Why does he hate Americans so much?'

She gave a strained little laugh. 'That's just it. I honestly have no idea. I mean, there's stories in the paper every now and then about GIs getting drunk and starting brawls or breaking shop windows, but that's not exactly exclusive to Americans, is it? And I suppose there's all the uproar about Jennie Pearson, but Father was against the Americans before all that happened—'

'Who's Jennie Pearson?'

'A girl I used to go to school with. She was seeing a soldier up at the camp and, well…' She flushed. 'Let's just say she got herself in a spot of bother, and instead of marrying her like he should have done, the soldier's dropped her like a hot potato. I feel awfully sorry for her – he's got away scot-free while she's being gossiped about all over town.'

'Well, I'm pretty sure that sorta thing ain't exclusive to Americans either,' I said drily.

'Oh, you don't need to tell me that! But it's not exactly helped change Father's mind.'

'Well, I guess. But even if he did find out about us he can't stop you seeing me, right? I mean, you're what? Twenty?'

She made a face. 'He is *not* going to find out about us. And, goodness me, no. Nowhere near. I just turned nineteen.'

'Really? When?'

'Last Sunday.'

'So it was your birthday the day after the dance? You shoulda said!'

She shrugged. 'It doesn't matter. It's always a quiet sort of day.'

'Jeez. I turn eighteen in January and I'm gonna…'

Crap. I shut my mouth with a snap.

Ruby frowned at me. 'Don't you already have to be eighteen to join up? Or is that only over here?'

I couldn't meet her gaze.

'Sam?'

'I lied,' I said. 'Paid some guy to sign a form saying I was of age. So did my pal Jimmy. Listen, Ruby, you can't tell anyone – if they find out, I'm done for. They'll send me back, court-martial me, maybe even throw me in jail. And I *need* this. Otherwise there'll be no money to send Ma and Meggie. They'll starve—'

'Of *course* I won't tell anyone! Why would I? Gosh, Sam, don't look so worried. Your secret's safe with me!'

I let out the breath I hadn't realised I was holding. 'Thanks.'

She leaned back, crossing her legs and hooking her hands around her knee. I took out my notebook. 'Stay like that, I wanna draw you,' I said. There was something about the way she was sitting that had me itching to get her down on the page. A shaft of sunlight was slanting into the cave, making a halo around the edges of her hair.

'I didn't know you were an artist,' she said as I sketched.

'I'm not. It's just a – a *thing*. Don't you have a thing?'

She frowned, although she didn't move. 'A thing?'

'Like drawing, or music, or writing, or—'

Her frown deepened. 'I do like to read, I suppose – it's why I wanted to work at the paper. I thought I might want to be a writer once upon a time, but...'

I sketched the slope of her nose, the tilt of her chin. Toffee reappeared, tail wagging, then rushed off again. I tried to capture him too, a few quick lines in a corner of the page.

'I used to write poems,' she continued, haltingly. 'But I – I showed them to someone and they – they didn't think they were very good.'

'What? Who? And who the hell do they think they are?' The words burst out of me before I could stop them. 'Sorry. It's none of my business. But – for real?'

She lifted one shoulder in a tiny shrug. 'I'm sure he was right. If I *was* any good, I'd be allowed to write proper stories for the paper, not be consigned to typing up adverts and obituaries. Here – let me see.' Before I could stop her, she snatched my sketchbook. 'What do you mean, you're not an artist? That's *fantastic*!'

'Aw, no.' As she flicked through the pages, my face grew warm.

'Oh, I *love* these!' She'd reached the pictures I drew for Meggie that day in the barn before I joined up. 'You should illustrate books!'

Now it was my turn to shrug. 'One day, maybe.'

'One day, *definitely*.' She handed the sketchbook back to me.

Smiling, still embarrassed, I shoved the sketchbook back in my pocket.

'What does your mother think about you joining up?' she said. 'Doesn't she worry about you?'

My gaze slid away from hers again. 'I didn't tell her, exactly. I mean, she knows now, because I send her a check every time I get paid. That is – I send them to the guy I used to work for and ask him to pass them on. If I sent them to the farm my stepfather'd drink 'em away and not give her a cent.'

'I'm sorry,' Ruby said. 'It must be difficult, being this far away from her.'

I hunched my shoulders. 'It's Meggie I worry about. She's so young, and Ma don't protect her like she should – she's too scared of Kirk, I guess. As soon as I've got enough dough and they let me go back home, I'm getting them both outta there, and that bas—' I stopped myself from swearing just in time. 'That *guy* can go jump in the Rappahannock River.'

We were silent for a moment, listening to the crashing of the sea. I looked up at the roof of the cave again. 'You ever wish you were someone else, living a different life?' I said.

'Oh, gosh, all the time.' Ruby's tone was so vehement, it made me look round at her again. 'Don't get me wrong, I love Father,' she added hastily, her cheeks flushing, 'but the older I get, the more I feel responsible for him, and it sounds awful but sometimes the thought of looking after him for the rest of my life makes me want to *scream*. It's like someone tightening a chain around my neck, just a tiny bit each day.'

I was going to say, *What's he gonna do if you get married?* but then I caught sight of my watch. I jumped to my feet. 'Jeez – I gotta get back.'

I reached down to help Ruby up. As she took my hand, I caught her eye, and suddenly the air between us was crackling with that same electricity I'd felt the first time we met. It was exciting – dangerous – as if anything could happen.

In a blur of ginger fur, Toffee appeared and barged between us, tail wagging frantically. The electric feeling melted away.

'We'd better leave separately, just in case,' Ruby said. 'You go first – I'll follow. And about the dance, Sam – I don't know if I can make it. Probably not, to be honest. I'm sorry.'

'That's OK. But hey – we can do *this* again, right?'

One corner of her mouth lifted in a smile as she bent to clip the dog's leash onto his collar. 'I don't see why not. After all, Toffee *does* need his walks. Especially on Sundays.'

'Don't let anyone else look at those adverts first. I'll send a message as soon as I can.'

Her smile widened into a grin. 'I won't.'

'Oh, and Ruby?'

She looked expectantly at me.

'Write your poems.'

'Oh, no, really—'

'Whoever said you weren't good enough, screw – I mean, don't listen to him. Here.' I took my sketchbook from my pocket again and carefully tore out my drawing. 'Write *me* something. I'll give you this as an advance payment.'

She folded the piece of paper carefully, as if it were a hundred-dollar bill, and slid it into the pocket of her skirt. 'All right,' she said. 'I can't promise anything, but I'll try.'

II

RUBY

October–November

Back at the cottage, I put Sam's drawing in Alfie's box, folding it into a tiny square and burying the box in my underwear drawer again. Sam's words echoed in my head and I remembered the day I'd shown Alfie my poems – a day I'd tried hard to forget.

It was a few weeks after the war had broken out and I'd started working at the newspaper. Alfie and I had gone for a walk through town to the gardens; his mother had taken in two evacuees, so he took every opportunity he could to escape.

In my pocket was an old exercise book. I'd spent the evening before going over some poems and short stories. They needed work, but I didn't think they were *too* bad. I'd already been quite friendly with Vera by then, and had been wondering if I dared ask her to read them – and if she might know somewhere I could send them when they were finished.

To bolster up my courage, I'd decided to show them to Alfie first.

We'd sat down on a bench near the fountain. I'd watched him flick through the pages, half sick with a swirling mixture of panic and hope. What would he think? *Were* they good enough?

Soon – too soon? – he'd shut the book with a slap and handed it back to me.

'Are – are they OK?' I'd asked him.

He'd given me a smile. 'Oh, yes, they're fine.'

'F – fine?'

'Yes – *fine*. I mean, it's something you do for fun, isn't it? Like knitting. Or whittling sticks.'

I'd known he didn't mean to be unkind; I'd tried to smile back at him, but all the hours I'd poured into those words between the covers – all those pieces of my soul – had turned to cinders at his words. Back home, I'd dropped the notebook into the stove, my eyes brimming with tears. Apart from my work at the *Herald*, I'd not written a word since.

I'd wanted to, of course – at times, it felt as if I might burst with it – but every time I thought about trying again I remembered what Alfie had said. *Fine. Fun. Like whittling sticks.*

The next day, at work, I found an old accounts book, only half used. 'Oh, take it,' Vera said. 'I won't tell anyone about it if you don't.' But every time I opened it, that same old paralysis crept over me, and the unused pages in the book remained blank.

Then the letter from Grandmother arrived.

All our post went to the main house. Father brought the letter home one evening, and I recognised the looping handwriting on the front at once. My stomach twisted. At dinner, I waited, holding my breath, while Father slit the envelope with his butter knife and read the single, thin sheet of paper inside.

'I'm afraid it rather looks as if Mother is coming to visit,' he said, handing it to me.

My dearest Cecil, the letter said. *I write to you with terrible, terrible news. The Allied forces are coming to Tyneham. They say they wish to use the surrounding area for training, and we are all to be turned out of our homes like vagrants.*

When I think of all I have done here and the years I spent in service up at Tyneham House I could weep, but of course that means nothing to the people who have posted horrid notices up everywhere telling us that we must leave by 19th December as it will no longer be safe for us to remain.

I do not know when I will be able to return so I ask that you extend your hospitality to me for as long as you feel able. Of course if you are too busy with your work to accommodate me I shall try to make arrangements to go elsewhere, but where that might be, I do not know.

I eagerly await your reply by return of post.

Yours in hope,

Mother

P.S. I hope the child is well.

The child. She didn't even mention my name. Inwardly, I sighed; it was no more than I'd come to expect from Grandmother, yet it never failed to sting.

I gave the letter back to him. 'But where will she sleep?'

My heart sank as I waited for his reply, because I already knew exactly what he was going to say.

He gave me a small, apologetic smile. 'I'm afraid she'll have to share your room. There's nowhere else, not if she's staying for an indefinite amount of time, and there's no question of putting her in the main house – we're full up with patients, and there are more coming in every day.'

I knew it was useless to argue, or to point out that Grandmother had managed perfectly well on a truckle bed in the parlour when she'd visited before. How long would she be staying this time? Until the end of the war, I expected – and who knew when that would be?

'I shall write back and tell her she must come here as soon as possible,' Father said, sounding as resigned as I felt, and folded the letter neatly back into its envelope.

'Can't you put her, I dunno, in your air raid shelter or something?' Sam said, his breath turning to clouds of vapour in the chilly air. It was the following Sunday; we were sitting in the cave.

'Of course not!' I said. 'There's no light – no way to keep warm – a permanent puddle of water in the bottom – even rats, sometimes—'

'I was kidding!' Sam held his hands up. He had a khaki muffler around his neck, his collar turned up and his cap pulled down low over his eyes. It had been raining steadily all morning. The coast path was cloaked in fog, and although it was dry inside the cave, I was so cold my fingers had gone numb.

'Oh. Sorry.' I hunched my shoulders.

'She's really that bad, huh?'

I gave a bitter little laugh. Where to start? For most of her adult life, Grandmother, who had brought Father up alone after my grandfather's death, had worked as a lady's maid for the Bonds, the family who owned Tyneham Manor. She was still, as she liked to tell anyone who would listen, a *pillar of the community*, with neatly curled hair – now snow-white – and a penchant for twinsets in muted tones of heather and brown. Although Tyneham was a primitive sort of place compared to Bartonford – there was only one house with running water, and the school had closed years ago because there weren't any pupils – she kept her cottage as neat as a new pin, the gardens front and back filled with flowers and vegetables.

Ever since I was old enough to notice the way she looked at me – suspicious and watchful, like a cat with a mouse – I'd known she wasn't a bit like other people's grandmothers. She didn't hug me, read me stories, or bring me toys or sweets. I was the reason her son had the unbearable burden, as she had had, of bringing up a child alone. But even worse, I was a girl, one who carried the double affliction of being clever *and* plain. 'Look at her with her nose in a book!' I'd heard her complain to Father on more than one occasion as I sat in a corner, trying not to be noticed. 'She'll never marry, that one!'

I tried to explain some of this to Sam. It sounded rather feeble, but he nodded, as if he understood. 'Maybe you should lock her up in that hospital somewhere,' he said. Another wry smile told me he didn't mean that either; not quite.

I tried to smile back.

'You're shivering.' He stripped off his coat and wrapped it

around my shoulders. It smelled like him: a comforting blend of damp wool, cinnamon gum and tobacco. 'Here.'

I tried to give it back. 'I can't – you'll freeze!'

'I'll be fine. I need to toughen up anyway, for when...'

He trailed off.

'Do you know when you'll be going over to France?'

He shook his head. 'Next year sometime, I reckon. No one's telling us anything much.'

I frowned. After the British Army were evacuated from Dunkirk three and a half years ago, the trickle of patients arriving at Barton Hall had, briefly, turned into a flood, and although Father always discouraged me from having any contact with the patients, it had been impossible to avoid them. I'd see them in the grounds or the workshops, or being wheeled about by nurses: men with arms and legs missing, or their faces half hidden by bandages to cover terrible wounds and scars. Then there was the ones Father treated – the ones so traumatised by their experiences that it was their minds that had broken. What if that happened to Sam? What if he was maimed or killed? What if he was driven mad?

Some of this must have shown on my face, because Sam shrugged and said, 'Anyway, I'm not gonna worry about it. Whatever's happens, it's ages away.'

Then he sneezed three times in quick succession.

Despite his protests, I made him take back his coat. 'We can't carry on meeting here,' I said. 'It'd be fine if the weather was warmer, or if there was a stove we could light or something, but if we carry on like this we'll both end up with pneumonia!'

'Couldn't we light a fire?'

'Someone might see the smoke. Anyway, isn't it dangerous to light a fire inside a cave?'

'Where can we go, then, if you don't want anyone seeing us?'

I tried to think. Town was out of the question, of course. And I couldn't go up to the camp on my own, even during the day – tongues would soon start wagging. If word got back to Father about Sam...

'Of course!' I cried. 'The old lodge! Oh, why didn't I think of it before?'

'Where's that?'

'At Barton Hall, from when it used to be a house. It's at the edge of the grounds, well away from the main hospital and the staff cottages – no one's lived there for years and years, but I think the roof's still OK. And at least we'd be inside, and dry.'

'How do I get there?'

'I'll draw you a map.'

'Here.' He took his sketchbook from his coat pocket, and a pencil. 'Better do it now. They open our mail sometimes – not that I ever get any, but if they find a map they might start asking questions.'

Although I still couldn't feel the ends of my fingers, I managed to sketch a passable diagram of Barton Hall's grounds. 'The main drive, where you come in off the lane, goes right past the main house and the staff cottages where I live, so that's no good,' I said, pointing. 'If anyone sees you they'll want to know what you're doing. You'll need to come through the woods at the edge of the estate, over here. There's a track that leads off the coast path and then there's a wall –

it's broken down in places so you should be able to get over it. If you do get caught you can just say you were going for a walk and got lost.'

'Got it,' Sam pocketed the sketchbook again, one corner of his mouth quirking up in a smile. 'So, where's this poem you were gonna write me?'

My shoulders sagged. 'I... I haven't managed anything yet. Sorry.'

'Hey, don't worry. You don't *have* to do it. Just don't let other people stop you doing something you love, that's all.' He sounded so fierce, I looked up. Our gazes met, and there it was again: that zing of electricity. I wasn't imagining it, was I?

The wind picked up, sending an icy gust howling into the cave. Sam sneezed again. 'Dammit. We'd better get going, before we really do catch pneumonia or something.'

'I'll go and look at the lodge as soon as I can,' I promised.

I called Toffee, clipping his lead back onto his collar. As always, I left first, so if there was anyone out on the path above the cove they wouldn't see us together. As I walked away, I glanced back to see Sam standing in the cave entrance, watching me. He raised a hand in farewell and I waved back. Even though I was wet and cold, and Grandmother's imminent arrival was hovering over me like a dark cloud, I smiled, because just for that moment, none of that mattered at all.

12

SAM

I walked back to the camp in a daydream, hardly noticing the rain or the wind. All I could think about was Ruby.

The camp was deserted, everyone down at the beach on exercises or sheltering inside from the weather. I still had a couple of hours left before I was back on duty so I made for my hut, my head down against the rain, which was heavier now, slanting sideways. I didn't see someone step out in front of me until it was too late. We collided hard and both of us went sprawling in the mud.

It was Freddie Gardner. *Damn*. He lay on his back with his white helmet over one eye, spluttering in surprise and anger. I jumped to my feet and reached down to help him up.

'Chrissake, Archer, look where you're going!' he barked, shoving my hand away, his feet slithering in the mud as he scrambled up too. He yanked his helmet back into its correct position, scowling.

'I'm sorry, sir.'

'Papers.'

'But you know who I am, sir.'

'Show me your goddamn papers, soldier,' he spat. '*Now.*'

I held them out and he snatched them, smearing them with mud. He scanned them before thrusting them back at me. 'Where have you been?'

'For a walk.'

He looked me up and down. Cold mud was seeping through the seat of my pants; Gardner looked like he'd been taking a bath in it. I struggled to keep a straight face – it was more than my life was worth to laugh right now. 'In this weather?' he said.

'Yeah. I mean, yes, sir.' I tried to keep my tone civil; I wanted to get back to my hut, change my uniform, get warm and go find something to eat.

Gardner narrowed his eyes. 'You know, Archer, I been watchin' you. And there's something about you that don't sit right with me.'

Oh yeah? I wanted to say. *Well, the feeling's mutual, buddy.* But my stomach clenched. Had he figured out I was underage? Nah – there was no way – all my documents said I was twenty, about to turn twenty-one. And he didn't know me or anyone I knew, although I'd been worried at first that he might. I'd thought he was just guessing about my age.

He shook his head. 'Don't think I've forgotten the way you and that girl were laughin' at me at the dance a few weeks ago, 'cause I haven't.'

My shoulders sagged with relief. Was that all it was?

'We weren't laughing at you, Fre— sir,' I said. 'We were talking, is all.'

'You said somethin' to her. She woulda wanted to dance with me otherwise.' His chin was jutting out, like he was a kid who'd dropped a bag of candy. I bit back another bark of laughter. Damn, I never thought I'd see Freddie Gardner *sulking*.

Ruby'd never want to dance with you. She's got too much class, and besides, she knows what a fucking bully you are, I told him inside my head. 'Perhaps you can ask her next time, sir,' I said levelly.

'Yeah, maybe I will.' He looked me up and down again in a way I didn't much care for. 'Maybe I will,' he repeated slowly. Then his gaze focused on something behind me. 'Hey, that yours?'

I looked round and saw my notebook lying in the mud. *Shit*. It must have fallen out of my pocket when I bumped into Gardner. I snatched it up. 'Yeah.'

'What is it?'

'Just drawings, sir.'

'Show me.'

Wasn't there a caricature of Gardner in there? And Ruby's map... 'It's nothing, sir.'

'Give me that notebook, soldier, *right now*. Unless you wanna get written up?'

Heart sinking, I handed it to him, and watched as he flicked through the pages. 'Whew-ee,' he whistled when he saw the sketches of Ruby I'd done from memory, trying to capture her smile, the way the corners of her eyes crinkled when she laughed, how she moved her hands as she talked like she was weaving the words out of the air. 'You got it bad for that British girl, ain't ya? She got it bad for you too, or is this just wishful thinkin'? You know all those girls from town are only after one thing, right?'

I gritted my teeth. He meant the women who hung round the perimeter fence, chatting and checking their reflections in their compacts, the bolder ones calling out to the guys as they came and went. They looked casual, like they were just hanging around with their pals, but you could sense the desperation under their lipstick-rimmed smiles and carefully set hair. Ruby couldn't have been less like them if she tried.

Thank *God*, Gardner lost interest after that. He slammed the book closed and tossed it at me. It bounced off my chest and fell into the mud again. I grabbed it, wiping it on my pants.

'This ain't the end of it, Soldier,' Gardner growled. 'I'm gonna be keepin' a real close eye on you from now on.' He stalked away.

'Goddamn Gardner,' I said to Jimmy once I was back in my hut, struggling out of my mud-caked uniform as Duke Ellington blasted out of the wireless nearby.

Jimmy glanced round. 'Careful. That guy's got ears and eyes everywhere.'

I yanked off my socks, scowling. *Who gives a damn?* I told myself. *As long as he doesn't find out how old I am, Gardner can do what the hell he likes.*

Later – much later, in France, and in the camp – those words would come back to haunt me. But I had no idea what was waiting for us there. None of us did.

I wonder what we'd have done if we did.

13

RUBY

I'd planned to slip over to the lodge that evening for ten minutes, but at dinner, I noticed Father kept coughing, his handkerchief pressed against his mouth. 'Are you OK? Do you need your tablets?' I asked, but he waved me away distractedly.

I decided it would be better to stay at home and keep an eye on him. I didn't like the sound of that cough, and anyway, I had a whole week before Sam and I were due to meet again; I could do a recce around the lodge tomorrow. In the meantime there were the shirts to iron, my shoes to polish, and I was on duty at seven o'clock.

While I was heating up the iron on the stove – and wishing we could have one of those new electric irons that plugged into a light fitting; Father didn't trust them – I made plans for the lodge. It was years since I'd last been inside. I expected it would be rather dusty, even if the roof was still all right. I'd have to tidy up. Perhaps I could sneak a broom out with me when I went over there. I hugged my arms around myself, smiling in anticipation.

★

By the next morning, it was clear Father's cough was a chest infection. He always got one at this time of year, and, as usual, feeling it coming on, he'd tried to work through it until he was too ill to continue. Abruptly, my world shrunk back down to the *Herald* offices and home. The cottage walls echoed with Father's hacking as I ran up and down the stairs with brown glass bottles of medicine, hot water bottles, towels and bowls of steaming water. I couldn't walk Toffee – I couldn't even do my ARP shifts, although thankfully they were understanding about it.

On Wednesday, Sam's message arrived like clockwork. *Sunday, 2 p.m., Lodge?*

That evening, as I was wondering frantically if I could slip out to the lodge for half an hour, Mrs Blythe brought the post over from the main house. 'I thought I'd save you the trouble, my lovely, with your pa being so poorly and all,' she said. 'There's two letters, and a telegram.'

A telegram? I frowned, wondering who it could be from. Father was sleeping, so I put the letters in his study and turned the telegram over. My heart jolted. *LEAVING TYNEHAM EARLIER THAN PLANNED. WILL BE ON 2.30 BUS SUNDAY. PLEASE ARRANGE TO MEET ME. HAVE SENT BELONGINGS ON AHEAD. ALL MY LOVE MOTHER.*

Panic gripped me like a fever. Grandmother was coming on Sunday? *This Sunday?* That was less than four days away – Father was ill – nothing was ready – there wasn't even a bed for her yet! And what about Sam? I wouldn't be able to get away to meet him. Could I send a note up to the camp?

'Are you all right, my lovely?' Mrs Blythe was watching me

closely. 'You've got a phizog on you like you've seen a ghost. Bad news?'

'I – well, no, not exactly,' I said. 'Grandmother's village is being evacuated. She's coming here, and she'll be arriving sooner than I thought.'

A strange expression flitted across Mrs Blythe's face when I mentioned Grandmother, but it was gone so fast I was left wondering if I'd imagined it. I handed her the telegram.

'Now, don't you worry about a thing,' she said briskly when she'd read it. 'We'll have this place sorted out d'reckly.'

And she kept to her word. The following evening, she enlisted the help of Alfie and one of the kitchen boys to bring a spare bedframe over from the hospital, which they wedged into my bedroom alongside my own bed, and over the next few days, when I wasn't at work, I helped her clean the cottage from top to bottom until the windows sparkled and there wasn't a cobweb to be seen, not even in the outhouse.

We finished just in time. On Saturday, I returned from the *Herald* to find a pile of bags, suitcases and boxes in the kitchen. 'Looks like she's bringing everything bar the kitchen sink,' Mrs Blythe said drily when she popped over that evening to check the cottage was ready. She helped me stack everything in the parlour, out of the way, and as I looked at it all it finally hit me properly that, by this time tomorrow, Grandmother would be here – and that she'd be staying. It made me feel as if a hand was closing around my throat.

Sighing, I straightened my shoulders. 'Thank you for all your help. I don't know how I'd've managed without you.'

'Oh, you're welcome, my lovely.' She put her broad arms around me and gave me a hug. I stiffened slightly – I wasn't used to physical contact – before squeezing her back.

'If it all gets a bit too much for you, you know you're welcome at our'n. Our Alfie and Annie would be right glad to see you. Come down any time. I mean it.'

'Thank you. I will.'

'And our Wilf'll drive you down into town tomorrow to meet 'er nibs.' Mrs Blythe winked, pitching her voice lower in case Father, still in bed, was awake and listening. 'Wouldn't want 'er having to walk, would we?'

I spent the next day in an awful state of suspense, waiting for Mr Blythe to drive me down to meet Grandmother's bus. It was almost an hour late. At first, when everyone got off, I couldn't see her, and I felt a small, irrational burst of hope that she wasn't coming after all.

Then she stepped down off the bus, immaculate in a lilac coat and matching hat, looking around her with her usual slightly sour expression.

'Ah, Ruby.' Hurrying over to me, she planted a cold, feather-light kiss on my cheek. She had to stand on tiptoes; I was taller than her now. 'What a dreadful journey that was, squashed on there with all those people. I thought it would never end! Where's your father?'

'He's ill,' I stammered, suddenly realising I'd forgotten to reply to her telegram. There'd been too much to do.

'Ill? Why wasn't I told?'

'I'm sorry, Grandmother—'

'Take me to him at once!'

Mr Blythe stepped forward, clearing his throat. 'Who's this?' Grandmother said, her mouth compressing into a flat line.

Mr Blythe tipped his cap. 'Good afternoon, Mrs Mottram.'

'This is Mr Blythe – you've met him before, remember?' I said, a little desperately. 'He's going to drive us home.'

'In that?' Grandmother eyed Mr Blythe's van, which had *Blythe's Engineering Works* painted in ornate script on the side. 'Oh, dear me.'

'It's an awfully long way to walk, Grandmother.'

She sniffed. 'One must make do, I suppose, with this war on.' Straightening her handbag on her arm, she allowed Mr Blythe – whose moustache was twitching suspiciously, as if he was trying not to laugh – to open the door and help her up into the cab. I clambered in beside her.

Just as Mr Blythe was about to shut the door, I saw a flash of khaki out of the corner of my eye. Two soldiers were crossing the road – Sam and his friend Jimmy. Suddenly, I realised I'd forgotten to reply to Sam, too. He glanced our way and our gazes met. He raised his hand and started to come over. I shook my head quickly, sharply: *No.*

His face fell.

'Do you know that young man?' Grandmother said as Mr Blythe slammed the door. My heart sank. She missed nothing.

'No, I don't think so.' It was a struggle to keep my voice even.

'I should hope not. Isn't he one of those Americans?'

'I don't know, Grandmother.'

'Dreadful people. *Dreadful.* The stories I've heard!'

Oh for goodness' sake, don't you start going on about that too, I thought drearily. I wondered what she'd do when she found out about Jennie Pearson; it wouldn't be long, I was sure. As Mr Blythe drove away, it took everything in me not to turn my head and look back to see where Sam had gone.

★

'Are you all right?' Vera said when she came into the office on Monday morning and found me almost in tears because my typewriter ribbon had jammed.

'No,' I said. 'I'm not. Grandmother arrived yesterday and she's behaving as if it's all my fault Father's ill. I can't so much as blink without her criticising me and there isn't room to swing a cat because of all her *things*. She's forever moaning about *those awful Americans who've taken over this town* and I've had no bloody sleep and I was supposed to meet Sam again yesterday and I couldn't because—'

Tired and muddled, I remembered, too late, that I hadn't actually told Vera about Sam yet.

Vera put her head on one side. 'Sam? As in, Sam Archer? Soldier Sam? What do you mean, you were supposed to meet him *again*?'

I felt my face getting hot.

'Right.' She handed me a hanky so I could wipe my ink-stained fingers. 'I'm going to make you a cup of tea and then you're going to tell me *everything*.'

I didn't try to argue. Resisting Vera when she was in this sort of mood was like trying to dig your way out of an avalanche with a mustard spoon. I drank the tea she made me, which was hot and reviving, sweetened with not one but two spoonfuls of sugar ('Ask me no questions and I'll tell you no lies,' she said, winking, when I asked her where she'd got it), and spilled the beans about me and Sam.

She grinned at me. 'Well, you sly little thing! And there was I thinking you were such a mouse. Good for you!'

Relieved she wasn't annoyed with me, I grinned back.

'Personally I think you're doing the right thing, keeping away from the camp,' she said. 'It wouldn't do for that father of yours to find out about Sam, or your granny if she's so dead set against the Americans too. But you'll need to let Sam know that you've got to be a bit more careful about seeing him, and that it might be difficult for you to get away. Why not write him a letter and post it, for goodness' sake?'

'Because Betty Lowe works at the post office, and her mother is matron at Barton Hall – you know what terrible gossips they both are.'

'OK, why don't I take a message up to the camp for him myself? I'm going up there tonight – they're showing a film, and Stanley asked me to come.'

'Who's Stanley? What happened to George? Or was it John?'

'Oh, him.' Vera waved a hand dismissively. 'He wasn't up to much. Stanley's much more my type. He's a journalist too – before the war he worked for one of the big papers back in Washington. Anyway, enough about him. What about a message for this Sam of yours?'

I scribbled a note, folded it and wrote Sam's name across the front. Vera pocketed it. 'I'll make sure he gets it. And if you want to use me as a go-between from now on, I don't mind.'

'*Thank* you.'

'No need to thank me. It's about time you had a bit of fun. Fancy another cuppa? And let's change the subject – I'm sure I can hear Alfie coming up the stairs.'

She was right; a few moments later, he came in with the post, handing it to me with a shy expression.

'Poor boy,' Vera said when he'd gone. 'It'll break his heart if he finds out about Sam.'

'Don't!' I felt suddenly, absurdly guilty. 'I've got enough to worry about without adding Alfie Blythe's feelings to the list!'

After that, I tackled the typewriter ribbon with renewed determination, desperate to take my mind off the misery that crept over me every time I thought about going home and Grandmother being there. I'd always been able to cope with her previous visits by telling myself that she'd be going home soon; this time, who knew how long it would be?

After work, I took my time going home, wheeling my bicycle the long way through town instead of riding straight back to Barton Hall. Perhaps it was just my mood, or the dreary winter weather, but I couldn't help thinking how drab everything looked. In a few weeks it would be Christmas, and some of the shops had decorations hanging in the windows, but the tape criss-crossed across the glass and the sandbags heaped on the pavements spoiled the effect. They were a stark reminder that we were at war, which wouldn't be stopping for Christmas or for anything else. I sighed softly to myself. When would all this end?

'I've as much right to shop here as anyone else, you know!' I heard someone say suddenly, their voice sharp and edged with tears. Startled out of my gloomy musings, I turned and saw a woman who had come out of the greengrocer's a moment before; the door had just slammed shut in her face, the bell jingling. The woman had mousy brown hair, inexpertly waved beneath the tired-looking felt hat she wore, and her coat, in a matching shade of dull green, hung open despite the chilly weather. As she turned towards me, I saw why.

'Hullo Jennie,' I said, trying to tear my eyes away from the slight, but all-too-obvious swell of her belly beneath her frock. 'How are you?'

Jennie Pearson's face was a dull pink, her mouth pinched into a tight line, her eyes bright with unshed tears. 'Oh, Ruby,' she said, tossing her head. 'I'm fine. Never better. How are you?'

'I – I'm fine,' I stammered, becoming aware of the people inside the greengrocer's staring through the window at us, all wearing identical expressions of disapproval.

Following my gaze, Jennie glanced round at them and her face went an even deeper shade of pink. 'Apparently there's a problem with my coupons or something,' she said, shifting the empty basket on her arm to a more comfortable position. 'I'm to try somewhere else.'

I wanted to offer her some word of kindness or reassurance, but I had no idea what to say.

'Well, I'll be seeing you, then,' Jennie said when the silence between us had stretched out for just that bit too long.

And before I could answer her, she'd turned and walked away, shoulders slumped and head down.

14

SAM

November–December

'What's wrong?' Jimmy said as he came into our hut. 'You look like you lost a dollar and found a cent. Ain't you coming up to the rec hall to watch the film?'

I slumped on my bunk and sighed. 'I'm not in the mood.'

'Is this 'cause of Sunday?'

'I don't get it. Why wasn't she there? And what was she doing in town?'

I'd followed her map across the fields and through the woods to Barton Hall, and found the lodge just where she'd marked it, a squat building with arched windows and two clusters of narrow chimneys. A couple of small stone figures stained with moss and algae – they looked like dragons or something – crouched at either end of the sagging roof. I'd called Ruby's name softly and tapped on a couple of the boarded-up windows. But no one answered.

Around back, one of the boards across the windows was

loose, and there was no glass in the frame. I'd managed to pull the board aside and make a big enough gap to climb in. 'Ruby,' I'd called softly. 'You here?'

But there'd been no answer.

Snapping on my army-issue torch, I'd prowled around the lodge for a bit. The window I'd climbed through was at one end of a long sitting room with a sofa and chairs still arranged around the fireplace. Next door was a bedroom, empty except for an iron bedstead, and a kitchen with a range and a table and chairs. There was dust everywhere, the paper stained with damp, and in places the plaster had come down from the ceiling. It looked as if no one had been in here for a very long time. And there was no Ruby.

Climbing back outside, I'd sat down on the wall to wait, keeping an eye out in case someone else came along and I had to duck behind it. Maybe she'd gotten held up.

Fifteen minutes had turned into thirty, and then to an hour. Eventually I'd walked back into town where I'd met Jimmy, and seen her getting into that van.

'Something came up, that's all,' Jimmy said placidly.

'Yeah, so why didn't she try and get a message to me?' I stared at the ceiling, remembering the look on her face when she'd seen me and the way she'd shaken her head at me, almost scowling.

Jimmy clapped me on the arm. 'Forget about it. There's a million other girls round here who'd give their right arm to spend time with you – why don't you go out with one of them?'

'Because I don't want to.'

He sighed. 'C'mon.'

Reluctantly, I followed him to the rec hall. The film was just starting – some Charlie Chaplin thing. We slipped into the back of the room and grabbed the last couple of spare chairs.

'Sam. *Sam.* Psst!' someone whispered, and touched my arm. I looked round and in the semi-darkness, saw a woman sitting on the other side of me with Stanley Novak: Ruby's pal Vera. She leaned towards me, holding something out. 'I've got a message for you from Ruby.'

I tucked it into my shirt pocket, not wanting Freddie Gardner or any of his goons, across the room, to see. Vera gave me a grin and a thumbs up.

I slipped outside again to read the note.

Dear Sam, it said. *I am SO SORRY. My father is ill and Grandmother arrived on Sunday afternoon, a whole three weeks early! (She says it's because she couldn't bear the thought of still being there when the Allied forces began moving in to take over the place.) There was no question of me getting away, even to the lodge, and when you saw me in town I'd just met Grandmother off the bus so I had to pretend I didn't know who you were.*

We'll have to be very careful from now on. Vera has agreed to bring my messages up to the camp now (I hope you don't mind that I told her about us!) so as soon as Father is better and things have settled down a bit with Grandmother I'll arrange a time when we can meet. Look out for my next message!

R x

I tore a page out of my notebook and scribbled a reply.

Dear Ruby, don't apologise. Hope everything's OK and sorry to hear that things are a bit difficult at the moment. I don't mind waiting at all. Get in touch when you can.
   Sam

I thought about adding an *x* of my own, but I hesitated – what if she thought it was too much? Instead I drew a little sketch of a soldier leaning on an American-style mailbox, an eager grin on his face. Back in the rec hall, I sat down next to Jimmy and leaned over to tap Vera on the arm. 'Here,' I whispered, handing her the note.

'I'll make sure she gets it,' she whispered back, putting it in her handbag. She murmured something to Stanley, who was watching us. He nodded, grinned, and gave me a wink, whilst Jimmy looked on, a curious half-smile on his face.

The very next day, there was a letter waiting for me, but it wasn't from Ruby. It took me a moment or two to recognise the handwriting on the envelope; I tore it open with shaking hands.

Dear Sam,
   I know you didn't want me to know where you are but I begged Mr Addison to tell me until he gave in. Please don't worry, I have not told Kirk or anyone else and I will not try to make you come home, but I wanted to say thank you for the money you have sent. Mr Addison is letting me keep it at the store. It is a real load off my mind to not have to worry about food or paying the bills. Kirk has not noticed yet and I am being very careful.

*Meggie is doing well. She is growing fast and her teacher
tells me she is top of the class at her school. She keeps
asking where you are. I don't want her to worry so I have
told her that you have gone away to find work.*

*Please stay safe, Sam, and write back to me when you
can.*

Your loving Ma (and kisses from Meggie)

The letter was dated almost a month ago, but that didn't
matter; I sat down on the edge of my bunk, relief washing
over me. Ma and Meggie were OK! And Ma was getting
my money. Thank God. Thank *God*. I wrote her back that
evening, addressing my reply to Mr Addison's store and
including an extra check so she could buy Meggie something
nice for Christmas.

The next day, mine and Jimmy's unit was put on night
exercises, going out in convoys to remote stretches of coast
in the south of the county. After that, we had a few days off.
There'd still been no word from Ruby so, reluctantly, I agreed
to go to Rainbow Corner, the American Red Cross Club near
Piccadilly Circus in London, with Jimmy, Stanley and another
pal of ours, Davy Manganello.

London was quite a change from sleepy Devon. It was
jarring to see bombed-out buildings and piles of rubble
everywhere, while inside the club and the shops there were
Christmas decorations hung up and we were going to dances
and dinners and listening to bands play. How did people
cope, living amongst such destruction? Everyone seemed
excited that we were there, especially the women, but I
wasn't interested in any of them; the only girl I had eyes for

was Ruby. I missed her terribly. What if there was a message waiting for me back at the camp?

On our second day in the city, I found myself wandering through a narrow little back street near the club. Jimmy and the others were still there, playing cards and eating donuts, but I needed some fresh air so I'd made my excuses and ducked out for a while. I wasn't planning on going anywhere in particular, but up ahead, I caught sight of a crooked, narrow little building with a hand-painted sign above the door: *Second-hand books bought and sold.* As I climbed the steps and pushed the door, a bell jangled madly, reminding me of Mr Addison's store.

The bookstore was a dim, hushed labyrinth of book-laden shelves, the air filled with the smell of ink and dust. I breathed in deeply, marvelling that such a place could exist right in the middle of a place like London. *Ruby would love it here*, I thought as I stood in the middle of the floor, looking round at it all in wonder.

'Finer than wine, that smell, eh, young man?'

A voice behind me made me jump. I looked round and saw a guy with a white moustache and beard standing behind me. He was like something out of a Dickens novel. 'That's the smell of words,' he said. 'Nothing better. What can I help you with?'

'I – er – I'm looking for a book for someone, sir,' I said.

'Who's someone? Yer mother? Yer sister?'

'No, er, a girl.'

'Ah.'

Under his moustache, his mouth crinkled into a smile. My face heated up.

'What sort of thing does she like?' he said, turning to scan the shelves.

'Um, I dunno. Poetry, maybe?'

'What sort of poetry?' He moved towards the back of the shop, where there was a ladder leaning against the wall.

'Hey, you want me to go up there?' I asked as he carried it over to a set of shelves nearby and put a foot on the bottom rung.

He waved me away. 'No, no, I'm quite all right.'

I watched, a little alarmed, as he hauled himself up the ladder. 'I'm guessing you don't want any of that soppy, romantic stuff,' he grunted as he reached the top. 'I know what young people are like today. Now, let me see. Hm...'

Eventually he clambered back down, a slim volume with a blue cloth cover and gilt-edged pages under his arm. 'Try this. She was an American, like you.'

The book was by someone called Emily Dickinson. I'd never heard of her, but as soon as I started flicking through the pages I knew Ruby would love her.

'I'll take it,' I said.

The man beamed. 'An excellent choice.'

I paid for the Emily Dickinson, tucking it into my jacket with my notebook, and wandered back to the smoky basement at Rainbow Corner.

'Where you been, man?' Jimmy crowed as I sat down. 'I'm raking it in!'

'No you ain't.' Davy Manganello slapped his cards down on the table.

Jimmy looked at them and his face fell. 'Aw, that ain't fair.'

Davy grinned and scooped up the pile of coins and notes sitting in the middle of the table next to a half-empty bottle of brandy, while Jimmy scowled and Stanley shook his head good-naturedly. I thought of telling them about the bookshop, but something stopped me. Stanley might get it, but I wasn't sure Davy or Jimmy would.

Later that day, we caught the train back to Devon. The others were playing cards again, but I gazed out of the train window, thinking about how every tree and telegraph pole sliding past took me closer to Ruby. I couldn't wait to see her again.

15

SAM

When we got back to the camp, I sent a message to Ruby straight away, asking if she could meet me that coming Sunday afternoon, at three o'clock.

Vera delivered her reply via Stanley the following day.

Will do my best to get away. Father better now but Grandmother being difficult. Will try to be there for 3 – if I'm more than an hour late assume I'm not coming. But I will try. R x

'Jimmy,' I said that evening, after dinner. 'Help me with something?'

He grinned wryly at me. 'What now? You're not after any more dog leashes, are you?'

I shook my head. 'Nothing like that.' From across the dining hall, I spotted Freddie Gardner watching me, his eyes narrowed. 'And don't say anything to anyone,' I added, lowering my voice.

'But what—'

'Tell you in a bit, OK?'

Thirty minutes later, he met me around the back of the dining hall. 'If anyone sees us, we're on a secret exercise,' I told him, handing him a broom. I had one too, and a couple of oil lamps.

'What the hell?' he said.

I slung my broom across my shoulder like a rifle. 'I'll explain on the way. C'mon.'

'Huh,' he said when I'd told him what I wanted to do. 'You really got it bad for that girl, haven't you?'

'Shut up.' I was glad it was dark enough that he couldn't see me blushing.

'Jesus fucking Christ, Sam,' he grumbled as we walked across the fields, mud sucking at our boots. 'If you wanted to go on a midnight hike, why not just say?'

'We can't go through the front gates. It's a goddamn military hospital. Unless you wanna get arrested?'

That shut him up.

Just as we reached the trees at the edge of the hospital grounds, the air raid siren started to sound in town.

'You think we oughta go back?' Jimmy said. I could just see his silhouette; he was looking up at the sky. Across the fields, back towards the sea, searchlights sprang into life, shining up into the clouds. I strained my ears, listening for planes, but it was impossible to hear anything over the siren.

I shook my head. 'Nah. If the Krauts start dropping bombs right now, we'll be caught out in the fields. Come on.'

We pushed on through the woods, followed by the wail of the siren. When we got to the lodge we climbed in through the window at the back. I lit the lanterns and set them on the floor.

'Wow. This place is a mess,' Jimmy said, looking round.

'Yeah, well, that's where you come in.' I picked up my broom again.

He shook his head. 'You owe me for this, Archer. *Big* time,' he said, but he was smiling. Five minutes after we'd got to work, the all-clear sounded. Guess it was a false alarm this time, or they were just on a photographic mission. Thank God for that. We swept the floors, piling the dust into a closet in the hall, and straightened everything up. We returned to the camp two hours later, tired out, our uniforms smudged with dirt.

There was no Christmas paper to be had anywhere, so the next day I liberated some brown paper from the camp kitchen, drew holly leaves and bells all over it and used it to wrap the Emily Dickinson book, tying a tag to it with Ruby's name on.

On Sunday, I arrived at the lodge early, climbing in through the window I'd got in before. I wondered if Ruby had been here since Jimmy and I had come to clean up. I didn't think so; it had that same deserted feel as before. I dropped my pack, which was full, onto the floor, and spent the next half an hour getting the place ready.

When I was done I sat down in one of the armchairs to wait. How long had it been since I last saw Ruby? I counted on my fingers: two – no, two and a half weeks. And now it was less than seven days until Christmas. I checked my watch. *Come on... come on...*

Three o'clock came. There was still no sign of her.

I got up and paced around the room. *Face it, she's not gonna make it. That grandmother of hers caught her trying to leave and stopped her. Or she decided it wasn't worth the risk.*

Then I heard a noise at the window. 'Sam? Are you there?' Ruby whispered. 'I've got Toffee.'

'I'm here!' I rushed over to help her lift the dog through the gap in the board over the window, and she climbed in after him.

'Thank you,' she said, brushing cobwebs out of her hair while Toffee bounded around my feet, overjoyed to see me. I bent down and unclipped his leash, rubbing his ears. Ruby was flushed and breathing hard, her hair coming unpinned. 'Oh, gosh, I'm so sorry I'm late. I ran all the way over. I—'

Then she looked round her, and her mouth dropped open.

'Whaddya think?' I said, grinning, as she took it all in. I'd found some candles in the camp stores, and now they were on the mantelpiece and some of the windowsills, filling the room with a flickering, rosy glow. I'd also found a paraffin heater, which made the temperature in here just about bearable – if you kept your coat on, anyhow – and there had been an ancient gramophone in the bedroom closet, which now sat on a table in the middle of the room. On another table, one I'd fetched from the kitchen, was a picnic: chicken salad sandwiches, cake, and a thermos flask of coffee. And in the corner was the tiny Christmas tree I'd bought in a department store in London, small enough for me to bring back in my suitcase but big enough to hang with a few single strands of tinsel and some miniature paper decorations.

Ruby's face was a picture. 'What – where – *how*?'

'You like it?'

'I *love* it!'

'I got you this, too.' I handed her the brown-paper-wrapped Emily Dickinson.

'Oh dear – I haven't got you anything yet.'

'Don't matter.'

I watched, holding my breath, as she unwrapped it.

'Sam!' she breathed. 'How did you know?'

'How did I know what?'

'That she's one of my favourite poets!'

'She is?' I wondered if the old guy in the bookshop was some sort of wizard. 'I haven't written anything in it – I didn't want you to get into trouble if your dad finds it, or your Grandmama.'

'Thank you. *Thank you.*' She flung her arms around me and hugged me, and it was like Christmas had come already.

'You're welcome,' I said. How I kept my voice even, I have no idea. I felt as if every nerve ending in my body was on fire. I led her to one of the armchairs, where a rug was folded over the arm. She sat down and I tucked it over her knees. Then I wound up the gramophone. Soft classical music filled the air. 'I dunno what this is,' I said. 'The label's damaged and it's the only one I found that wasn't completely wrecked. But I thought it was kinda nice.'

'It's Bach, I think,' Ruby said. She smiled and gazed round again, her face still full of wonder. 'I can't believe it. It's like something out of a fairy tale. Where on earth did you get that tree! I didn't even think I'd get a Christmas this year.'

'Things are that bad, huh?' Suddenly I noticed how weary she looked, despite her smile.

Her smile vanished. '*Worse.* You have no idea. Grandmother disapproves of me going out to work and sighs, and the way she looks at me every morning when I'm getting ready to leave – you can't *imagine* those looks. According to her, I should be married by now and bringing up a family, like she was when she was nineteen. And oh, Sam, she *snores*. You should hear her! I haven't had a proper night's sleep since she arrived!'

'Can't your pa do something?'

'No. He won't stand up to her at all. It's awful.'

Not knowing what else to do, I poured coffee and handed her a sandwich. 'Well, she ain't here, is she?' I said gently. It's what I always told myself about Kirk when he'd really gotten under my skin. *Forget him. He's not here. Think about something else.*

Ruby sighed, her shoulders relaxing. 'You're right. She's not. Anyway, what about you? Won't your family miss you this Christmas, with you being so far away?'

I shrugged. 'We never really celebrate. When I was a kid Ma used to try and make something of the day, but Kirk put a stop to all that. He thinks Christmas is a waste of money – in other words, he don't want Ma spending money on me and Meggie that he could use to go out and get drunk.'

'I'm sorry. You must miss them,' she said.

I nodded. 'Yeah. But at least Ma'll be able to get Meggie something this year with the money I've been sending home.'

We worked our way through the sandwiches and cake, feeding Toffee the scraps, and listened to the music until the record ran out. I got up to put it on again and held out a hand. 'Care to dance, ma'am?'

As Ruby stood, grinning, I realised she was right: it *did* feel like something out of a fairy tale in here. There was no Hitler; no bombs; no war; no Kirk; no bossy, interfering grandmother. As Ruby laid her head against my shoulder and I slid my other hand around her waist, my heart was beating so hard I was scared she'd be able to tell.

I could feel the warm weight of her body pressed against mine, the softness of her. She smelled of woodsmoke and something faintly flowery – her shampoo, maybe. The music was still playing, but we didn't move. I looked at her, and saw she was looking right back.

'Happy Christmas, Sam,' she said softly. She tilted her face towards mine, and we kissed.

PART TWO

1944

16

RUBY

January

If it hadn't been for Sam, Christmas and the New Year would have been unbearable. It was always a quiet affair, even before the war, but Father and I would decorate our little artificial tree – one we'd had for years that was starting to look decidedly tatty – and stood it on the parlour bureau with a few sprigs of holly cut from the hospital gardens, I'd cook lunch, and we'd exchange presents. Usually I'd get a book or something useful, like handkerchiefs, for me, and I'd give him a tie or a pen, though in recent years I'd often had to resort to something home-made because of the difficulty in finding anything suitable in the shops in Bartonford or Ilfracombe. And on New Year's Eve, we'd stay up and listen to the wireless, toasting in the first of January with a mug of cocoa. It was perhaps a little dull as far as Christmases and New Years went, but it had always been pleasant enough.

Grandmother's presence had changed all that. She had never spent Christmas with us before, claiming she preferred the comfort of her own home to 'being a burden on relatives', but of course, this year, she'd had no choice. She hovered over me as I decorated the tree ('What a shame your father couldn't get a real tree instead of bringing out that old thing! Although with this war on, I suppose one must make do...'), and tried to scratch together a suitable lunch from ingredients procured using hard-saved coupons and a gift of some vegetables from Alfie Blythe's father ('This *dreadful* war – I'd never have imagined I'd be eating *rabbit* for Christmas lunch. What a pity you couldn't manage to find a goose!'), until I was ready to scream.

'Oh, thank goodness *that's* over!' I exclaimed the Sunday after Boxing Day, flopping down on the old horsehair sofa in the lodge. Sam had already been there when I arrived, coaxing the little primus stove into life; with Christmas and Boxing Day falling on the previous weekend, I hadn't been able to get away, so it had been a fortnight since I'd last seen him.

'That bad, huh?' he said. After he'd sat down beside me, we'd kissed, and I felt all the pent-up tension inside me melt away as I relaxed against him.

'Worse.'

He got up again to make two mugs of tea – real tea he'd "borrowed" from the camp stores, which even had a spoonful of sugar in it, although we still had to make do with powdered milk.

'Let me guess. Nothing was good enough for the old dragon and she made sure you knew it.'

I sighed. 'In a nutshell, yes.'

He sat down again and we snuggled closer together, pulling a blanket across our legs. It was chilly, even with the paraffin heater burning. The tea warmed me, though; I sipped at it gratefully as we sat in companionable silence. It was one of the things I liked best about being with Sam; I didn't have to scramble for conversation. We could just *be*.

'Did you have a nice Christmas?' I asked him at last.

'Yeah... it was all right.'

There was a sad note in his voice. I remembered what he'd said about missing his mother and sister, even though they didn't really celebrate because of his stepfather, and sighed. Why were families so difficult, and so complicated? Did anyone really have Christmases like in the articles in Vera's magazines, the ones with pictures of everyone sitting around the tree smiling and laughing? Even Alfie, whose family all got on famously, had had a grumble to me about his various relatives descending on the Blythes' tiny cottage.

'Oh! I nearly forgot!' I sat up again, reaching for my satchel. Inside was a small parcel, wrapped in a piece of the paper Sam had made for me with holly leaves and bells drawn on it. 'I'm sorry it's late. And I hope you don't mind me reusing your paper – I hadn't anything else.'

'That don't matter,' he said as he unwrapped it. 'Jeez, Ruby, you shouldn't have.' He gazed at the small tin of drawing pencils with a grin. 'Where did you get these?'

'That's for me to know, and you to find out,' I said with a mysterious smile. I'd actually enlisted Vera's help to get them; as always, she'd managed to come up with the goods.

'I love them. *Thank you.*' He tucked them in his inside jacket pocket, still grinning.

'You nearly didn't get them, you know. Grandmother found them and *oh*, the grilling she gave me!' I shuddered, remembering. 'You should've heard her. *'I didn't know you sketched, Ruby. Where did you get these – weren't they dreadfully expensive? I hope you've not been wasting coupons!'*

'Huh,' he said. 'What business is it of hers anyway?'

'Oh, Sam, she's just *awful*. And the worst thing is that it's driving a wedge between me and Father. Oh, I know he can be difficult at times, and looking after him is sometimes a bit – a bit *suffocating*, but we've always rubbed along together OK. Grandmother's changed everything. *She's* the visitor, but I feel as if I'm the one who's not welcome there anymore. Oh—' I rubbed my eyes. 'I don't even know if I'm making sense.'

'No, I understand,' Sam said. 'It was a bit like that with me and Ma. Before Kirk came along, things weren't easy, exactly, but we were happy enough. We were a team – a unit, you know? Then he turned up like a bad smell and I'm the one who got pushed out.'

'I just wish we didn't have to sneak about like this,' I said. 'I wish we could be like Vera and Stanley, going to the pictures and out to dances and dinner and not having to worry one bit about who sees them or what they might think. Drat Father for believing everything he reads in the papers. And double-drat the soldier who got Jennie Pearson pregnant and made Father even more paranoid about the Americans!'

'What's happened to her?'

'She's being sent away somewhere to have the baby. Plymouth, I think. After that, goodness knows. I'd be surprised if she came back – the gossip's been dreadful.'

'Damn small-town narrow-mindedness. It's the same the world over.' Sam sighed. 'I know it ain't quite the same thing, but everyone back home judges me 'cause of Kirk, and we're not even related.'

I squeezed his hand, then gave a little laugh. 'Gosh, aren't we being melancholy today? It's the second day of nineteen-forty-four – we ought to be looking forwards. Perhaps this is the year the war will end!'

'I hope so. I hope it ends tomorrow so I don't have to go to France and leave you behind,' Sam said, a little fiercely.

I laid my head on his shoulder. 'Wouldn't that be something?'

He picked up his mug. 'Let's make a toast to it.'

'To the war ending tomorrow,' I said, and touched the rim of my mug against his before taking the last mouthful of my now-lukewarm tea.

'To the war ending tomorrow.'

'And now let's talk about something else – something cheerful.'

'I've got a better idea than that.' Sam kissed me, then got up and went over to the gramophone. His pack was leaning up beside it; out of it he took a record in a cardboard sleeve and he put it on the turntable. He wound the gramophone, and the record began to turn: not classical music but jazz, a stream of bright notes tumbling from the speaker.

Sam held out a hand and smiled. 'Ms Mottram, will you dance?'

He whirled me around the room, using silly, exaggerated moves until I was breathless, both from the dancing and from laughter. Had I ever laughed with anyone the way I laughed with Sam? If I had, I couldn't remember. Eventually, we collapsed onto the sofa again, still giggling, Grandmother and the war all but forgotten.

17

SAM

February–March

At the beginning of February, the weather changed. There was a brutal cold snap, which went on and on for weeks. The ground was hard as iron and the air was so cold it bit into your lungs when you breathed. Ruby's father got sick again, and a lot of the guys got sick at the camp, too, so many that the medical bay was overrun and the whole place echoed with the sound of their hacking coughs.

'Goddamn,' Jimmy wheezed as we hustled along the beach one morning at the beginning of March, weighed down by our packs and guns. He wasn't long out of the sick bay himself, and still looked pale. 'If this is winter in England, it can goddamn keep it.'

'You can say that again,' I grumbled. So far, I'd been lucky and escaped whatever it was that was going round, but every headache or tickle in my throat had me worrying I'd be next. I was worried about Ruby, too. Because of her pa, I hadn't seen her in two weeks. Was she all right?

That Sunday we were finally able to meet up again. When I got to the lodge, Ruby was already there, bundled up in her coat and scarf as she dozed on the sofa with the blanket pulled over her. She woke when I walked in, looking disorientated. 'Oh, Sam,' she said. 'Sorry. I just sat down for a moment – I didn't mean to fall asleep.'

'You'll freeze to death!' I said, hurrying to light the paraffin heater. It was as cold in here as it was outside, our breath making clouds of white vapour in the air.

'Well, if I do, at least I'll be able to get some sleep,' she said, sounding bitter. I lit the lamp too and saw how white and drawn she was, purple shadows under her eyes.

'Hey, don't say that!' I sat down beside her, drew her into my arms and kissed her. 'Are you OK?'

She didn't answer me. As I brushed a strand of hair out of her face, I saw her eyes were brimming with tears.

My stomach clenched. 'Your pa – is he—?'

'Oh, he's getting better now, no thanks to *her*.' Ruby sniffed fiercely, and took the handkerchief I offered her. 'She hasn't lifted a finger to help look after him, even though she's his mother. She says it's *vital* she gets her rest because she's so busy with all her volunteering work for the WVS and the Red Cross. Meanwhile I'm up all night, every night, taking Father hot water and his medicine and fresh pyjamas, and changing his sheets. It doesn't seem to occur to her that *I* might need some rest too!'

'Miserable old witch,' I said. 'Who the hell does she think she is?' Not for the first time, I found myself wishing I could wave a magic wand and change things for Ruby – take her far away from here and from that hideous grandma of hers.

She must have been thinking along the same lines, because

suddenly she said, 'One day it won't be like this. I'll have a place of my own, and I'll stay in bed until eleven o'clock in the morning if I want to.'

'What sort of place do you want?' I said, trying to keep my voice light. I reached for my cigarettes and lit one, then settled down beside her more comfortably, trying to get warm.

'I don't know... something modern, not like that damp old cottage,' she said. 'Red-brick, with a little wooden fence outside, and lilac and rose bushes in the garden. There'd be blue-and-white check curtains at the window, the wireless would always be on and oh! I'd have to have at least two dogs – I can't have my own here because they make Father wheeze – and I'd be somewhere with a view of the sea... *Not* Bartonford, though.'

'You can have any sort of house you like, and as many dogs as we can fit in it,' I said, gently winding her hair through my fingers, and then my heart leapt, because she'd been talking about *her* house and I'd said *we* without even thinking about it. But she went on as if she hadn't even noticed.

'I'd paint the kitchen green – no, yellow, so it always looks sunny. And I'd have a proper bathroom, *inside*. And a study full of books, with a big, squashy armchair next to the fireplace and a little table with a typewriter on it next to the window, where I can sit and look out at the view when I'm wondering what to write next.' She gazed up at me, smiling. 'What about you? If you could have any sort of house at all, what would it be like?'

That one you just described sounds pretty good to me, I wanted to say, but I wasn't quite brave enough.

I dragged on my cigarette, blowing a stream of smoke into the air. 'I dunno,' I said. 'Somewhere out in the country, but not like Kirk's farm. I guess it would be a bit like yours, actually – a house with a view of the sea, where Meggie can run around and Ma can have a garden and a place to sit and read, like she used to.'

'That sounds wonderful,' Ruby said.

I didn't answer. I was thinking about the house, imagining not just Ma and Meggie there but Ruby too...

Was it even possible? I hadn't thought much about what would happen after the war ended; my only plan had been to join the army and make enough money to get Ma and Meggie away from Kirk someday. How I'd actually manage that, I still had no idea. And I hadn't factored meeting a girl into my plans at all, never mind one who lived a whole ocean away.

And what if you don't make it through the war? a nagging little voice in my head spoke up. *What then? What will happen to them – to Meggie, and Ma, and Ruby?*

'You look very serious,' Ruby said, breaking into my thoughts. 'What are you thinking about?'

'Oh – nothing much.' I couldn't find the right words to tell her.

She snuggled into my chest and murmured something else, so quiet I didn't think I'd heard her right at first. 'Hmm?' I said.

She looked up at me. 'I love you, Sam Archer.'

I felt a jolt go through me. 'I love you too,' I said, burying my face in her hair.

Somehow, I'd make this work. I *had* to.

18

RUBY

Early May

'The Welcome Club?' I said. 'But Grandmother, I thought—'

She fixed me with her usual flinty stare. 'You thought *what*, Ruby?'

'Well, that you weren't awfully keen on the Americans.' I gazed at my bowl of tapioca pudding, moving the lumpy mixture around with my spoon.

Grandmother sniffed. 'How I personally feel about the Americans is of no consequence. Dorothy Blythe asked us to assist her at this party, which the Welcome Club are throwing on Sunday afternoon for the evacuees, and assist her we shall.'

I sighed. The Women's Voluntary Service had set the Welcome Club up just after the GIs arrived to promote cordial relations between them and the townspeople and, despite her intense dislike of all things American, it hadn't taken Grandmother long to involve herself. I glanced across the kitchen table at Father, who had his spoon in one hand and was making notes with the other, so absorbed he didn't even look up. I was beginning to suspect he used his work to escape Grandmother's incessant nagging as much as anything else.

'I – I don't know if I'll have time, Grandmother,' I said, feeling slightly desperate. Sunday was mine and Sam's day – I *couldn't* let her take that away.

'Nonsense. One has to *make* time. This war won't be won by people sitting around doing nothing. Now, wash the dishes for me, please, Ruby, and before you report for duty I'd like you to help me unravel some old seaboot stockings. The Naval Comforts Committee in Exeter have sent them to Bartonford WVS to re-knit them into jerseys for the men.'

Sighing inwardly, I heaved myself out of my chair and went over to the sink, trying to keep my resentment off my face.

'Perhaps she'd like you to stick a broom up your backside and sweep the floor while you're at it,' Vera said at work the next day when I grumbled to her about it.

'Vera!'

'Well, it's true.' She plonked a mug of tea down in front of me. 'I know we all need to do our bit, but this is *ridiculous*. You already have a job *and* all your ARP stuff, and that granny of yours has got you volunteering with the Red Cross and the WVS on top of it all too. Now the Welcome Club party! When are you supposed to sit down? Or sleep?'

'I *do* sleep.'

'Could've fooled me. And what about those awful men she keeps trying to introduce you to?'

'Oh, don't,' I groaned. 'It was only one awful man.'

'Only one *so far*. What was his name again? Hubert?'

'Humbert. Humbert Spriggs.'

'*Humbert*. Oh, Lord!'

I shook my head, remembering Humbert, a bank clerk from Ilfracombe and the son of one of Grandmother's Red Cross ladies. She'd invited him to lunch last Sunday and it had been *hideous*. He'd had a nervous sniff, and had been wearing so much hair cream you could have scraped it off his head and used it to grease tank axles. That afternoon, sitting in the lodge with Sam, we'd both cried with laughter as I told him about the barely disguised look of horror on Father's face when Humbert had launched into a detailed tale about his mother's gout, thinking he'd be interested, and Grandmother's desperate attempts to steer the conversation onto safer ground.

'What did your father make of him?' Vera asked.

'He *loathed* him. Said he's never met such a stupid young man, although not within Grandmother's earshot of course. I'm not sure Grandmother will try to pull a trick like that again, even if she is desperate to get me married off and out of hers and Father's hair.'

'I wouldn't be so sure.' Vera's expression grew serious. 'You don't think she's found out about Sam, do you?'

'No! How could she? I only see him once a week – sometimes not even that – and I always take Toffee with me and walk the long way round to the lodge through the fields and the woods. I'm sure she'd like to stop me doing *that*, too, because she hates dogs almost as much as she hates the Americans, but she can't because it's Helping Someone in Need.'

I knew I should feel guilty about sneaking off to see Sam, but for some reason, I didn't – not a bit. Those snatched, precious hours with him kept me going, through Grandmother's "little jobs", Father's coughs and nightmares and the long nights on ARP duty as I trudged up and down the streets until my feet ached, looking for chinks of lights around the edges of people's windows. And they kept me going through the days when it had felt as if we'd be locked in winter forever, and everyone had been holding their breath as the news from Europe grew steadily worse and the Germans kept trying to pound us all to bits. Now spring was here, but it still felt as if this war would never end. Sam's training was getting more intense, and sometimes, at the lodge, he'd be so tired he'd fall asleep in one of the armchairs, quite suddenly, as if someone had flicked a switch. I'd be talking, he'd go quiet, and I'd look over to see him with his head back, his eyes closed, snoring softly. I didn't mind, of course, but it was a reminder that the day the war would take him away from me was drawing closer, and I was dreading it.

'Anyway,' I said to Vera, wanting to change the subject. 'How's Stanley?'

She smiled – a dreamy smile; it was utterly unlike her. 'He's very well, thank you.'

I shook my head and smiled too.

'*What?*' Vera said, narrowing her eyes.

'I never had you marked as the settling-down type, that's all.'

'No,' Vera said thoughtfully. 'Neither did I, to be honest.'

Alfie arrived with the post. Things were a little easier between me and him again now. Just after Christmas, he'd started going out with a girl from his father's works, Maud Tinney, and the little gifts he used to bring me – the eggs and, once, horrifyingly, a bunch of snowdrops from his father's garden – had stopped. I suppose he gave them to Maud instead. It was a relief, being able to go back to being old school friends.

Sunday soon came around. I'd given Vera a message to take to the camp for Sam, explaining why I wouldn't be at the lodge that day, and had received a mysterious reply: *Don't worry about a thing, you're in for a surprise.* As I dressed and made breakfast, I veered between scowling at Grandmother whenever she wasn't looking, filled with resentment, and wondering what on earth Sam meant.

When we arrived at the Bartonford Arms Hotel, there was already a crowd of soldiers in smart khaki uniforms gathered at one end of the ballroom, arguing good-naturedly with a group of women as they helped them set up tables of food. Others were blowing up balloons and stringing paper streamers across the room, and on the stage, there was a band, tuning their instruments. I was surprised to see that these men had dark skin, as I knew that in the camp, black soldiers were segregated as they were in America, living in a separate camp from the white soldiers. Here, however, relations between them and the other soldiers seemed quite cordial – they called out to one another, joking and laughing, and the atmosphere was carefree. When Grandmother saw them, she sniffed, but all she said was, 'Hm. I do hope they're not going to play any of that awful jazz rubbish.'

I was relegated to a side room with a group of women who were all around Grandmother's age, helping prepare the rest of the food. Mrs Blythe was there, and Barnaby Sykes's and Tom Bidley's wives. 'Just look at it all,' I heard Mrs Bidley say as I came in. 'All come from the Americans, that has. I can't remember the last time I saw a nice bit of ham like that!'

'Lucky devils,' Mrs Sykes grumbled.

'I don't know,' Mrs Blythe chipped in. 'If I was being sent off to fight Jerry I'd want feeding up too.' She saw me and smiled. 'Oh, hello, Ruby love. Come with that grandma of yours, have you?'

'Hello, Mrs Blythe,' I said. 'Where d'you want me?'

As we finished making sandwiches and cutting cake, I heard the band strike up a jaunty tune and the air swelled with excited shrieks and laughter. The children had started to arrive.

'Bless 'em,' Mrs Sykes said. 'I'm glad some of them evacuees 'ave got a chance to 'ave a bit of fun. Can you imagine what it must be like for 'em, so far from home, and not even knowing if they're gonna have a home to go back to? Poor little tykes.'

Mrs Bidley snorted. 'Poor little nothing. That pair that're stayin' with me got into the hens yesterday and let them all loose. Took old Tom almost an hour to round 'em up again.'

Mrs Blythe and I exchanged glances and smiled. Her evacuees had gone back to London after their parents had decided it was all a fuss over nothing and that they wanted them home again. (Father had been exempted from taking anyone in because of living at the hospital, a relief to us both.)

The party was riotous, with games of pass the parcel, pin the tail on the donkey and musical statues – and dancing, of course. I was so busy helping serve the food that I didn't realise Sam was there until almost halfway through the afternoon when, suddenly, I spotted him standing near the stage with Jimmy, Stanley and another friend of his, a man with dark curly hair who I vaguely remembered him telling me about – Davy, I think he'd said he was called. Heat flashed through my body and I almost smiled and called out. So *that's* what his message had meant! Just in time, I remembered where I was. I turned away, wondering what on earth I was going to do if he tried to talk to me.

A little later, I was sitting with Grandmother at the side of the hall, resting for a moment, when a familiar voice, American with a distinct British twang, said, 'Would either of you two ladies care to dance?'

Another wave of heat went through me as I looked up and saw Sam standing in front of us.

'No thank you.' Grandmother's tone was positively dripping with frost. 'I don't dance.'

'How about your daughter, ma'am?' Sam said, equally politely, and I realised, with a little jolt, that he was pretending not to know me. *Thank you*, I telegraphed to him with my eyes.

I could see from the look on Grandmother's face that she was fighting her disdain for the Americans with being flattered someone would call me her daughter. 'That's up to Ruby,' she said at last. She didn't try to correct Sam's "mistake".

I smiled innocently at Sam. 'I'd love to dance, thank you. You don't mind, do you, Grandmother?' I added, putting a slight emphasis on the last word.

She waved me away, looking cross.

'I'm Sam Archer, ma'am,' Sam said as he led me away, loud enough for Grandmother to hear. 'And you're Ruby—?'

'Ruby Mottram. Nice to meet you.' Sam's mouth was twitching, as if he was trying not to grin; I bit back a smile too.

'I'm glad you're here,' he murmured in my ear as we twirled around the room to a Glenn Miller tune. 'I couldn't put this in a message in case it got intercepted, but I can't get away next Sunday – we're going down to south Devon for some sort of big training exercise a couple of days after, and they've cancelled all our time off. I think they're worried someone'll spill the beans.'

My heart sank a little at the thought of being stuck at home with Father and Grandmother next Sunday. I could still take Toffee out, of course, but it wouldn't be the same. 'Does this mean they'll be sending you to France soon?' I murmured back, trying not to let my disappointment show on my face.

'I dunno. I guess the top brass know, but they're not saying anything to us.'

We spent the rest of the dance in silence. I wanted to lean into him like I did when we danced at the lodge, our bodies fitting together like two puzzle pieces; take in deep lungfuls of his tobacco and cinnamon gum scent; kiss him until we were both breathless and giddy with it. But with Grandmother's gaze on us the whole time, we had to keep our bodies apart, and I could only rest my hand lightly in his.

When the dance ended, I was overtaken by a sudden, irrational wave of terror. 'You will be careful, won't you?' I said quietly as he released me. 'This weekend, I mean?' I couldn't shake the feeling that something awful was going to happen to Sam down in south Devon and this would be the last time I saw him.

He nodded, looking slightly puzzled. 'Course I will. I'll be back before you know it.' He gave my hand a little squeeze. Heart hammering, I glanced round, praying Grandmother hadn't seen, but she was engrossed in conversation with Mrs Blythe.

Nearby, a little girl in a brown frock started wailing. She was about six or seven years old, with bobbed, mousy brown hair. Sam crouched down beside her. 'Hey, honey, what's wrong?'

'I don't fe-e-el well,' the girl sobbed, tears streaming down her face. 'I want my mu-u-ummy!'

Sam grinned at me. 'Too much candy and ice cream, I bet.' He took the girl by the hand. 'C'mon, let's go find your mommy. What's she look like?'

I watched him lead her across the hall, wishing I had the same easy way with children that he did. I always felt so awkward around them; I couldn't imagine ever having any of my own. His sister, Meggie, was about the same age as that little girl, wasn't she? Whenever he talked about her – and he talked about her a lot – I could hear how desperately he missed her.

'Ruby!' I heard Grandmother call sharply. I jumped, realising I was still watching Sam.

'Stop mooning over that soldier and go and help clear the tables,' she snapped when I went back over to where she was sitting. 'You look like a complete fool.'

I bowed my head demurely, so she wouldn't see the anger in my eyes. 'Yes, Grandmother.'

19

SAM

After I'd delivered the kid to her mother, the party started to wind down. There was a lot of clearing up to do and by the time we'd finished, Ruby and her grandma had gone. Her parting words echoed through my head. *Be careful.* What had got her so worried? It was a training exercise, not the real thing. They probably wouldn't even give us live ammo.

Davy gave me a nudge. 'Hey, that was risky, wasn't it, dancing with your girl in front of her grandmama like that?' I'd told him and the other guys about Ruby's situation, warning them not to acknowledge her if they saw her in town so she didn't get into trouble.

I shrugged. 'What was I supposed to do, ignore her all afternoon?'

'She's hot stuff.' He winked at me, elbowing me in the ribs. 'You two – you know – yet?'

It took me a minute or two to figure out what he meant. 'Aw, that ain't none of your business,' I said, going red.

'Lookit him,' Davy crowed to Jimmy and Stanley. 'I bet they're at it like—'

Stanley shook his head good-naturedly. 'Leave the kid alone, Davy. Just because you think with your balls, it doesn't mean the rest of us do.'

I didn't hear the rest; I was already on my way outside to have a smoke and let my face cool down. Leaning against the wall outside, I gazed out to sea, thinking about what Davy had said. In recent weeks Ruby and me had gotten close – real close – a few times, but she always pulled away, breathless and flushed, her hair in disarray, saying, 'I'm sorry, Sam, but we mustn't. Not yet.' I had to admit, it was kinda frustrating, but I didn't want her to think that was all I was after.

I blew smoke into the air, remembering the conversation we'd had in March about the houses we wanted to live in one day. It all still felt like an impossible dream.

After the party, Jimmy and I ended up in the hotel bar with the guys from the band: Walt, Arthur, Wilson and Godfrey. They set up their instruments around the piano and soon the locals were singing along and we were having ourselves a second party. Everyone kept offering to buy us drinks, but I stuck to water. 'You professionals?' I said to Godfrey after last orders had been called, and we were getting ready to leave at last.

Godfrey shook his head. 'Not me. Walt, though, he was playing before he was even out of diapers.'

Walt, the saxophone player, didn't look much older than me or Jimmy. He grinned bashfully.

The six of us walked down the steps at the front of the hotel together. 'Hey, what are you boys doin', leavin' by the front entrance?' a voice drawled. *Shit.* It was Freddie Gardner and another of his goons, a guy called Moran, both of them wearing their MP uniforms.

'Oh, man,' I heard Wilson mutter behind me.

Freddie stepped forward, holding his truncheon. 'And what are *you* kids doin'?' he asked me and Jimmy. His eyes were slightly glazed and his breath stank of whisky. Guess he'd been having himself a party somewhere too. My stomach twisted. That mean look on his face reminded me of Kirk. That old, familiar feeling of anger, mixed up with fear, began to simmer inside me. 'There a problem?' I said before I could stop myself.

Jimmy gave me a sharp nudge. '*Shut up, Sam.*'

'There sure is.' Gardner came even closer, pushing me and Jimmy out of the way. 'But I'll deal with you later. I want a word with these boys first.' He narrowed his eyes at Walt, Arthur, Wilson and Godfrey.

'Hey, what do you think you're doing?' someone said as Gardner and his pal backed Walter and the others against the side of the hotel. I looked round, and saw one of the old boys who'd been with us in the bar, a guy with a white moustache.

Gardner gave him a wide, shit-eating grin. 'Nothin' to worry about, sir. We're just makin' sure these boys ain't been botherin' anyone.'

'What the bloody 'ell are you talking about?' the man said in his thick Devon drawl. 'Of course they bloody 'aven't. You leave them alone!'

'This is military police business, sir,' Moran slurred. 'Please step away.'

The man's moustache bristled. '*You* bloody step away. Who the bloody 'ell d'you think you are, ordering me around like that?'

His friends had come out of the hotel behind him. They came down the steps and formed a ring around Walt, Arthur,

Wilson, Godfrey, Gardner and Moran. White Moustache jabbed a finger into Gardner's chest. 'Those lads haven't done nothin' wrong. They're as welcome 'ere as anyone else, aren't they?'

He looked round at the other men, who nodded. 'Course they are, Tom,' one of them said.

Gardner raised his truncheon. 'Listen, you stupid old—'

'Hey, don't you bloody threaten my dad!' a younger man cried. He gave Freddie a hard shove, sending him stumbling backwards. Freddie roared, and swung at him with his truncheon.

All hell broke loose. Before long, there was a pile of men brawling in the street, with Gardner and Moran at the bottom of it. Jimmy and I helped Walt and the others rescue their instruments, and they fled.

Jimmy and I glanced back at the fight, and scarpered too.

We left the camp for the south coast just over a week later, thousands of us packed into the back of chugging, canvas-covered lorries headed for Torbay. There, we were going to board destroyers, then sail round the coast to practise beach landings at a place called Slapton Sands.

Usually the guys would have been singing, laughing, cracking jokes, but the rumours that had been circulating round the camp for the past few days were on everyone's minds, and the lorry was silent. Last week, another division had been practising beach landings in the same place when something had gone badly wrong – most of the men hadn't come back. No one knew what had happened, exactly – some said there'd been an attack by the Germans, some said it was friendly fire – but the higher-ups had forbidden anyone from asking questions. It hadn't stopped us talking about it amongst ourselves, though. The words Ruby had said to me at that party echoed round my head: *You will be careful, won't you?*

'Think Jerry'll have a go at us too?' Jimmy asked from the bench opposite as we bounced along the narrow Devon roads. It was a few minutes past dawn. I could only just make him out.

'They said hundreds died. *Hundreds*. What a screw-up,' Davy Manganello, next to me, said, dragging on a cigarette.

'We don't know anything,' Stanley Novak said on my other side. 'If so many guys died, what the hell would they have done with all the bodies? How would they have gotten rid of them without anyone finding out?'

You could tell Novak was a journalist; he sounded so calm and matter-of-fact, you'd think we were on our way to a church picnic. Taking a battered hip flask out of his pocket, he passed it across to me and Davy. 'Here.'

The neat whisky burned a fiery trail from my throat to my stomach, warming me, although it didn't do much for my anxiety. It had been a crappy week already, and I was exhausted. When news of the street brawl outside the hotel reached the top brass at the camp, Gardner had been hauled in front of them to explain himself. He didn't get in too much trouble because of his daddy, but he got enough of a scolding that he'd been sour as hell about it afterwards, and he spent the rest of the week doing everything he could to make life miserable for me and Jimmy: stuff going missing from our hut, only to turn up again damaged or covered in mud; getting jostled in the queue at the canteen hard enough to make us drop our trays; shit like that. This morning, he was in another lorry, thank God.

After the long, jolting ride, we were marched on board our destroyer, joining a convoy of other ships travelling around the coast. I snatched a few hours of uneasy sleep, dreaming of Ruby. In the early hours of Wednesday morning, with Slapton Sands in sight, we were packed into shallow landing craft. Thank God the sea was calm, because I didn't even wanna think what being on board a tin can like this would be like if it wasn't. Even so, some of the guys got sick, leaning over the sides to lose their breakfast to the waves. I turned away, trying to close my ears to the sound of their retching, my own stomach clenched in sympathy.

Despite everyone's nerves, the landings passed off without a hitch. We scrambled out of the landing crafts and splashed through the shallows onto the beach, sergeants barking orders and shells screaming over our heads. The smoke made my eyes and throat burn. *Next time I do this it'll be for real,* I thought as we headed for a shingle bank guarded by units pretending to be German soldiers. *I hope it's this goddamn easy next time.*

Men were stretched out on the sand, acting as casualties as medics wearing uniforms with crosses on the shoulders worked their way across to them, ducking at the sound of booming gunfire from the ships anchored out to sea. Another shell screamed over and I lay down too, keeping myself as low as I could.

As I crawled forwards with Jimmy, Stanley and Davy either side of me, my fingers caught something half buried in the churned-up sand. It was a watch, US army issue. As I dug down, I found more bits and pieces: a handful of spent bullet casings; a button; a shred of khaki cloth. Where the hell had all this come from? The face of the watch was smashed, and there was a brownish stain on the piece of fabric that looked like blood.

I remembered what Davy had said in the lorry yesterday, and a shudder wrenched up my spine. Maybe those rumours weren't rumours after all.

'Sam, come on!' Jimmy yelled. The others were leaving me behind. I shoved the watch, bullets, button and cloth back down into the wet sand, burying them as deep as I could, and scrambled up the beach after the rest of my unit.

20

RUBY

14th May

'Father? Grandmother?' I called as I went up the front garden path, edging past the furniture haphazardly arranged across the path. 'Is everything all right?'

Grandmother met me at the cottage door. She was wearing a faded pinny – goodness knows where she'd found it – and a look of long-suffering martyrdom I was growing to know all too well. Her hair was wrapped in a scarf, and she was clutching a broom. 'Ah, I'm glad you're home. You can help me take the curtains down to wash them before your father gets back,' she said briskly.

When I went into the parlour, I discovered everything that was too heavy to carry outside had been pushed against the walls, and all the pictures had been taken down. The piano was covered in a grubby sheet and Mother's photograph lay face down on the windowsill. In a panic, I rushed upstairs; as I'd feared, everything had been turned upside down and inside out up here as well. In the bedroom Grandmother and I now shared, the contents of the bureau had been tipped out onto the bed, including my underwear drawer, where I kept the box Alfie had given me last year – the one I kept Sam's drawings in – and my book of Emily Dickinson poems. Frantically, I raked through the piles of clothes, my shoulders sagging with relief when I found them.

I tiptoed back down the stairs and out to the Anderson, placing the box on a shelf inside, and tucking the Emily Dickinson into my cardigan pocket. Then, with a glance over my shoulder, I took my bicycle and cycled back into town, feeling mulish. Blow Grandmother and her spring cleaning!

Oh, if only I could see Sam! I thought as I pedalled. He was back from his training now, but Sunday was three days away, and going up to the camp was, of course, out of the question. When I reached the town gardens I dismounted, intending to find somewhere to sit and read for a while.

I didn't notice the hunched figure sitting on a bench beside one of the ornamental flower beds – flower beds now filled with cabbages and potatoes instead of pansies and geraniums – until they called my name. 'Ruby!'

I jumped. It was Alfie, wearing his post office uniform, his own bicycle propped up beside him.

'Oh, hullo, Alfie,' I said.

'Hullo, Ruby.' He sounded fed up. His hair was standing on end, as if he'd been running his fingers through it.

I leaned my bicycle against the railings behind us and sat down beside him; there wasn't really any other option unless I wanted it to look as if I was avoiding him. 'Are you all right?'

'Not really. Maud chucked me.'

'What? Oh, no. I'm so sorry, Alfie.'

He looked round at me. 'She was seeing one of *them* behind

my back – an *American*. Can you believe it? I can't *stand* it. Nothing's been the same since they arrived. *Nothing*. They've taken over – turned everyone's heads! It makes me sick, seeing them swanning round town in their flashy cars and jeeps, and all the women throwing themselves at their feet. Oh, I know they're supposedly going to help us win the war and all that, but *really*. Who in their right mind would want to get involved with a load of show-offs like that?!'

I sat very still; I didn't say a thing. He was wheezing slightly. 'We had a terrible argument, Maud and I. She said I was dull. And – and… there were other things, too.'

I frowned. 'What other things?'

'She – she wanted me to do things. Things which weren't—' He swallowed, his Adam's apple jerking, and as I watched, a flush suffused his whole face. 'You know – gentlemanly.'

'Oh.' Now my face was going pink too. 'Gosh.'

He dug the toe of his boot savagely into the grass. 'I suppose that's why she went behind my back with that soldier. I suppose *he* does anything she wants him to. And after that she told me I was a coward for not joining up.'

'Oh, nonsense! You *can't* join up – what about your chest? They won't let you!'

'*I* know that, but she said she thought it was an excuse. She said if I really wanted to, I'd find a way, bad chest or no bad chest.'

'Alfie, she was just saying that to hurt you – to make herself feel better for being such a worm. I mean, is my father a coward? He can't join up either, because of *his* chest.'

'Yes, but he *did* fight in the last war.'

I wanted to shake Alfie. Who *cared* what an idiot like Maud Tinney, with her brassy-coloured hair and her way of laughing in a patronising and ever-so-slightly-sarcastic way at whatever you said, thought? I'd only met her twice, and after she'd begun yet another sentence with *When we lived in Exeter...* I'd found myself wanting to shake her, too. 'She doesn't know the first thing about you. She's not even from round here – didn't her family move from Exeter after they got bombed out? And anyway, if she was asking you to – to do things you didn't want to, then she's not the girl for you, is she?'

We sat there for a while in silence until my stomach growled, reminding me I'd not had my supper yet. Did I dare return to the cottage? I stood up and patted his arm. 'Forget her, Alfie. Plenty more fish in the sea.'

'Yes, but what if those fish aren't interested?' His tone was so gloomy I had to bite back a laugh.

'Oh, I'm sure one of them will be! Keep your chin up.'

As I wheeled my bike back to the gates, I glanced round and saw him gazing after me.

I took the long way home, ignoring the hunger gnawing away inside me; when I finally returned to the cottage, it was almost nine o'clock. To my relief, the furniture had been taken back inside and everything was more or less in one piece again. Father had shut himself away in his study and Grandmother was thumping around in the parlour. I didn't go in there to see what she was up to. I ate some bread and margarine standing up in the kitchen, went upstairs and slid the Emily Dickinson under my mattress. As I washed my face, brushed my teeth and got into bed, I was thinking about what Alfie had said about Maud Tinney – how she'd wanted him to do things he hadn't wanted to do – and about kissing Sam on the old horsehair sofa at the lodge.

I wanted to go further – wanted it more than anything – but I was scared Sam would think I was easy, that that was all I wanted him for, like the women who hung around the camp gates. I'd never realised how lonely I was before Sam came along. He made me feel as if a lamp had been lit inside me, one I didn't even know was there, filling all the dark corners of my soul with light and laughter and warmth. I was terrified of getting it wrong – of scaring him away.

Perhaps I should ask Vera about it; no doubt she was as knowledgeable about these things as she was about everything else. But even thinking the word *sex* made me blush to the roots of my hair. I couldn't imagine saying it out loud, not to Vera, not to Sam, not to *anyone*. Perhaps if Mother had been around, she might have talked to me about these things. I had a vague picture of lovemaking in my head, pieced together from stories and novels, but they were all very clear it was something strictly reserved for after you were married, and what about babies? How did you stop *that* from happening?

When I was with Sam, at the lodge, these worries never seemed to bother me; it was when we were apart that doubts came creeping in. We'd talked a few times, in a roundabout way, about the future, but the reality was that Sam would soon be sent off to war, and I had no idea if or when I'd see him again. And then there was the problem of Father, who couldn't manage without me...

Hearing Grandmother coming up the stairs, I turned my face into my pillow, pretending to be asleep. I heard her sniff as she got into her own bed, but she didn't say anything. Once she'd started snoring, I rolled over again and lay staring up at the ceiling, turning the same old thoughts about Sam and Father over in my mind, until I was exhausted with them.

21

SAM

28th May

'You OK?' I asked Ruby.

'Yes, of course.' She pushed a curl of hair out of her face and smiled at me. 'Why wouldn't I be?' Turning away, she busied herself looking through the stack of records next to the gramophone – I'd bought some over from the camp. 'What would you like to listen to next? There's Glenn Miller, or Mozart—'

'I don't mind,' I said. 'You choose.'

It was the first time we'd seen each other in three weeks. Our time off was being cancelled left, right and centre as our training ramped up, and although the high-ups weren't saying as much, word around the camp was that the invasion of Europe was imminent. A lot of the guys were excited about it. I wasn't sure how to feel. Part of me wanted it over with; mostly I was dreading it, wondering what was waiting for us on the other side of the English Channel and knowing that when it happened I'd have to leave Ruby behind. And I was scared what would happen to Meggie and Ma if I got killed.

I watched as Ruby picked up a record, put it down again. 'Look, you sure nothing's bothering you?'

'I *said*, I'm fine.'

Her sharp tone stung me. 'Well, you're not acting like it.'

'What's that supposed to mean?'

'What I mean is, you've been like a bear with a goddamn sore head ever since I got here. I thought you'd be glad to see me.'

She put the record down with a sigh. 'I am. It's just – oh, I don't know.'

'So tell me.'

'This.' She waved a hand around. 'Us. *Everything.*'

'What about us?' A cold finger was tracing down my spine. We'd been apart for too long – she'd been thinking – changed her mind.

'What's going to happen to us, Sam? After you go to Europe, I mean?'

'Well, I dunno. I guess I'm gonna try my best to make it back over here to you. And then we can make plans, if that's what you want.'

'I *do* want that – of course I do – but then what?'

'What do you mean?' I said.

She sat down, her shoulders slumping. 'How are we going to make it work, Sam? With Father, I mean? I'll have to tell him about us, and—'

'So what's he gonna do? Tell you you can't see me? Ban us from getting married?'

The word slipped out of my mouth before I could stop it. Ruby's face kind of froze. But I'd said it now; there was no going back. 'I mean, is that what you want? For us to get married? Because you're nineteen. He can't stop us.'

'He can. You have to be twenty-one here to marry without parental permission. *You'll* be all right – on paper you're old enough already – but—'

I got up and went over to her, crouching down in front of her and taking her hands in mine. What had only been a vague, unspoken thought – a hope for some distant time in the future – was suddenly real. 'We'll find a way,' I said.

'When? *How?*'

'I dunno, but we will. If you can sort something out, I can make arrangements with the camp chaplain. Some of the other guys have done it already. They're giving us special dispensation because of us going off to war. It would only take a few days.'

She looked kind of dazed, as if she couldn't quite take in what I was saying.

'Is there any way – any way *at all* – you can get round having to ask your pa if we can marry?' I said. 'If you can, we don't even have to tell him. Not until I come back. And then I could take you to America with me – find a job and someplace for us to live, if you don't mind my ma and Meggie staying with us for a while.'

'Of course I don't,' she said.

'So could you?'

'I don't know. There might be a way – I'll have to think. But do you really mean it?'

'I can't think of anyone else I'd want to spend my life with,' I said.

I searched her gaze, praying I hadn't overstepped the mark. A smile spread across Ruby's face, like the sun coming out from behind a cloud, and a dimple appeared in one cheek. 'I'm not doing anything unless you ask me properly,' she said.

I climbed out of the window. Underneath it, in a spot of shade, there was a patch of white flowers with narrow white petals shaped like elongated hearts, nodding on slender stems. I picked one and fashioned the stalk into a ring, clambering back inside.

'Ruby Mottram,' I said, going down on one knee in front of her chair. 'Will you marry me?'

Back at camp, I headed for the canteen. I wanted to whoop, holler, punch the air. She'd said yes. *Mrs Ruby Archer!* I could hardly believe it.

As I went in, I tripped over a strategically stretched-out leg; Freddie Gardner. He grinned nastily at me. I ignored him, grabbed a coffee and a slice of pie from the counter, and headed over where Jimmy and Stanley were sitting with Davy Manganello and a couple of others, playing a game of Crazy Eights. There was a pile of notes and coins in the middle of the table.

'Feeling lucky, Sam?' Stanley said with a grin as I sat down.

I grinned back. 'You could say that.'

'Don't. He's cleaned me out already.' Davy looked at the cards he was holding in disgust.

'Yeah, I'm out too,' Jimmy said.

'Nah, I'm OK.' I shovelled the pie into my mouth, suddenly realising how hungry I was.

'Lookit him.' Davy narrowed his eyes. 'There's something he ain't telling us.'

'You been with your girl?' Jimmy asked.

My mouth was still full of pie, so I just nodded.

'You look like you asked her to marry you and she said yes,' Davy said.

I shrugged.

'You did, didn't you?' A grin spread across his face. '*Shit, Sam—*'

'When?' Jimmy demanded.

I swallowed the pie. 'Dunno. Soon as we can. I was gonna go and talk to the camp chaplain.'

Stanley frowned. 'You can't marry her here, in town. Not if her family are as bad as you say they are.'

Crap. I hadn't thought of that.

'I know a guy in Ilfracombe, though,' Stanley went on. 'Reckon he could do it, if you got the right papers.'

'Yeah?'

'I'll get in touch with him, see what he says.'

Grinning again, I clapped Stanley on the arm. 'You're a pal.'

'Bagsy I'm a witness!' Jimmy yelled.

'You can all be witnesses,' I told them. 'So don't start quarrelling like a pack of goddamn kids.'

By the following afternoon, thanks to Stanley and his contact, it was all organised. Ruby and I had an appointment at the registry office in Ilfracombe at eleven o'clock on Sunday morning. I sent a message to the *Herald* offices, and she sent one back saying Vera had agreed to be her witness and that she had got around having to ask her pa for permission – she didn't say how.

Now all I had to do was pray she didn't change her mind.

On Saturday night the camp was busier than usual, jeeps everywhere. As Jimmy and I went to get dinner I saw a group of top brass, stripes on their sleeves and medals across their chests, walking from the officers' mess hall to one of the big recon huts.

I turned, watching them go. 'Huh, why d'you reckon they're here?'

'I dunno,' Jimmy said, frowning after them. 'Maybe Stanley will. If anything's happening he's usually the first to know about it.'

But he shook his head. 'No idea, sorry. A meeting or something, I guess.'

'Or they're gonna bust your chops for being a goddamn card cheat!' Davy said. Laughing, Stanley swiped his hat off his head.

As we ate, I tuned the rest of the guys out, thinking about Ruby again. In less than twenty-four hours, she'd be my wife.

'Sam. *Sam.*' Someone nudged me sharply in the ribs.

'Huh?'

Jimmy was looking at me. 'I *said*, when do you think they're gonna send us over there?'

'Over where?'

'Holy mackerel, he's got it bad,' Davy said. '*France*, you knucklehead.'

'Oh, I dunno.'

'Reckon it'll be soon.'

'You do?' Stanley mopped his plate with a hunk of bread. 'I heard the weather's gonna be pretty bad over the next week or so. Reckon they'll hold off for now.'

The conversation turned to other things. I went back to thinking about Ruby, and that house we were gonna live in – that one with the roses and lilacs in the yard.

Despite Stanley's gloomy predictions about the weather,

Sunday dawned fine and clear. I was too nervous to eat, so I skipped breakfast and headed for the camp gates. Stanley, Davy, Jimmy and I were leaving for Ilfracombe in an hour or so and I wanted to take a walk to clear my head. My uniform was clean and pressed, my boots polished to a shine.

I saw a group of soldiers coming towards me. They looked pissed off.

'Don't bother,' one of them said to me, shaking his head. 'They're not lettin' anyone out.'

My stomach lurched. 'What?'

But he and his pals had already gone past.

I ran down to the gates. 'Sorry, Private,' the guard said. 'Camp's closed. No one in or out. Orders came last night.'

'But I've gotta go – I'm getting married!'

He shook his head. 'Sorry. There's nothing I can do.'

I went back to my hut and slumped onto my bunk, staring at the floor. Soon, Ruby would be at the registry office – and I wouldn't. What was she gonna think? Jimmy, Stanley and Davy came in and I watched their faces fall as I told them what had happened. 'I'll try and get hold of Vee,' Stanley said, turning on his heel and rushing out again. Before long, he came back, looking ashen. 'They won't even let us make phone calls,' he said. 'I'm sorry, Sam. There's nothing I can do.'

Shortly afterwards, we were all called to the parade ground, and given our orders.

We were leaving for the embarkation camp at Portsmouth tonight.

22

RUBY

'Oh, darling, I'm sorry,' Vera said again, trying to put an arm around me as the bus bumped back through the lanes to Bartonford. I shrugged her away, staring out of the window, my eyes bright with unshed tears.

We'd waited and waited outside Ilfracombe Register Office, me wearing the smart cream blouse and fawn skirt, jacket, hat and shoes I'd borrowed from Vera, Vera similarly attired in dark blue. Eleven o'clock had come and gone – half past eleven – then the town hall clock had struck twelve, and I'd finally been forced to admit defeat.

'This means they're on their way to France, doesn't it?' I'd said as we walked back to the bus stop. 'It must do – Sam wouldn't change his mind like that. And even if he had and he was too scared to tell me, surely Stanley would have let you know he wasn't coming.'

Vera had squeezed my hand. She'd looked pensive, biting her lower lip, and despite my own crushing disappointment I'd realised she must be worried too. We'd walked the rest of the way to the bus stop in silence.

When we got back to Bartonford, we returned to her flat so I could change back into my ordinary clothes. Then I sat on the edge of her bed and cried. Vera brought me tissues and tea, and a cold flannel to wipe my face. 'I'll go up to the camp this afternoon,' she said, 'and see if I can find out what's going on.'

Later, back at the cottage, I took Alfie's box out of my underwear drawer. The stitchwort flower ring Sam had made me, shrivelled now, was inside, wrapped in a piece of tissue, next to the drawing he'd given me that first time we'd met at the cave. I gazed at it, biting back another sob.

I was supposed to be Mrs Ruby Archer by now, I thought bitterly. It wasn't fair. It wasn't *fair*. This *bloody* war. After all the trouble we'd gone to! I'd got around the problem of asking Father's permission to marry Sam by typing a letter myself on a piece of headed notepaper I'd stolen from his study, and forging Father's signature by copying it from some notes he'd left on his desk. I hadn't been proud of myself, but Sam was right – I didn't need to tell Father yet. For now, nothing had to change, and what he didn't know wouldn't hurt him.

The rest of the day passed in a daze. Every minute seemed to take an hour; I didn't know what to do with myself – couldn't settle inside my own skin. Whenever I thought about Sam it was as if someone was twisting a knife into my stomach, a physical pain that took my breath away. Where was he? Was he all right?

On Monday morning, I lay dozing, pushing away the moment of complete awakening; of remembering. Then, in an unpleasant rush, it all came back to me. Slowly, drearily, I sat up and swung my legs out of bed.

When I went outside after breakfast, it was drizzling, and my bicycle had a puncture. I shouldn't have been surprised; both wheels were more patch than tyre these days and it needed new ones really, but – like with so many things – they were impossible to find. Perhaps Sam could—

That pain stabbed through me. *Oh, Sam, please be OK*, I thought.

As I walked down the hill into town, the streets seemed unusually busy, everyone standing round in little groups on the pavement instead of queuing to go into the shops.

'Yes, they've gone, every last one of them!' I heard a woman outside the fishmonger's say.

'Who has?' I asked her.

'The Americans! The camp's empty!'

I ran the rest of the way to the *Herald* offices, where I almost collided with Vera, who was in the hall putting on her coat and hat.

I didn't need to say anything; I could see from her face that she already knew. She'd chewed all her lipstick off.

'Howler wants me to go up there and report on it. Are you coming? Don't worry about your work – I'll help you catch up later.'

I didn't need asking twice.

'I went up yesterday afternoon and they were still there, but no one would tell me anything – the guards weren't letting anyone in,' she said as we hurried back through town, following a crowd of people making their way up to the camp.

It was just as the woman outside the fishmonger's had said: the camp was empty, the gates standing open. The sandy ground outside the fence was churned up with tyre tracks, all of them fresh. On the other side of the wire were piles of food:

tins and boxes, fresh fruit, meat and bread. *They've left it for people to take because they won't be needing it anymore*, I thought, and a cold hand squeezed inside me.

Squabbles broke out as everyone fell on the food, desperate to grab whatever they could. Vera squared her shoulders. '*Herald* reporter, coming through!' she said in a shaky voice, brandishing her notebook. The crowd parted and we pushed our way through into the camp.

I shivered, remembering how full of life and noise the place had been when I came to the dance last year. Now, it was like walking through a ghost town. Vera pushed the door to one of the soldiers' huts open and we peered inside. The beds were unmade, books and packs of cards scattered everywhere, and in one corner, a wireless was still playing. Vera marched in and turned it off. The silence was deafening.

'It looks like they could come back at any moment.' Vera's face was paler than ever, and she was gripping her notebook so hard her fingers made dents in the cover.

Eventually, we returned to the *Herald* offices, leaving the crowd still fighting over the food at the camp gates. We spent the rest of the day at our desks, trying, not very successfully, to work.

That evening, after supper, Father turned the wireless on for the BBC news bulletin. He'd heard about the Americans leaving too, from one of his colleagues at the hospital.

'What on earth's wrong with you?' Grandmother said sharply, noticing the way my fingers were clenched around my knitting needles.

'Nothing, Grandmother.' I marvelled at how even my voice sounded. 'I was just wondering if there was any news about the Americans – the camp's empty, you know.'

'Well, we all knew this day would come eventually. And it's not just the Americans we need to think about. Our boys are over there too.' Then her tone sharpened. 'What were you doing up at the camp, anyway?'

'Please will you both be quiet,' Father pleaded. 'I'm trying to listen.'

Grandmother sniffed, pursing her lips. I pretended to concentrate on my knitting. There was nothing much on the news about the Americans, and once it was over, Father switched the wireless off.

Later, in bed, I lay awake, listening to Grandmother's snores and the thudding of my own heart. It was no good. Quietly, I got out of bed, bundling up my bedclothes so that if Grandmother should wake and light the lamp, she'd look over and think I was burrowed underneath them. I padded across to the door in my bare feet and slipped out onto the landing, holding my breath as I pushed the door closed behind me. I crept down the stairs and into the parlour, feeling my way across to the wireless and turning the volume right down before I clicked it on.

I didn't have long to wait. Just after midnight, a broadcast came through.

'This is Richard Dimbleby speaking from an aerodrome in England on the night of June 5th,' a faint, crackling voice said, *'and reporting the fact that the first aircraft carrying the first parachutists who are going to land on the fortress of Europe in the beginning of our great attack tomorrow morning, are taking off from this air station at this moment quite fast...'*

I pressed my ear to the speaker, listening to the grumble and roar of plane engines firing in the background.

'Eight machines have gone – a ninth – the tenth – the

eleventh – the twelfth – and up to something like a score are coming round the aerodrome, one after the other…'

This was it. *This was it.* But what about the soldiers on the ground? Where were they? Where was Sam? I waited for Richard Dimbleby to mention them, but when the broadcast ended, I was none the wiser.

When I got to work the next morning, Vera had a wireless set on her desk, an ancient, monstrous thing with its cracked case held together by tape and string. 'Howler dug it up from somewhere. I told him we'd listen and take notes.' She tried to smile at me, but her face was as pale as it was yesterday and she'd forgotten to pencil in her eyebrows. 'I didn't get a wink of sleep last night, did you?'

I shook my head, and took the Benzedrine tablet she offered me.

Half an hour later, Alfie arrived with the post. 'What d'you think's happening over there?' he said breathlessly. His eyes were shining, his cheeks flushed.

'They're giving Jerry what for, I hope,' Vera said.

Alfie sighed. 'I wish I was there with them.'

'No you don't!' My tone was so sharp that both Vera and Alfie look round at me, startled. 'It's dangerous – men are going to get killed. You can't want that!'

He scowled at me. 'It's different for you. You're a *girl*,' he said, and stalked out without another word.

'Oh dear,' Vera said as the door to the street slammed below us, hard enough to make the building shake. 'I don't think he took that very well.'

'Oh, blow him! It's that Maud Tinney – you know she's chucked him, and told him he was a coward for not joining up?'

Vera's eyes narrowed dangerously. 'Silly cow. I'll give her what for if I see her round here again.'

It wasn't until midday that the announcement we'd been waiting for came crackling over the airwaves.

'Here is a special bulletin, read by John Snagge,' the announcer said. 'D-Day has come. Early this morning the Allies began the assault on the north-western face of Hitler's European Fortress...'

We listened in tense silence.

'Oh, Ruby, do you think they'll be OK?' Vera said in a trembling voice when it was over.

She reached for my hand and I took hold of it, squeezing her fingers tightly. 'They'll have to be. They *must*,' I said. I was trying to sound strong, although I wasn't sure if I really believed it.

Would we ever see Sam and Stanley again?

23

SAM

Eight hours earlier

'Jesus,' Jimmy groaned. 'Dunno if I can take much more of this.'

I shot him a sympathetic look, too far gone myself to speak. On the other side of me Stanley was retching into his steel helmet; everyone had long since used up the vomit bags they'd handed out to us before we embarked.

It was the early hours of Tuesday morning and we'd been anchored out in the English Channel in a flat-bottomed landing craft for hours now, packed shoulder to shoulder with the other men. A short while ago there'd been a bombardment, planes roaring overhead. The noise was terrific, like nothing I'd ever heard before. *I shoulda been married by now*, I thought miserably.

As dawn broke, the landing craft engines shuddered into life. Our boat surged forwards and we approached Omaha Beach under a sky like an iron lid, crouched in the bottom of the boat to avoid enemy fire. The swell hurled us up into the air and back down again. I was soaked and freezing, my teeth clacking together, and I needed to urinate. I'd never felt so scared in my life.

More guns boomed overhead. Then I heard the *sip-kiss* of a bullet whistling over our heads. 'What the fuck, man?' Davy said behind me.

Jimmy bobbed up, just long enough to take a look at the beach up ahead of us. 'Oh, *shit.*'

I took a quick look over the side of the landing craft too – I didn't want a bullet through my neck before I'd even got off the damn boat. We were about a hundred yards from the beach, maybe a little less. The bombardment just before our crafts launched was supposed to have destroyed the beach defences and create shell holes and craters we could shelter in when we landed.

But there was nothing there: no craters, no shell holes, nothing. Just virgin sand, stretching as far as the eye could see, and all the beach defences were still intact.

I crouched down again. 'What the fuck are we gonna do?' Jimmy shouted over the cacophony all around us. 'There's no cover! We'll be dead meat!'

The guys near us heard him and panic ran through the troops like a shock wave. Several of them stuck their heads up to look too, ducking again and swearing as sniper bullets cracked through the air.

All of a sudden there was a tremendous jolt, throwing us all off balance; we'd hit a sandbar, fifty yards from the shore. The British Navy officer crewing the landing craft tried to get us off it, grinding the engine, but we were stuck fast. 'Lower the ramps!' our CO barked.

I held my breath, trying to remember everything I'd learned.

I'd heard about guys drowning during training exercises when they tried to go over the end of the ramp and got crushed underneath it. *Go over the side, go over the side*, I repeated to myself, checking I had my pack, my gun, ammo, lifebelt, more to give my hands something to do than anything else; I didn't want anyone to see how badly they were shaking.

More orders, the ramps clanged down, and the world exploded around us.

Shells and mortars screamed overhead; bullets zipped past; men were mown down by machine-gun fire before they even made it off the ramps. I could see Jimmy yelling something at me but I couldn't hear him. Stanley was on my other side, shouting too. The press of the men behind me pushed me forward and then I was in the water up to my armpits, surrounded by floating bodies and equipment.

As Jimmy, Stanley, Davy and I began to wade towards the shore, holding our guns above our heads, the landing craft next to us took a direct hit, black smoke pouring from the bow. A guy jumped screaming over the side, his uniform in flames. There was nothing any of us could do. We had to get out of the sea; the water was freezing, slicked with oil from the damaged landing craft, and all around us the snipers' bullets were zipping and cracking through the air. Somewhere out there, there were four of them with our names on them, and unless we got ourselves under cover somehow, we were gonna get it.

My foot hit something on the seabed – a rock, a body, a piece of equipment that someone had dropped, maybe – and I staggered, fell face first into the water and couldn't get up again, weighed down by my own equipment and my saturated uniform. The damn life vest I was wearing, shoved up under my arms, was no use whatsoever – it kept me afloat, but I couldn't turn over to get my mouth and nose out of the water. I sucked in oily water and began to choke, my gun slipping out of my fingers. *This is it*, I thought as black spots began to dance in front of my eyes. *This is how I die. Not because I got one of Jerry's bullets through my head but because I'm too damn heavy to swim. Sorry, Ruby, I guess I won't be seeing you again after all.*

Then someone hauled me upright by the webbing on my pack. At first I thought it was Jimmy or Stanley but when I looked round, coughing up water, it was Wilson, one of the fellows from the band who played at that party. Christ, that felt like a lifetime ago.

Wilson had a medic's badge on his arm. 'You OK?' he yelled in my ear. I couldn't speak for coughing but I managed to nod. He clapped me on the arm and, before I could thank him, carried on wading to shore. When I'd finished spewing up seawater I felt around for my gun, but it had gone. So had Jimmy, Stanley and Davy – I couldn't see them anywhere. I was sure only seconds had passed since we were given the order to disembark, yet half the 116th Infantry Regiment seemed to be lying in the water, shot to pieces or drowned.

Nearby a soldier was floating face down, his helmet gone and blood pouring out of a hole above his ear. My stomach turned over, thinking it might be one of the guys, but when I lifted his head it was a fellow from another unit who I'd never seen before. I yelled at him, '*Hey!*' just to make sure, but he was a goner all right. 'Sorry, pal,' I muttered as I pulled his gun off over his head. A big wave came in, almost knocking me off my feet again. As the water sucked back, I saw it was red, and it took me a moment to work out why.

You know those dreams where you're running but you're not going anywhere? That was what it felt like as I splashed through the shallows, ducking and flinching as the bullets and mortars whizzed over my head. Up ahead I could see men floundering onto the sand and taking shelter behind the beach obstacles. More men lay at the edge of the water, dead or injured, or half drowned, too weak to crawl any further. *Just get there*, I told myself. *All you have to do is get there.* But the beach was still a hundred miles away. It would take a miracle for me to make it out of here alive.

24

SAM

With one last effort I hurled myself forwards through the shallows and onto the wet sand, collapsing behind one of the beach defences, a structure made out of heavy wooden posts with sharpened ends that had been driven at angles into the sand. I used my hands to try to scoop out a shallow foxhole, burrowing down as far as I could.

As I lay there, I found myself wishing I could go back, warn myself what I was letting myself in for. But then there would be no Ruby; did I really want to change that? I wondered if she knew where I was right now, what was happening.

The tide was creeping in, washing bodies up onto the sand; that was stained red too. After a while, the waves began lapping at my feet. I needed to move, but there was no one giving orders. Everyone who hadn't been killed was just lying here, like me, pinned down on the beach. There was nowhere to go. Nowhere that was safe.

I heard a gurgling sound. A soldier had washed up beside me, lying face down in the shallow water; the poor sonofabitch was drowning. I raised my head and yelled. '*Medic! MEDIC!*'

The only response was a hail of machine-gun fire from Jerry. I had to press myself flat against the wet sand again, praying that bastard up on the cliffs wasn't a good shot. When it was over, I slithered over to the soldier, keeping as close to the sand as I could. I reached out, trying to push his head sideways to get his face out of the water, and swore.

It was Jimmy.

He was half conscious, the skin around his lips turning blue. 'C'mon, Jimmy,' I said, pushing his shoulder. 'C'mon. Wake up. Wake *up*.'

He groaned. I swore again. Looking round, I saw another soldier nearby, watching us: Freddie Gardner. His helmet was gone, and his bluster with it. He was white-faced, wide-eyed.

'Help me get him out of the water!' I shouted at him.

Gardner whimpered and shook his head.

'Help me get him out, or he's gonna fucking die!'

But Gardner just closed his eyes and turned his head away, gripping his gun so tight his knuckles turned yellow.

I spat at him. 'Fuck you, you piece of *shit*.'

I got slowly to my knees, every muscle in my body taut as a violin string as I tried to pull Jimmy clear of the waves. He was too heavy, his uniform and equipment saturated with water. I grabbed the knife off my belt and cut his pack away. With it gone, I was able to drag him a little way up the sand. I shook him again, patting the side of his face. 'Jimmy, it's Sam. Wake *up*.'

He groaned again, his eyes rolled up to the whites.

Zip! A bullet flew over my head, practically parting my hair. I flattened myself to the ground again. 'Jimmy,' I say in a firmer voice. '*Jim*. C'mon, buddy. Speak to me. *Wake the fuck up*.' I was halfway between laughing and bawling my eyes out.

Jimmy's eyes flickered open. 'Hey, Sammy,' he croaked. 'We're in deep shit, aren't we?'

'We will be if we don't get off this damn beach. You hit anywhere?'

He coughed weakly, spitting seawater. 'Don't – think – so.'

An impossible distance away, I could see a sea wall at the foot of the bluffs, wounded men lined up along the bottom. The position of the wall meant they were safe from German fire, and there were medics moving among them, treating their wounds. If Jimmy and I could get up there, he'd get the help he needed.

'Jim,' I said, pointing. '*Jimmy*. You see that wall?'

He nodded.

'That's where we're gonna go. Me and you together, buddy, OK? But we'll have to stay low so we don't draw fire.'

He nodded again.

'OK. Follow me.'

I began to crawl forward, using the beach defences for cover as I wriggled across the sand. All around us, men lay dying or dead – I'd never seen so many goddam corpses. Every so often I looked round to check Jimmy was still with me, and I could see the effort it was costing him; he had to keep stopping, coughs racking through him, and there was bloody froth on his lips.

Somehow we made it up the beach until we were only a hundred yards from the sea wall. Some of the men there spotted us and start calling to us, waving. 'When I say go, we're gonna run,' I said through clenched teeth as Jimmy and I lay there, side by side. 'We just gotta get over there and we'll be safe. OK?'

Jimmy didn't answer me. He was grey with exhaustion and cold. His eyes kept closing.

'*Jimmy*. Fucking stay with me, man.' I gave his shoulder a hard punch and his eyes flew open again.

'Sorry, Sam,' he slurred. 'So... tired...'

'You can sleep in a minute, buddy, OK?'

He nodded.

'*Go!*' I scrambled to my feet, pulling Jimmy up with me. As we ran a hail of machine gun bullets spattered into the sand all around us. We were nearly there now – fifty yards; thirty; twenty; ten—

Jimmy went down like a puppet with its strings cut, screaming and clutching his knee.

I hauled him to his feet again and half dragged, half carried him the rest of the way to the sea wall to where the medics were waiting. One of them was Wilson. He started working on Jimmy immediately, slapping a field dressing on his leg while another guy prepared a morphine injection. I collapsed with my back against the wall, gasping for breath. 'You hurt?' Wilson said over his shoulder. I shook my head.

'Shit, man, I thought you were both gonna die out there.'

'Me too,' I gasped.

Stanley Novak crashed down next to me. 'Jesus fucking Christ, am I glad to see you. What the fuck is happening? Why the fuck didn't they take out the defences?'

'I don't know,' I say. 'You all right?'

'I think so.'

'Jimmy got hit.' I jerked a thumb at him. He was moaning, but then another medic injected him with the morphine and he went still. 'You seen Davy anywhere?'

Stanley shook his head. 'We gotta get the fuck off this beach.'

'How?'

'I have no fucking idea.'

We stayed at the foot of the sea wall for what felt like hours, trapped there with the battle raging on all around us. More men joined us, until we were a little group of twelve. Among them was Freddie Gardner. He ran his hands through his hair until it was standing on end. 'Shit,' he kept saying, staring at the bodies lying on the beach, at the smoke pouring from the crippled and half-sunken craft still out at sea. '*Shit.*'

'Shut the fuck up,' someone told him at last.

Eventually an officer I'd never seen before made it over to our little group and we began to get organised. He ordered us to start climbing the bluffs. As I forced myself to scramble after Stanley, Gardner and the others, digging my fingers and toes into sandy rock that crumbled away beneath them, a sniper spotted us and began firing. I heard someone cry out but I didn't look back to see who it was. I was running on pure adrenaline now. *It wasn't supposed to be like this*, I thought. *We were supposed to storm this place in a blaze of goddamn glory.*

Because there was no glory here. It was a nightmare, one that felt as if it would never end, and I was praying and praying I'd wake up and find myself back in my hut at the camp or at the lodge with Ruby sitting in the armchair opposite, the lamplight making a halo around the edges of her hair. Or maybe, if I couldn't have that, back home with Ma and Meggie.

As bullets whipped around me, I kept climbing, wondering if I'd ever see any of them again.

25

RUBY

10th June

For the past four days, it felt as if the whole of Bartonford had been holding its breath. People kept asking me and Vera what was happening, perhaps thinking that, because we worked for the *Herald*, we were privy to information they were not, but we only knew what everyone else did: that the British and Americans had met fierce resistance on the French beaches, managed to push through in the end, albeit with enormous casualties, and were now fighting their way across France.

Everywhere you went, people were talking about it. Vera was sent to write a story about Richard Bland, the butcher's son, who was in the navy and whose ship had been sunk in the channel by the Germans before he could even reach the shore. No one was sure what had happened to him; hearing his name made me feel sick. What if Sam was one of those whose boats had been sunk too, or one of those who hadn't made it off the beaches?

Vera was equally worried about Stanley. She bought the

Telegraph daily, and we combed through the names of the dead. So far, Sam and Stanley hadn't been among them, but I was constantly gripped by terror that it was only a matter of time.

'What on earth's wrong with you?' Grandmother snapped at dinner one evening, as I listlessly pushed my food around on my plate.

'Nothing, Grandmother,' I said automatically.

'You're looking awfully pale. And thin. *Please* don't tell me you're moping over those Americans!'

Oh, if only you knew, I thought bitterly. I stabbed my fork into a piece of carrot. 'I'm not moping, Grandmother.' I tried to keep my voice level, but I couldn't quite manage it.

Grandmother threw her hands in the air, wearing her long-suffering look. 'Oh, the way she talks to me, Cecil!' she said to Father. 'And I suppose you're just going to let her get away with it?'

'Mm?' Father glanced up from his notes.

'Your daughter is being unforgivably rude to me, Cecil!'

Father blinked myopically at us both. 'I – er – oh dear.'

'*Cecil*,' Grandmother thundered.

Father frowned at me. 'Er, apologise to your grandmother, please, Ruby.'

I'd had enough. Wordlessly, I stood, scraping my chair across the floor, and went out, thumping the door closed behind me and cutting off Grandmother's '*Well!*'

I hunted round for my shoes and cardigan, choked with fury. I didn't know where I was going to go or what I was going to do; all I knew was I couldn't stay here a moment longer, not with *her*.

Grandmother's voice coming from behind the kitchen door, raised and shrill, made me turn back.

'This is your fault, Cecil! If you'd sent her away to school when she was younger, like I told you to—'

'I did what was best for Ruby at the time, Mother.'

'And look where it's got her! She's such an *odd* girl. Always got her nose in a book – and so wilful – no man's going to want *that*!'

That's what you think! I wanted to burst in there and yell at her, but I stayed where I was.

'When I was her age I was married – I had a good job—' Grandmother continued.

'Ruby has a job, Mother.'

'Huh! Making tea and changing typewriter ribbons – some job *that* is!'

'Mother, will you *please* stop giving Ruby such a hard time?' Father's voice was sharper suddenly; his tone took me by surprise.

'And now he turns on me too! So this is the thanks I get!'

'*Mother.*'

'*Everything* I did for you was for your sake, Cecil. I gave up *everything* for you. And you *abandoned* me.'

'I did not *abandon* you, Mother! We had to move to Bartonford because of my work, and we came back to visit you regularly. But you didn't like Ellen – didn't approve of her – nothing she said or did was ever good enough—'

'Because she *wasn't* good enough! She was flighty, unstable – you of all people should have been able to see that – and as for what she did with that *man*—'

'Shut up!' Father roared at her. 'Just SHUT UP!'

I stared at the kitchen door, mouth open in shock.

A few moments later, Grandmother stormed out of the kitchen. She pushed past me as if I wasn't even there, stalking out of the cottage and slamming the front door behind her hard enough to make the whole house shake. She wouldn't return until almost midnight; goodness knows where she'd been.

I went into the kitchen. Father was breathing hard, staring at his notes, his pencil gripped in his fist.

'Father?' I said, aware of a faint ringing sound in my ears. He didn't answer me.

'Father, what did she mean?' I said. 'What did Mother do?'

Father shook his head. 'I don't want to discuss this. Not now.'

'But, Father—'

This time, it was me he shouted at, making me jump almost out of my skin. '*NOT NOW, Ruby!*'

He began to cough, his shoulders shaking. I brought him a glass of water but he pushed me away. 'Leave me alone, damn you. Why can't everyone just bloody well leave me alone?'

I ran upstairs, my eyes stinging with tears. Father had never spoken to me like that before, not even when I was a small child.

Sitting down on the edge of my bed, I gazed at the worn rug beneath my feet. What had Grandmother meant? Who was *that man*?

Oh, Sam, I wish I was here so I could talk to you about it, I thought, with a burst of longing and despair.

Suddenly, I was struck by a chill certainty that I would never see him again: the same awful feeling that had come over me that day at the party when he'd told me he was going away to south Devon on training exercises. I told myself not to be so stupid – that I couldn't possibly know that. We still needed to get married – we had our whole lives together in front of us. He'd be all right. He *had* to be.

But that night, I lay awake, gripped by fear, unable to quiet the anxious thoughts running through my mind.

26

SAM

11th June

'You sure you're gonna be OK?' I asked Stanley Novak, who was lying next to me in a pile of straw, a blanket rolled up under his head. He nodded, sucking in his breath sharply.

'You want some water before we go?'

'That would be good, yeah.'

'I'll go find you some.'

I got to my feet, rubbing my eyes, which were gritty from lack of sleep. Then I realised we were alone. *Dammit*, where had Gardner got to now? We'd made the decision last night to try and get back to the beach today, find out where our unit had gotten to and send help for Stanley. Freddie wasn't too happy about it; he'd gotten comfortable here, even though he was the only one out of the three of us who was in decent shape. He'd looked at me incredulously and said, 'Why the fuck would I want to go out there? I'll get shot to pieces by the Germans.'

'We leave it any longer, we'll get court-martialled for desertion,' I'd told him, and he'd gone quiet. Clearly, even he wasn't dumb enough to think his daddy could save him from that.

Now, I went to the stable door. It felt as if years had passed since Omaha, even though it was only a few days. As I'd scrambled up the bluff that afternoon, another two fellows had been picked off by the sniper; I hadn't known who either of them were, but I'd never forget the look on the face of the guy beside me when a bullet smacked into his shoulder, or the sound of him screaming for his mother as he tumbled backwards onto the shingle. As I made it to the top, I'd taken one last look over my shoulder at the beach.

Bodies had been strewn across the sand and floating in the sea, where crippled landing craft and tanks stuck out at jagged angles from the water. The sky had been thick with smoke from burning fuel and the damaged ships. *How the fuck are we even still alive?* I'd thought. For a moment, I'd been frozen, my fingers dug into the crumbling, sandy rock. Then Stanley had reached down and pulled me over, and I'd sprawled on my stomach on the ground at the top of the bluff.

The officer who'd joined us at the sea wall had been barking orders. Soon our little group was up and running in formation towards the road above the cliffs. We'd pushed our way through tangled hedgerows and across fields, keeping low, trying to move as fast as we could. As night fell we'd come across a German platoon and there was a fierce firefight; two more of our guys had bought it, cutting our number down to seven, but the rest of us got away.

By nightfall we'd reached a little village. None of us had a map, so I still didn't know what it was called. We'd thought we might be able to find food, somewhere to rest up, but the place was in ruins. We'd searched anyway, and found a bottle of wine, the label too dusty to read, which we'd shared between us – it was vinegary and thin – then we'd snatched a few hours' sleep amongst the rubble of someone's basement, taking turns to keep watch.

I'd been sure only minutes had passed when I was shaken awake again. Our CO wanted us to keep moving inland, try and join up with other units if we could find them. My heart had sunk. I was so goddamned *tired*, and I couldn't get the things I'd seen that day out of my head. Even when I'd been asleep they'd haunted me – I'd had nightmares about being back in the water, drowning, choking on blood and oil, all mixed up with desperate dreams of Ruby who was standing with Ma and Meggie on the beach, all of them shouting something at me that I couldn't hear.

This time we'd stuck to the roads. We'd been walking for quarter of an hour or so when we reached a castle – an actual, goddamn castle, looking like something out of a fairy tale. That had been the only fairy-tale-like thing about it, though; the place had been crawling with Germans dug down in trenches. We'd opened fire, tossing grenades, but we were hopelessly outnumbered. In the end, only Stanley, Freddie and I had managed to get away. We'd run like hell, scrambling across more fields and hedgerows, and it wasn't until we'd reached the farm where we were now that I'd realised Stanley was shot in the thigh, his pants soaked with blood.

'Shit, man, why didn't you say something?' I'd hissed at him as we entered the yard, guns raised and ready.

'Didn't – want – to – slow – you – down,' he'd jerked out

from between gritted teeth. Even though it was dark I'd been able to see he was at the end of his strength.

'Gardner, help me, Goddammit,' I'd hissed. 'Stanley's hurt.'

Grudgingly, Freddie had come around the other side of me, and we'd helped Stanley into a stable where there was a solitary horse dozing in a stall near the door. It snorted when we came in but I was able to soothe it, stroking its nose and talking softly to it until it calmed down again. We'd put Stanley in the stall at the other end of the stables and then I'd torn a strip off my shirt and tied it around his thigh to try and stem the bleeding. To my relief, it had worked. I'd collapsed beside him in a heap of dirty straw, too exhausted to carry on. I'd fallen asleep again almost immediately and, despite the nightmares, I'd slept until the morning when I woke up to find the farmer's daughter, a girl about mine and Ruby's age, staring down at us with her mouth open. I'd tried to reassure her, although I didn't speak a word of French, and I'd started coughing. I'd got a raging fever; I guess those hours on the beach, soaked to the skin and freezing cold, had taken their toll.

That had been five days ago; we'd been here ever since. The farmer and his family were part of the resistance; they'd been looking after us, and tried to get a radio message through to the British to let them know we were here, although they hadn't managed it so far. I was starting to feel a little better now, although I was weak and couldn't shift this damn cough. Stanley was still real sick. His wound had gotten infected even though we'd used our supply of sulphanilamide bandages on it and tried to keep it clean, and he couldn't put any weight on his leg at all.

I looked out of the stable door. The yard was empty save for a few hens pecking around in the dirt. After checking again that the coast was clear I went over to the house and knocked on the door. There was no answer. Perhaps the farmer and his family were out in the fields. I pushed the door and it creaked open.

I was about to step inside when, from the nearby barn, I heard a woman's voice. Although I couldn't make out the words, I recognised the tone: pleading, slightly panicked, but low, as if she didn't want anyone to hear. *Shit*. Had the Germans found us?

As quietly as I could, I went over there. The door was closed but there was a window in one side without any glass in it. I crouched down, and peered over the sill.

It was the farmer's daughter, Isabelle, and there was a guy in there with her. Freddie. He'd got her backed up against an old horse cart with a broken wheel.

'*Non, non, monsieur. S'il vous plaît,*' Isabelle was saying. She was struggling to push him away, her face streaked with tears. Freddie shoved her back again, pinning her in place with his legs. 'No you don't.'

He yanked her skirt up roughly, exposing her thighs. 'I got *needs*, sweetheart. Shut up and do your bit for the goddamn war effort.' With his other hand, he was fumbling with his belt. Isabelle was sobbing loudly now. Anger flooded through me, making black spots dance in front of my eyes as I remembered all those times I'd listened to Ma begging Kirk not to hurt her through my bedroom wall. Grabbing my pistol from my belt, I burst in there.

'You bastard! Leave her the fuck alone!' Freddie sprang away from her, his pants half undone, his face a picture of surprise. His expression quickly changed to an angry sneer.

'Sammy boy. I might've known. Come to take your turn, have you?'

'You piece of shit,' I said as Isabelle yanked her skirts down and fled, pushing past me and out of the barn. 'You're no better than the goddamn Krauts.'

Freddie did his pants up again, his face flushed and furious. 'That's goddamn rich, coming from you.' He didn't seem to have noticed or even care that I was pointing a gun at him.

'Fuck you, Freddie.' I spat in the dirt at his feet.

His face flushed a dull purple, and he launched himself at me. We grappled on the barn floor, months of mutual hatred finally boiling over. I was still holding my pistol, trying to keep it out of his reach as he attempted to wrestle it away from me. He punched me in the side of my head, making me see stars; with my free hand, I landed a blow right on his mouth, mashing his lips against his teeth. I wasn't seeing his face. I was fighting Kirk, and every blow I landed was one for Ma, and for Meggie.

Freddie grabbed my wrist and my gun flew out of my hand, hit the floor and went off, the bullet ricocheting up into the rafters above us and sending a flock of doves roosting up there fluttering out through the half-open door in panic.

We both scrambled to our feet. I stared at Freddie, panting and coughing, noting the blood coming out of his mouth and nose with satisfaction, even though one of my eyes was swelling shut and it felt as if my lungs were tearing themselves apart.

'What's the matter?' I said when I could speak again, and he still hadn't moved. 'You scared, you goddamn bullying piece of shit?'

He didn't answer. He was staring past me at the door. I saw my gun lying nearby, and stepped forward to pick it up.

'*Halt!*' a voice barked. I froze, my fingers just inches from the gun.

'Put your hands up and turn around,' the voice said in precise, heavily accented English. A dog began to bark. Slowly, I turned, and saw a German soldier standing in the doorway, pointing his Luger straight at our heads.

27

RUBY

3rd July

Slowly, my days slipped back into their old, pre-Sam routine: I got up, went to work, came home, ate supper, and went to bed or out on ARP duty.

I was existing, but I wasn't living.

The war ground on, with no word from – or about – Sam or Stanley, although Vera had written to the Red Cross, begging them for information. Sometimes I found myself wondering if Sam had even existed, or if the past ten months had been some long, wonderful dream I'd managed to convince myself was real. The only thing I had to remind me of him was the Emily Dickinson, and his drawing, and the shrivelled remains of the flower-ring. I hadn't looked at them since he'd gone; I couldn't bear to.

I didn't talk about how I was feeling to anyone, not even Vera – I didn't want to burden her with my own worries when she was so upset about Stanley. Grandmother kept plying me with various nasty-tasting tonics, saying I looked under the weather, but really, I knew they were her way of getting back at me for causing the row with Father. I had to force myself to eat, my waistband becoming so loose I began fastening my skirt with a safety pin.

A few days later, at work, Vera had popped out to the lav when Alfie arrived with the post. 'There's one for Vera,' he said.

'Oh, put it on her desk; she'll be back in a sec,' I said, sifting through my envelopes, which were all addressed to *Announcements* or *Advertisements, the Bartonford Herald*, and dividing them into the usual piles on my desk.

Alfie coughed. I looked round at him; he was twisting his cap in his hands.

'Father's having another dance at his works the first Saturday of August. I was wondering if this time, you might be free to go with me. I know your father doesn't approve of dances,' he rushed on, 'but you see, I've already got permission from your grandmother – I met her in the lane when I was on my way to work this morning and asked her, and she said it was all right to speak to you about it. I hope you don't think that was terribly forward of me but I – I'd really like you to come.'

Going to a dance with Alfie was the last thing on earth I wanted to do, but I hadn't the heart to turn him down flat. 'I – I'll think about it,' I said. 'Is that OK?'

He nods, his cheeks going pink. 'Thank you.'

Vera returned. 'Oh, hullo, Alfie.'

'H – hullo,' he stammered. 'B – bye, Ruby.' He dashed out of the room.

'What's got into him?' She sat down at her desk and picked up her letter, frowning at the handwriting on the front.

'He wants me to go to a dance at Blythe's with him next month,' I said dully.

She reached for a letter opener and slit the envelope, pulling out a single, thin sheet of paper. 'Oh. Will you?'

'I don't know. He's asked Grandmother and apparently she's quite happy for me to go, but I'm not—' Then I noticed the way she was staring at her letter, her face suddenly chalk-white. 'Are you OK?'

'I – it's from Stanley,' she croaked.

My heart gave a great, painful jolt. I stood up. 'I'll leave you in peace to read it.'

'No, don't!' She grabbed my hand. 'Please – stay.'

I sat back down, watching as she scanned the page. Her eyes grew bright with tears, but she began to smile. 'He's OK. He's in hospital, but he's OK!'

Then her face grew grave again.

'Vera? What is it?'

She turned the letter over. 'It – it's Sam.'

'What about him?'

'I – he—' She shook her head and, with a hand that trembled slightly, passed me the letter. 'I think you'd better read it.'

My dearest Vera, it began. *I am writing this to you from my bed at the Queen Victoria Hospital in Netley, Southampton – yes, I'm back in good old Blighty, and a lot sooner than I thought I would be! I am sorry it has taken me this long to write to you. I am wounded, pretty seriously I'm afraid, and I've been very sick, but now I am finally on the mend I wanted to let you know that I am OK. Hopefully this will make it past the censor.*

I don't know what you've heard about the invasion ("D-Day") over there but the Germans put up a hell of a fight. It was...

The next few lines had been blacked out.

A group of us made it over the bluffs later that day and inland, the letter continued. *After a few more skirmishes with the Germans we reached a little village, and sheltered there for a few hours before moving out again. Our CO was pretty keen for us to find another unit – strength in numbers, I guess. What we hadn't counted on was stumbling across a whole nest of Germans, who were waiting for us in the castle just outside the village. The fight was terrific – most of the guys bought it and I got shot through the leg. Eventually I managed to escape with Sam and a guy called Freddie Gardner.*

I shuddered, remembering the grinning, arrogant soldier who'd cornered me in Ropewalk Alley, and leered at me at the dance. How long ago that seemed! Poor Sam, getting stuck with him.

We staggered around the countryside the rest of the night until we were thoroughly lost, Stanley continued, *and I was half out of my mind with pain. Eventually we stumbled across a farmhouse, right out in the middle of nowhere, and hid in a stable. I was good for nothing and by the next day, Sam was sick with a fever and cough – we'd all spent most of the previous day...*

Another blanked-out section. I held the paper up to the window, but the censor had used indelible black ink in great thick strokes, obliterating whatever was there.

For the first couple of days, the farmer and his family looked after us, Stanley continued. *I had a nasty infection in my leg, which was getting worse, and in the end Sam, who was starting to feel better, made the decision that he and Freddie would go and look for our guys and send help. But something went wrong – I'm not sure what, because I was laid up in a stable, unable to move, but Sam went to fetch me some water before they left and next minute I heard shouts in English and in German.*

Somehow, I found the strength to haul myself up into the rafters of the stable, where I hid myself just minutes before the Germans came pouring in. There seemed to be hundreds of them, although in reality there can't have been more than twenty. They searched the stable, jamming their bayonets into the pile of straw where I'd been lying, but I guess God was on my side that day because they didn't look up. A guy in a commandant's uniform came in and barked something in German. After taking the horses, his men filed back out into the yard. I heard the farmer's wife sobbing, pleading with them. Then shots – five of them.

I don't recall much after that, except that I smelled smoke and heard more shouts before everything went quiet. I hid in those damn rafters until nightfall, then crawled out into the stable yard. The Germans had ransacked the farmer's house and burned it to the ground. The barn too. Only the stable was left – maybe they'd run out of fuel. There was a pile of something in the middle of the yard, smouldering too – bodies. Nearby was a jacket. I managed to pull it towards me. It was torn and covered in blood. In the inside pocket were some papers. They were Sam's.

I wanted to go and check the bodies to make absolutely sure, but as I tried to crawl across there my strength left me and I lost consciousness. I was found a few hours later, still lying in the yard, by a British platoon. They got me back to the coast and onto a ship for England, which was pretty hairy too, as during the crossing an enormous storm landed right on us. We made it in one piece, though, and I've been here at Netley ever since. It looked for a while as if they might have to take my leg off but they think they might be able to save it after all, thanks to this new miracle drug they call penicillin.

Please tell Ruby about Sam. And make sure you tell her he is one of the finest men I ever knew. I am so sorry.

I will write again soon,

Yours,

Stanley xx

My ears began to ring, the letter slipping out of my fingers to the floor. Somehow I found myself in my chair, my legs turned to India rubber, dark spots flocking in front of my eyes. 'Put your head between your knees and breathe,' Vera ordered. 'I'm going to make some tea.'

She returned with two mugs a few minutes later, but I couldn't drink mine. Sam... *gone*. It was what I had feared all along, yet it still didn't seem quite possible. Vera kept asking if I wanted to go home, but having to hide how I was feeling from Grandmother was the very last thing I wanted or needed right now.

What about his mother and sister? Did they know? Should I try and find out where they lived and write to them? What were they going to do now, without the money he'd been sending home to them?

That evening, I cycled back to Barton Hall in a stupor. I got off at the gates and wheeled my bicycle the long way round through the gardens, still unable to face returning to the cottage. Men were sitting on the lawn in the evening sun – the numbers of patients at the hospital had swelled again after the invasion – but no one paid me any attention.

In the rose garden, I bumped into Mrs Blythe, who was on her way back to her house in the lane. 'You're lookin' right peaky, my girl,' she said in her kindly way. 'Not sickenin' for summat, are you?'

'I'm fine, Mrs Blythe, honestly,' I heard myself say, as if from a great distance. 'It's just this awful war. It's been going on for so long.'

'And you're missing that soldier of yours, no doubt.'

I stared at her. 'How did you—'

'Oh, goodness me, Ruby love, don't look so worried! I won't tell anyone. Saw you two sneaking into that old lodge one day, didn't I? Well, good for them, I said. It's about time that girl had a bit of happiness in her life, especially with that old dragon breathing down her neck at home.'

Suddenly, I remembered a day in April when Sam and I had arrived at the lodge and there had been an enormous bunch of wildflowers in a vase on the lounge table. He'd sworn he had nothing to do with them, but I'd thought he was being bashful, and had laughed his protests off. The lodge had always seemed so tidy, too, even though we were always far too preoccupied to think about sweeping the floors or dusting. Again, I'd put it down to Sam.

I burst into tears. 'Sam's dead, Mrs Blythe. The Germans shot him.'

The colour drained out of her face. 'Oh, Ruby, love.'

There was a little summer house in the secluded rose garden nearby, which was empty; she led me in there, sat me down and offered me a hanky. 'You have a good cry. Let it all out.'

I leaned against her, all the pain and anguish of the last few weeks pouring out of me in wrenching sobs. Mrs Blythe put her arm around my shoulders. 'There, there,' she kept murmuring. 'There, there.'

Eventually, I had no tears left. I sat up and blew my nose, swallowing hard, my eyes raw.

Mrs Blythe gazed out at the flower beds, which were a riot of scent and colour – pinks, reds, white, cream and lemon yellow. 'I had a fellow, before the last war. Dennis, he were called. He volunteered and got sent to France. *I'll be back before you know it, Dot!* he said before he got on that train. That were the last time I saw him.'

I looked round at her.

'But he also said to me, *If I don't come back, Dot, don't spend the rest of your life waiting for me. Don't make sense for you to act as if you're dead too. I want you to be happy. I want to know you'll be all right.* He made me promise, see?'

I wondered, numbly, what she was getting at.

'When I got that letter saying he was missing, it was the worst day of my life,' she said, 'but I remembered what he'd told me and I made up my mind there and then that I was going to keep my promise. I met Wilf a few months later and, oh, I knew I'd never love anyone like I'd loved Dennis, but we've been happy enough, Wilf and I.'

She gave me a motherly squeeze. 'Allow yourself to grieve, Ruby love, but don't spend the rest of your life pining away. Your Sam wouldn't have wanted that – I'm sure of it. And at least you know, one way or the other. There's so many that never will.'

Getting heavily to her feet, she gave me a pat on the arm. Then she was gone. All around me the air was heavy with the fragrance of the roses, and filled with the screams of the wheeling swifts that nested in the eaves of Barton Hall. I sat in the summer house for a long time, thinking about what Mrs Blythe had said.

28

RUBY

August

'I 'll come to the dance with you on Saturday, Alfie.'

It felt as if a stranger was moving my mouth, making me speak the words, but Alfie didn't seem to notice anything was amiss. A grin spread across his face and the tips of his ears went pink. I could see how relieved he was I'd finally made up my mind. Every day since he'd asked me, he'd come into the office with a hopeful expression; I could tell he was desperate to ask me if I'd decided yet, but, being the gentleman he was, he'd never said anything.

'I'll call for you at half past six,' he said, dropping a bundle of envelopes on my desk. 'Thanks awfully, Ruby!'

It was a warm day and we had the office windows open; as he went out onto the street below, I could hear him whistling.

Vera was frowning at me. 'Are you sure?'

I shrugged. 'Why not?'

Ever since Stanley's letter had arrived, I felt as if I had been split in two. There was a Ruby who lay awake into the small hours of the morning, with a lump in her throat and a pain behind her eyes from the tears she couldn't shed, and who, when she caught Father looking sorrowfully at Mother's picture on the never-played piano, wanted to say to him, *I know how you feel. I've lost the love of my life too.*

And there was another Ruby who got up every morning and made breakfast as if everything was as it always had been; who dodged Grandmother's barbs and placated her fretful father with her usual, long-practised ease; who went to work every day where she ignored Vera's concerned looks and dodged her gentle questions. Both of them were trapped behind a thick sheet of glass where no one could reach them.

Ever since that evening in the rose garden I'd been turning Mrs Blythe's words over and over inside my head: *Allow yourself to grieve, Ruby love, but don't spend the rest of your life pining away. Your Sam wouldn't have wanted that; I'm sure of it.*

My Sam. But he wasn't *my* Sam anymore, was he? He wasn't anybody's. He was gone. What was I supposed to do? Live like Father, my life blunted forever by grief? If I was going to survive, I had to let the other Ruby take over, and push the Ruby who couldn't cry – who felt as if a knife was twisting inside her every time she remembered the way Sam used to smile at her – deeper down inside. And that meant accepting Alfie's invitation.

On Saturday evening, Alfie called for me at half past six on the dot, as promised. He was wearing a suit that was slightly too short in the arms and slightly too tight across the shoulders, his hair slicked back with almost as much hair cream as the unfortunate Humbert Spriggs.

Blythe's Works were ten minutes away, at the edge of town. 'Dad offered to take us in his van,' Alfie said, 'but as it's such a nice night I thought you'd rather walk.'

I could tell he wanted me to take his arm, but I kept my hands down by my sides, not looking at him. How different he was to Sam – so serious! He always had been, even when we were children. It was impossible to imagine laughing with him until my sides ached and my eyes streamed, the way I had with Sam.

With a guilty wrench, I pushed the thought aside. It wasn't right to compare them; Alfie didn't deserve that. But when we went inside, I couldn't help making comparisons again, this time with the hall at the works to the one at the American camp. There was no band, only a wind-up gramophone on a table in the corner, and the walls had been decorated with paper bunting that did little to brighten the dingy paintwork or disguise the tape criss-crossed over the windows. And there were no pineapples or bottles of Coca-Cola.

STOP, I told myself. *You're being terribly unfair.*

To my relief, Alfie turned out to be a surprisingly competent dancer. He guided me around the dance floor, one hand resting at my waist. I didn't mind. That glass wall was all around me, shielding me from thinking, from feeling.

We were halfway through a polka when the air raid siren split the air.

'Oh, not *tonight*,' I heard someone groan.

We all went down to the air raid shelter in the cellar, which was dimly lit by gas lamps. 'You watch,' a man said to me over his shoulder. 'We'll get down there and the all-clear'll sound.' But it didn't, and pretty soon it looked like we would have to settle in for the night.

'Let's sit over here,' Alfie said, laying his jacket on the floor in the corner away from everyone else. I couldn't think of any reason to refuse, so I followed him over there. Someone started singing, a cheerful if tuneless rendition of 'On the Sunny Side of the Street', and soon everyone was joining in except for us. Alfie and I sat in silence; I glanced at him every now and then to see him watching me intently.

At last, he cleared his throat. 'Ruby.'

'Yes, Alfie?'

'I – er—' His ears had gone pink, like they had the morning he asked me to the dance – the morning I'd found out Sam was dead.

I waited, concentrating on my breathing. In, out, in, out. Wasn't it marvellous, the way our bodies worked without us even having to think about it? They kept going, like machines, even when it felt as if, inside, we were barely alive.

'The thing is—' Alfie cleared his throat again. 'I didn't ask you to come to the dance tonight as a friend. I wondered if – well, you see, I care for you, Ruby. A great deal.'

I looked at him. His expression was raw, earnest. I wondered what he'd say if I told him, *I'm sorry, Alfie. I don't feel the same way about you. You're a chum, but that's all.* How his face would crumple as my words hit home.

I couldn't do it.

And what else did I have? Night after night at the cottage with Father and Grandmother? Was that really how I wanted to spend the rest of my life?

Don't think about the future. Don't think about anything, I told myself. *It doesn't matter – none of it does.*

'If you want me to go out with you, Alfie, I will,' I heard myself say.

His eyes shone. 'D'you really mean it?'

I nodded.

'Oh, Ruby!' His face lit up with a broad smile. 'You've made me the happiest man in Bartonford tonight – in the whole of Devon!'

The all-clear sounded. Alfie got to his feet, still smiling, and helped me to mine. We spent the rest of the evening dancing together, and at the end of the night, he walked me back up the hill to Barton Hall. The hospital was in darkness save for a few lights burning in some of the windows, where the nurses were tending to the trickier cases, the ones who needed caring for throughout the night.

'D'you fancy the cinema in Ilfracombe one evening next week?' Alfie said as we parted.

'That would be nice.'

He leaned towards me. I turned my head slightly so that his kiss landed awkwardly on my cheek.

'Goodnight, Ruby,' he said.

'Goodnight, Alfie.'

In the moonlight, I watched him walk away, back down the hospital drive to the lane. He was whistling, a spring in his step. Then I turned and went inside the cottage, softly closing the front door behind me.

PART THREE

1945

29

SAM

9th February

'I love you,' I told Ruby, taking her hands in mine. We were back in the old lodge at Bartonford Hall, which had been restored, its mildew-speckled walls painted a bright white, the wooden floors gleaming, hazy sunlight pouring through the windows and turning her hair to spun copper.

She smiled at me – that smile I saw for the first time on the beach. 'I love you too, Sam. I always will. But I have to go. They're waiting.'

'Who's waiting? No – don't!' As she stepped away from me, I grabbed at her hands, trying to hold on to her. But there was no longer any substance to her; she was dissolving into the dust that danced in the shafts of sunlight, and even those were dimming to a dull, lifeless grey.

'Ruby!' I cried. But I was alone. The sun had gone, and all around me the lodge had become a ruin. The roof was gone, the walls reduced to piles of rubble as if they'd been shattered by a bomb. The smashed stones were dusted with frost, the air bitterly cold. A crow cawed, the sound harsh and rasping.

The sound turned into someone coughing. Slowly, the dream left me as I woke, drifting back to reality: not the lodge, but a squalid tent in a Nazi prisoner of war camp somewhere in Germany.

I was coughing too. Everyone in the camp was sick, thanks to a combination of the cold weather, the harsh conditions and lack of food. I rolled over on the pile of straw that I used as a bed, shivering. I felt wrung out and exhausted, even though I'd just woken up, as if a heavy weight was pressing down on me. Part of it was this damn flu or whatever it was that I couldn't get rid of; mostly, it was despair.

I'd been here for almost eight months now. When the Germans had caught me and Gardner at the farm, I'd tried to put up a fight, but one of them had wrestled me to the ground, tearing off my jacket and punching me in the face. Then the soldiers had killed the farmer and his family and ransacked the house, setting it on fire. I'd thought they were going to kill us too, but they'd taken me and Freddie to another farm where there were other American prisoners waiting, rounded up like sheep. A few hours later, we'd been on the move again. Gardner and I had been separated, and I'd not seen him since. Not that I cared; that chicken-shit bastard could go rot in hell.

The Germans had marched the captured troops – hundreds of them – along miles of country road with no food or water. As we passed one house in a tiny, bombed-out village, an old woman had emerged with a basket of apples and handed them out to us. They'd been last season's, old and shrivelled, but I'd never tasted anything so good. I'd been the last person to get one before a guard shoved her roughly back into her house, swearing at her in German. She'd jutted her chin out defiantly and slammed the door in his face.

Finally, we'd reached a railroad, where they locked us in boxcars for the slow, seemingly endless second leg of our journey. They'd let us out once a day to relieve ourselves; the rest of the time we'd had to use a steel helmet as a latrine, sharing it between eighty of us. The stink was terrible. As for food, if we were lucky we'd gotten dry bread and brackish-tasting water; most of the time there'd been nothing. The trains had only moved at night – I guess the Germans were afraid of them being spotted by the Allies and bombed – so it had been over a week before the train finally arrived at the prisoner of war camp. I'd been expecting to see rows of huts; instead, after we'd been interrogated and the officers separated from the privates, we'd been marched to a collection of big, circular tents.

'What is this, the goddamn circus?' one of the guys had joked, earning himself a crack across the head from one of the guards. It had turned out the huts were so full that there was no room for us. There were already thousands of prisoners at the camp, not only Americans but British, Dutch, French and Polish soldiers too. Each tent held around four hundred men, with nothing but our body heat to keep us warm.

At first, everyone had been scared to death. We all knew what the Nazis had been doing to the Jews, and others, too – how they'd been enslaving and murdering people. Some of the guys here were Jewish, but it turned out the camp was run by soldiers from countries the Germans had annexed, so a lot of the men who had been put in charge of the camp's day-to-day workings were prisoners who were Allied officers, mostly British. I guess the Germans wanted to keep their own guys to send into battle rather than have them stuck here doing all the boring jobs. The guards were German – kids mostly, all of them as miserable-looking as we were – but the officers running the place helped keep the Jewish prisoners safe and tried to keep things ticking over for the rest of us, too. There wasn't much anyone could do about the living conditions, though; from day one, I was dreading the weather getting colder. If it hadn't been for Davy Manganello, who I'd bumped into on my second day here, I'd've gone half crazy by now.

This morning, after breakfast – the usual crusts of bread and pale brown water they called coffee – I went back to the tent to wait for the work orders. It wasn't any warmer inside than it was out, but at least in here I was out of the wind. I sat down and took the book I used to sketch in out of the waistband of my pants. God knows how I'd managed to keep hold of it, but I had. I tore out a page and began to write.

Dear Ruby, I scrawled, muffling a cough with my sleeve. *How are you? I am fine and being treated well.*

I didn't tell her the truth; I knew better than that now.

What's been happening back in Devon? I continued. *Are you still working at the newspaper? I wish I could send you a message to let you know I'm OK. I hope that father and grandmother of yours aren't driving you up the wall.*

Can't write more now – no time. But I love you and I will make it back to you one day. Hang in there.

Sam xxxxx

I tore out another page.

Dear Ma,

I am sorry it's so long since I last wrote to you and that I haven't been able to send any more money. I hope you and Meggie are OK and managing to get by and that Mr Addison is still helping you. If you can, tell him I am not dead and that when I get out of here I will pay him back for any assistance he gives you with interest. I hope my letter gets through to you this time. I am OK and being treated well.

Sam xx

That was all the time I had. Another siren began to wail, signalling that we had about thirty seconds to get out into the yard and line up. I folded up the letters, scribbling addresses on the outsides, and scrambled out of the tent after everyone else.

A guard came down the line, stamping through the slush to collect letters from the prisoners who had them ready. Thanks to an agreement between the camp and the Red Cross, prisoners were allowed to write to their loved ones back home. *Please let them take them this time*, I prayed. *PLEASE*. I was desperate, especially about Ma and Meggie. I knew Ruby was probably OK, but the thought of Ma and Meggie not knowing what had happened to me – of the money I'd been sending home drying up – sent me half crazy with worry at times.

The guard took the pieces of paper I was holding out and unfolded them. He read them with one eyebrow arched – they read everyone's letters here, which is why I was so careful not to say anything bad about the camp. Then he shook his head. 'Not you,' he said, and tore them up, letting the pieces flutter down into the slush at my feet.

Anger and despair surged through me. *Damn.* It happened

every time, no matter how many lies I filled my letters with. Down the line, I saw Davy watching me sympathetically. They always did the same to him when he wrote letters home, too. It had taken me longer than it should have to realise we were still both being punished for last year when, a month or so after getting here, we'd tried to escape while we were on a work detail in a nearby town, clearing rubble after a bombing raid.

It had been Davy's idea. They'd only sent out one guard with us and after *Mittagessen* our group had gotten spread out, so when he left us alone we'd started walking, not looking back. We'd joined the railway tracks to the east of the town, planning on following them to the Czech border, but that night we were caught by a patrol and brought back to the camp, where we were beaten and put on latrine duty for a month as punishment. At first Davy had wanted to try again, but then winter came and with it, heavy snow. Davy got sick, and then I did. A couple of other guys, two Brits, had made a break for it anyway and were found about a mile away, drowned, in the middle of a frozen lake they'd tried to cross, not realising the ice was too thin. The guards had brought their stiff, blue, frozen bodies back to the camp and thrown them on the ground in the yard as a warning to the rest of us.

This morning, I was expecting to be sent on clean-up detail – a few nights ago there'd been a bombing raid on the railway yards in the middle of the city and I'd been part of the group sent out to clear the rubble, under careful watch from the guards this time. Instead, I was ordered to join a smaller group at one side of the yard with Davy, a Scottish guy called Harvey McLean who we were both kinda friendly with, and a couple of others.

I was about to ask if they knew where we were going when

another prisoner joined our group. Shock jolted through me. It was Freddie Gardner.

I stared at him. I'd not seen him since the day we were captured. There were so many of us here, and when we weren't out working we spent most of our time in our tents, sticking in little groups and trying to keep out of the way of the guards. Freddie looked very different to the guy who'd tried his best to make my life a misery back at boot camp and in England. His swagger was all gone, his cheeks hollowed out, his shoulders stooped. There were painful-looking sores at the corners of his mouth.

I tried to catch his eye, but the guard was ordering us into formation. I stayed with Davy and McLean. Gardner was at the back of the line.

Davy glanced back at Gardner too, and raised his eyebrows. 'Look what the cat dragged in,' he murmured, while my mind raced. If Freddie was here, what about Stanley? He wasn't here, so had he managed to escape the farm? Or was his absence because—

No, no. I didn't want to think about that. 'You know where we're going?' I asked Davy out of the corner of my mouth as we started to march, trying to distract myself.

'Soap factory,' he muttered back. 'Been there a coupla days already.'

'Damn.' I'd been hoping that we might get sent to a farm. You could scrounge vegetables sometimes – swedes or turnips or potatoes – and if you shared a few of them with the guards they'd look the other way while you filled your pockets.

We were marched through the melting snow to a collection of huts and buildings at the edge of the city, surrounded by tall barbed wire fences. It took us over an hour to get there and by the time we arrived my legs felt weak, my stomach already gnawing with hunger. I thought I'd gotten used to being hungry when I was living on Kirk's farm, but it had had nothing on this.

Me, Davy, McLean and Freddie Gardner were taken to a huge shed at the edge of the factory complex. 'What the hell's this? Are they making soap out of Goddamn cement?' Gardner said, scowling at an enormous pile of fine, grey grit. There was another pile of the stuff on the other side of the shed, two guys working away at it with shovels and piling it into barrows.

'Pumice,' McLean said. 'There's no fat to make soap the normal way anymore so they're using this instead. *That's* cement.' He jerked his head at the other side of the shed. 'Better not get 'em mixed up, eh, laddie?' He and Davy exchanged a glance.

I soon fell into a trance, shovelling pumice powder into barrows with Davy. Freddie and Harvey fetched the barrows and tipped them into the mixers. It was hard work, but the skin on my palms was thick with calluses and I'd learned to ignore the pain in my arms and back that set in after a few hours. *Do; don't think* was the only way to survive here.

'What's the cement for?' I asked Davy after a while. He was acting strangely – not nervous, exactly, but like he was on edge, watching for something – or someone.

'They're building some more sheds.'

He glanced round again. I knew that look.

'What's going on?' I asked him when we stopped for *Mittagessen*. The guard had his back to us, smoking a cigarette, and Freddie Gardner and Harvey McLean were sitting apart, not speaking to each other. Our skin and clothes were dusted grey from the pumice and I could even taste it in the bread we were eating, particles crunching between my teeth.

'Nothin', nothin'.'

'Pull the other one. It's got goddamn bells on it.'

His eyes narrowed. 'What's that supposed to mean?'

'You're jumpy as a jackrabbit. Just like you were when we were planning to escape.'

He looked over his shoulder at the guard, then said, 'Keep eating,' and bent his head close to mine.

'That cement—' he indicated to it with a flick of his eyes '—at about twelve hundred hours, one of the guys outside is gonna create a distraction. If it works, and the guard goes out, I gotta fill one of these barrows with it instead of the pumice.'

I frowned. 'Why?'

He grinned at me. ''Cause when they shut down the mixer tonight, it'll set and gum it all up. I know it sounds pretty dumb. We'll probably get a lot of flak for it, but it's worth it if it pisses the Krauts off and puts this place outta action for a coupla days.'

'You're nuts.' I was shaking my head, but I was smiling too.

'If anyone asks, you never heard nothin' about it.'

I nodded.

True to his word, about an hour later, there was a commotion outside: shouts, and a crash. The guard went running out.

Davy grabbed the nearest empty barrow, wincing as he did so; his back was bothering him.

'Here, I'll do it.' I ran with it over to the pile of cement and shovelled it into the barrow as fast as I could, choking as the fine dust rose into the air. I made it back to Davy's side just as the guard came back in, followed by Gardner. I was still breathing hard, and saw Gardner shoot me a narrow-eyed glance as he took the loaded barrow. *He blames me*, I realised. *He thinks us being here is MY fault because of the fight that got us caught by the Germans.*

Davy noticed the look too, and scowled after him. 'That sonofabitch. You wouldn't even be here if it wasn't for him.'

We worked for the rest of the afternoon in brooding silence, gathering outside the shed in the early evening with the other prisoners to begin the long march back to the camp. 'Did it go OK?' Davy asked McLean quietly, when the guard wasn't watching us. I remembered the glance I saw go between them earlier; he was in on it too.

McLean gave a brisk nod. 'Aye. Stuff wasn't mixing too well to start with, but we convinced the overseer it was a problem wi' the machines. He switched them off and we mixed the last few loads by hand. It'll be well set by the morning.'

'Great.' Davy grinned, his teeth very white in the middle of his dusty face. 'We'll do the other one tomorrow.'

The guard was looking at us again. Davy clamped his mouth shut.

The next morning, we were marched back to the factory. This time, Davy and I were sent to work the mixers, and Freddie and Harvey McLean were ordered to load the barrows. The overseer, a short guy wearing wire-framed glasses with little round lenses that flashed in the cold winter sunlight, ducked into a little outhouse next to the mixers to switch on the power. Davy and I glanced at each other, taking care to keep our expressions neutral. The first machine groaned into life. The second made a strange crunching sort of sound, then stopped dead. We heard the overseer swear. He hurried over to the machine and peered into it, and swore again. '*Nutzlose Maschine!*'

That was when I noticed curls of smoke drifting out of the outhouse doorway. I nudged Davy. His eyes widened.

A few moments later, the overseer saw the smoke too. He went running in there and came back out straight away, shouting '*Feuer! Feuer!*' I didn't speak much German, even after all these months in the prisoner of war camp, but you didn't have to be a genius to know what he meant.

Fire.

'Shit, the machines jamming up must've shorted out the wiring.' A mixture of panic and glee was fighting across Davy's face. 'Guess they didn't have proper fuses or something.'

The overseer had disappeared, to fetch help I guess. Smoke billowed out of the little outhouse, thick and dark and acrid-smelling.

'It's gonna blow.' Davy sounded nervous. We stepped back, out of the way. Behind us, Gardner and McLean came out of the shed and stared at the smoke. 'What the bloody hell's going on?' McLean asked as, from within the little outhouse, I heard a pop and a roar. Before I could answer him the roof was on fire, flames leaping into the air.

'Unexpected developments.' Davy was grinning now, but he still looked kinda worried.

The fire quickly spread to the other buildings. They were all built close together, the spaces between them barely big enough for a man to squeeze through. The place erupted into chaos as guards and the overseer ran about yelling, making prisoners fetch buckets of water. We might as well have been pissing on the flames for all the good it did. There didn't seem to be any hoses, and the heat was immense. When the guards realised it was hopeless, they hustled me, Davy, McLean, Gardner and the other prisoners into a small, fenced yard in the middle of the factory complex.

'If they ask who did it, don't say nothing,' Davy murmured

in my ear. 'I've already talked to some of the other guys who'd guessed we'd got something to do with it. They ain't gonna say nothing either.'

I nodded. 'No fear.'

I hadn't taken more than two steps forwards when a guy in a boiler suit strode through the gates, flanked by four guards. Davy's eyes widened slightly. 'Here goes,' he said out of the corner of his mouth.

'Who's that?' I muttered.

'The boss. *Kommandant.*'

The man barked an order in German. Everyone fell quiet. All I could hear was the roaring and crackling of the fire as it continued to tear through the factory complex.

'Who is responsible for this?' the foreman said in English. 'I know this was no accident.' Although his voice was level, his jaw was clenched.

A few people coughed and shuffled their feet, but no one said anything. I stared at the ground.

'I said, who is responsible? If you do not come forward now then you will all be severely punished.'

Still, no one spoke.

'In that case, you will all be beaten,' the foreman said. 'After that, you will give me your boots and march back to your camp in bare feet through the ice and snow. And you will have no food for the next two weeks. Not even stale bread.'

'It was them.'

My head jerked up. Freddie Gardner was pointing at me and Davy. 'They put cement powder in the mixers yesterday instead of pumice. I saw 'em do it.'

'You piece of—' Davy snarled at him. He lunged forward, but a guard grabbed him, pinning his arms behind his back.

Another grabbed me. A few of the guys called out in protest but were quickly silenced. We were hauled out of the yard and locked up in separate rooms in a little building off to one side of the main complex, which was far enough from the other units to have escaped the fire.

I slumped to the floor, holding my head in my hands. Shit. *Shit.* We'd burned down a whole goddamn factory. I didn't think the Germans were going to be content with giving us a telling-off and a few weeks on latrine-clearing duty this time.

I heard a tapping on the wall to my right. 'Sam, you in there?' Davy called.

'Yeah. Right here.'

'Shit, man, I'm sorry. I had no idea those fuses were gonna blow, honest to God I didn't. I thought maybe we'd jam up the machines and piss 'em off, is all.'

I let out a humourless bark of laughter. 'Well, we managed that, all right.'

'I'll tell them it was all my idea, OK?'

'Don't be dumb. I helped you. This is my fault too.'

'Shit, man. If it wasn't for Freddie fucking Gardner—'

Someone hammered on the door. '*Halte den Mund!*'

Shut up.

Half an hour later, the local Gestapo arrived. As we were dragged outside again, there was a tremendous crash behind us. The main factory building had collapsed, throwing fountains of sparks and debris up into the air.

'*Yee-ha!*' Davy yelled, punching the air, a wild look in his eye.

We were slung into a van, the doors slamming closed in our faces.

30

RUBY

11th February

'You're leaving?' I stared at Vera, wondering if I'd heard her correctly. 'But you can't!'

She bit her lower lip, a line appearing between her eyebrows. 'Darling, I'm sorry. I didn't want to tell you until I was sure – I knew you'd take it badly – but everything's been confirmed now. And I would have told you – of course I would – but I promise you, it was an absolute spur-of-the-moment thing. When Stanley told me he was being invalided out of the army and would be sent back to the States next week, getting married was really the only thing we could do. I've got to go to some sort of transit camp for a few weeks, and then – if all the correct paperwork comes through and I've not got any awful diseases or anything – they'll stick me on a ship and take me over there too. Oh, Ruby, don't look so sad – I'll write to you as often as I can – and I'll come back and visit—'

I forced myself to smile. 'I'm happy for you, I really am. It's just—' I swallowed, hard. 'It'll be awfully lonely here without you.'

'But you've got Alfie.'

'Yes, I suppose so.'

'And once I've gone, Howler will have to promote you – you'll be a proper reporter, just like you always wanted!' She put her arms around me. 'Please don't let's fall out over this.'

I hugged her back. 'Don't be silly. I could never fall out with you!'

'We'll have a party before I leave – a real knees-up. You'll have to bring Alfie, of course.'

'Of course.' I smiled again, brightly.

'I'm awfully glad things have worked out between you two.' Vera sat down at her typewriter, briskly rolling a sheet of paper into it. 'I was so worried about you when we got the news about Sam. I honestly thought you'd never get over it.'

I was glad she wasn't looking at me; the smile stayed on my face, but I couldn't stop it from wobbling. 'Yes, well, life has to keep going, doesn't it?' I said lightly.

Later, after work, I walked down to Wreckers Cove. I hadn't gone back to the lodge since Sam had gone, but I spent a lot of time here. No one else knew, not even Vera or Alfie.

As usual, there was no one else around. A bitter wind was blowing off the sea, churning the waves that pounded the shore into white foam. The horizon and the sky were the same shade of steely grey, making it hard to see where one ended and the other began.

I tucked myself away in the cave where Sam and I used to meet before we started using the lodge, sheltered from the wind, at least, if not the cold, and took the little accounts book out of my coat pocket, and the pencil I kept in there with it. I'd finally started to write again: letter after letter to Sam.

Dear Sam,

I wonder what we'd be doing right at this moment if you were still alive. It's something I think about a lot, imagining us together – the life we might have had.

I know I should feel guilty for writing to you like this, like I'm being unfair to Alfie, but I know I'll never see you again, that you only exist inside my head now, and that makes it all right somehow.

I still miss you so much. I wonder if I'll ever stop missing you. I hope not. The thought I might forget about you one day scares me half to death. I'm already forgetting little details, like what colour your eyes were and how you sounded when you laughed. But I still remember what it felt like when you held me, and your smile. You had the kindest smile I've ever seen. I wish I had a photograph of you, or even a drawing. But we never got round to it. We thought we had plenty of time. But we didn't, did we?

If you're able to read this somehow, please don't worry about me. I'm OK. Life is OK. Alfie looks after me and he's very dependable. We go out two or three times a week to the cinema or to a dance, and Grandmother is happy too because she approves of him so she leaves me alone most of the time now – which is a relief, I can tell you! Father's buried in his work as usual – the hospital is bursting at the seams at the moment – so I'm not sure what he thinks, but I expect he doesn't mind. After all, he's known Alfie for as long as I have.

I think Alfie wants to ask me to marry him. And I think

if he does, I'll say yes. Now, that DOES make me feel guilty, because officially I'm still engaged to you. I hope you won't mind. But the alternative is spending the rest of my life alone, living with Father (and Grandmother while she's here), and I don't think I could bear that. If we buy a house I'm going to plant roses and lilacs in the front garden in memory of you (although I won't tell Alfie that of course!), but unfortunately a dog is out of the question because of his asthma. Do you remember that dog we were going to have? A greyhound with a black coat and a white chest and paws, and a red collar?

Oh – I almost forgot to tell you. Vera has married Stanley and she's off to America! It was a surprise – for her too, I think. I'm happy for her, really I am, but there's part of me that's sad, too – and, if I'm honest, a little bitter. First, I lost you, and now I'm losing Vera. Even though she's promised to write and visit I can't help feeling as if both of my best friends have been taken away from me. And she's living the life I thought I would have, when you came back from war and I moved to America with you. It all seems terribly unfair somehow.

I wish I could see you one more time, Sam. I wish I'd said goodbye.

And I hope, wherever you are, you know how much I will always love you.

R xxxxx

31

SAM

Dresden, 13th February

'Private Archer and Private Manganello, your sentence has been decided. You will be shot at dawn tomorrow.'

The officer who read out our sentence, speaking in English, could've been reading out a weather report. Somehow, I kept my expression neutral, the way I used to when Kirk was whaling on me, staring straight ahead with my hands down by my sides. I heard Davy, standing beside me, swear under his breath, but he kept still too. We'd already agreed that, whatever happened, we wouldn't give these Nazi bastards the satisfaction of knowing how we felt.

It was just after dawn. A short while ago we'd been brought to this little side room at the *Straflager*, the prison in Dresden city centre where we'd been locked up after the factory burned down, to hear our sentence. Seated behind a table were four German officers, wearing immaculate uniforms with swastikas on the sleeves. Davy and I were still wearing the clothes we'd been brought in. They were torn, stained with soot and pumice, and we were both crawling with lice.

'*Bring sie hier raus,*' the officer ordered one of the guards, his tone bored now. We were bundled out of the room and marched back to the main room of the *Straflager.*

The prison was in a large, circular building, bitterly cold, stinking and so crowded there was little space to move, or even to sit down. The main room had an enormous glass roof that made me wonder if it had been some sort of library or museum before the war. All the doors were bolted on the outside, and every morning, groups of prisoners were taken away, never to be seen again. Tomorrow, Davy and I would be among them.

We jostled for a space at the edge of the room. Davy slumped to the floor and buried his head in his hands. 'This is all my fault, man. All my fucking fault. I'm so fucking sorry.' His voice broke on the last word.

'Don't.' I put a hand on his shoulder, alarmed; I'd never seen him like this, not even after we were caught when we'd tried to run away. 'At least we screwed things up for those bastards, right?'

He didn't answer me. I thought about Ruby, Ma, and Meggie, wishing I could see them all one last time. How would Ma feel when I didn't come home? And Meggie? How had they managed all these months without the money I'd been sending home before I went to France? *I'm sorry, Ma*, I thought. *I failed you.*

And Ruby? Did she still think about me? Or was she already moving on with her life?

I realised that, despite everything, I felt strangely calm. At least I knew what was coming now. What else could I do but accept it? I sat too, hugging my arms around my knees and looking up at the glass roof. Through it, I could see the faint shapes of clouds moving across the sky.

As the morning went on, Davy cheered up, cracking jokes about the Germans. At noon one of the doors at the side of the room opened, and people surged forwards as guards brought in metal drums filled with soup. There were no bowls or spoons – everyone had to drink out of their cupped hands and scuffles broke out as people jostled for a place in line. I didn't bother; I wasn't hungry anymore.

I spent the rest of the day dozing, and listening to Davy, who was taking the mickey out of the other inmates now. 'Shut it, yank!' one guy, a Brit, called, but he sounded good-natured enough.

Eventually, darkness fell. There were no lights; the room was dark as a cave. I wondered what time it was, and how long Davy and I and whoever the other poor bastards they were taking with us tomorrow had left.

'You OK?' Davy asked. We were sitting back-to-back now, for warmth; the temperature was plummeting.

'Yeah.'

The air raid sirens started wailing. No one reacted. They went off most nights; nothing ever happened.

Suddenly, Davy sat up. 'What's that?'

I frowned into the darkness. 'What's what?'

'Listen.'

Over the wail of the sirens, I began to make out another sound: the deep bass drone of plane engines. It grew and grew, until the walls were vibrating with it.

I realised I could see the faces of the men around me. The sky through the glass roof of the *Straflager* was getting paler, illuminated by long ribbons of slowly falling light.

Davy leapt to his feet. 'Flares! *Shit!* They're gonna bomb the hell outta this place!'

People began jumping up, shouting, pushing to try and get to the doors, but they were still bolted shut; no one could get them open. I found myself separated from Davy, pressed against a wall as the light from outside grew brighter and brighter and the sky turned orange. There had been no explosions yet. The throb of the plane engines died away briefly, then returned, a deeper and more insistent sound, making the building shake so much I got scared it was gonna collapse around our ears.

The bombs began to fall.

They made a sinister rushing, whistling sound. I knew it was only a matter of time before the prison was hit. People were screaming, pounding on the doors to be let out, but no one came – the guards had already scarpered. An incendiary came through the roof, raining shards of glass and metal down on the people stuck in the middle of the room. It hit with such force that it broke up; no one who was directly underneath could get away and they were showered with lumps of whatever it was inside those things that made them burn. Their cries were awful, but no one could do anything; getting close would mean getting the stuff on you, too, and there was nothing to put it out with. I crouched into a ball, my arms over my head, my eyes screwed shut. *I'd rather have been shot by the Germans than go like this*, I thought. *At least it woulda been quick.*

The air around me was getting hotter and hotter. Suddenly, there was a tremendous explosion and something slammed into my back like a giant fist, sending me flying forwards. I sprawled on my hands and knees, debris raining down around me. The building had taken a direct hit.

As the smoke cleared a little, I saw the bomb had torn a gaping hole in the wall across the room. If we could get over there we could get out. I yelled for Davy but I couldn't even hear myself; the noise of the bombardment was terrific and my ears were singing from the blast. I clawed my way through rubble and bodies, looking for Davy, my nostrils thick with the stink of burning.

At last, I saw him, sprawled on his back. He looked peaceful, his eyes half closed; at first I thought he was asleep, and I couldn't work out how the hell he'd managed it with all this going on. Then my brain caught up with my eyes and I saw his lower half was crushed under an enormous lump of stone that had fallen from the roof, too heavy for me to lift. I shook him by the shoulder, yelling his name again. His eyes came open a little. They were unseeing, vacant.

He was dead.

Another bomb shook the building, more pieces of stone falling from the ceiling and crashing to the floor just inches away from where I was crouched next to Davy. The roof was about to cave in.

I passed a hand over Davy's eyes to close them again. 'Shit, I'm sorry, buddy,' I said, my voice cracking on the last word. I scrambled over to the hole in the wall.

Stepping into the street outside was like walking into an inferno – the whole city seemed to be on fire, the air thick with dust and smoke. Coughing, my eyes smarting and streaming with tears, I stumbled clear of the *Straflager*. I was just in time; seconds later, the roof and walls sagged inwards with a great roar, burying Davy and everyone else who'd been left behind.

I yanked off my shirt, tying it around my face to keep the

worst of the smoke out of my lungs, and staggered down the street away from the prison. There were people everywhere – ordinary German citizens trying to flee the carnage. But there was nowhere to go. The planes had gone but the fires roared all around us, great vortices of sparks and flame spiralling into the sky, which had turned a deathly red. Every so often, I'd hear the crash of another building falling. The heat was ferocious, printing itself onto my skin.

A woman stumbled out into the street in front of me, her face, hands and clothes blackened with soot and blood, her mouth open in a soundless scream. She was only a little older than I was. '*Helfen Sie mir, bitte!*' she pleaded with me, sobbing. '*Mein Kind!*' Then, in broken English: 'My child! Trapped!'

She tugged on my arm, and I stumbled after her, towards the ruins of what looked like some sort of store. Lumps of burning debris were scattered across the street. The woman began digging in the rubble, wailing, '*Monika! Monika!*' She turned to me again, her face wild with desperation. '*Bitte!*'

As I began to help her, I heard a faint cry from somewhere underneath the fallen stones. '*Mutti!*'

'*Monika!*' the woman cried. We heaved and pulled the stones aside, and I saw a pale shape below us – a child's face, streaked with tears. The woman began to sob.

I grabbed the girl under the arms. She was no older than Meggie had been when I left to join the army, wearing a torn blue nightdress, her hair a tangled nest of curls. She clung to me as I lifted her from the ruins of the building, calling for her mother. As I turned to hand her to the woman, there was another blast nearby. The shock knocked me flat; I felt a wave of tremendous heat pass over me as flames shot through the air, and I dropped the kid, throwing my hands over my head to try and protect myself.

Hearing screams, I scrambled to my feet, looking round for the woman and her child. They were nowhere to be seen. The building I'd rescued the kid from moments before was a ball of flame. I guess there had been an unexploded bomb in there, or a gas main had gone up.

Out of a fog of smoke, a shape lurched towards me. Monika. Her clothes and hair were on fire, her arms outstretched, her mouth open in a soundless, agonised scream. I grabbed her, trying to push her to the ground to put the flames out, but she panicked and fought me; she was surprisingly strong for her size. I grit my teeth at the sudden, searing pain as the flames caught my undershirt and I had to let go of Monika to beat them out.

I looked round desperately for water. There was nothing. I finally managed to wrestle Monika to the ground, but it was too late. She'd lost consciousness and gone limp, her eyes rolling up to the whites. There was no sign of her mother anywhere. No sign of anyone. 'Wake up,' I pleaded with Monika, shaking her gently. 'Dammit, *wake up*.' Her head flopped back and forth.

She began to have some sort of seizure, her back arching, her body stiffening. All I could do was watch. Finally, she went still. As I knelt there, staring at her, another building at the end of the street collapsed, sending flames leaping into the blood-coloured sky and an avalanche of burning rubble spewing across the street, cutting off my only escape route.

I was trapped.

32

RUBY

8th May

'*Yesterday morning at 2:41 a.m. at headquarters, General Jodl, the representative of the German High Command, and Grand Admiral Doenitz, the designated head of the German State, signed the act of unconditional surrender of all German land, sea, and air forces in Europe to the Allied Expeditionary Force, and simultaneously to the Soviet High Command...*'

I stared at the wireless set, which had taken up permanent residence in the office after D-Day – *my* office, since Vera was no longer here – listening to Churchill's voice crackling through the speaker. It was three o'clock in the afternoon. I should have been typing up a story about a stolen bicycle. But instead, everyone at the *Herald* was crammed in this tiny room to listen to the announcement being broadcast from London. Even Howler was here.

When the announcement had finished, he took off his

spectacles and polished them on a corner of his waistcoat. 'Well, thank goodness for that.'

'I have some brandy in my office,' Dobbsy said. 'I think, if the occasion permits...'

She went out, returning a few minutes later with a bottle and an assortment of glasses.

Howler lifted his in the air. 'To the defeat of the Nazis!'

'To the defeat of the Nazis!' I, Dobbsy, Charlie Hopkins and Robert Towle echoed.

Oh, Vera, I wish you could be here, I thought as I choked down the brandy. I wondered what she was doing right now in Washington. What time was it over there? Was she celebrating too? I'd had a letter from her a few days ago, telling me how homesick she was even though she was enjoying her new job at the *Washington Post*.

I didn't let myself think about Sam.

No one was in the mood to work after that, not even Dobbsy, so Howler let us all go home. Outside, crowds were spilling onto the streets, laughing, smiling, singing, chattering excitedly. *Is it really over... Still fighting in Asia, don't forget... Our boys will be home soon!*

'Ruby!'

Struggling to weave my bicycle through the throng of people on the pavement, I turned. It was Alfie in his post office uniform, waving at me and beaming.

'Did you hear the news?' he said as he reached me, and I was reminded of that day, all those years ago, when he'd come to find me on the beach to tell me war had been declared. We'd both changed so much since then. Everything had changed.

I took his hands, and shook my head. 'I can't believe it. It doesn't feel quite real. Oh, isn't it wonderful!'

He kissed me, right on the mouth. He didn't normally go for public displays of affection; it made me laugh. 'Why, Alfie!'

He flushed, but he was still smiling. Then, with a mixture of amusement and horror, I watched him go down on one knee.

'Will you marry me, Ruby?' he said, looking up at me earnestly, as people gathered round, watching us.

Panic clawed inside me. I began to stutter. 'I – I—'

'You can't turn him down, miss! Not today!' someone called.

Alfie was still gazing at me. 'I'll do it properly, of course – get a ring – and I'll have to ask your father – we'll need permission – but please say yes!'

The arguments for and against marrying Alfie whirled through my head like a swarm of bees. The *fors* were obvious: if I married Alfie, I could leave home – leave the suffocating little cottage and Grandmother – of course we'd stay in Bartonford, so I'd still be close enough to see Father every day and help him when he wasn't well, but I'd have my own space – my own home. Alfie wasn't Sam, but he was kind and I knew he loved me and would look after me. His family loved me too, and I them – Annie would be *thrilled* when she found out she was going to have me for a big sister. If I married Alfie, I wouldn't want for anything – wouldn't have to worry.

As for the *againsts*, there was only one: Sam.

And he was nothing but a memory.

Allow yourself to grieve, Ruby love, but don't spend the

rest of your life pining away. Your Sam wouldn't have wanted that; I'm sure of it. Heart pounding, face bright red, I took a deep breath. 'All right, Alfie. But get up, do! Everyone's staring!'

He stood, brushing grit off the knees of his trousers, and kissed me again, so hard he crushed my lips against my teeth. The crowd around us cheered.

We walked through town together hand in hand, back in the direction of Barton Hall. 'Should I come and speak to your father now?' he said.

I shook my head. 'He'll still be working – call round this evening.'

'OK. Will you come in for a while? We should celebrate!'

We went back to the cottage on Barton Lane. Alfie didn't say anything about our engagement – he wanted to talk to Father first – but I had another drink with his parents, whisky this time, and Annie put a record on. Mr Blythe swept Mrs Blythe to her feet and danced around the living room with her, while the rest of us watched them, Alfie and his sister grinning from ear to ear.

We've been happy enough, Wilf and I...

Would Alfie and I be *happy enough*? I hoped so.

When the record ended and Mr and Mrs Blythe had collapsed breathlessly into their armchairs again, I stood, a little dizzily. 'I must go.'

Alfie walked me to the front door. Out of earshot of the rest of his family, he said, 'I'll call round later – about eight?'

'Yes, that's fine.'

'Ruby—'

I looked round at him.

He grinned. 'See you later, Mrs Blythe!'

'Oh, Alfie!' I said, and laughed. I'd get used to being called that eventually, I supposed.

He kissed me on the cheek, chastely, and I went home.

'A letter came to the main house for you today, Ruby,' Father said at dinner, absently patting his pockets. 'Now, where did I put it? Ah – here it is.'

He passed me a slim envelope with my name and the hospital's address written on it in an unfamiliar hand.

'Who's that from?' Grandmother's face was sharp with curiosity.

'Something for work, I expect – perhaps they couldn't find the *Herald*'s office address.' I put the letter into my own pocket without looking further at it so it was safe from her prying eyes, and, glancing at the clock, pushed my chair back. It was five past seven – less than an hour before Alfie was due to call. For some reason, the thought of being here when he arrived made me uneasy. 'I must walk Toffee,' I told Father. 'I'll be back in a little while.'

When I went to Mrs-Baxter-down-the-lane's, she was beaming from ear to ear. 'I was so pleased to hear the news! All that dreadful fighting, over at last!'

'It's wonderful, isn't it?'

Her face grew sober. 'Although there's still all those terrible things going on in the Far East, of course.' She sighed. 'Someone's always fighting over something somewhere, aren't they? Anyway, don't let me keep you.'

I walked Toffee up to the coast path. When I reached Wreckers Cove, I remembered the letter in my pocket, and sat down on a rock at the mouth of the cave to open it. A strange little shiver went down my spine: the envelope had a Southampton postmark. There was one thin sheet of paper inside, typed. The letter was dated a week earlier and the address at the top said: *Royal Victoria Military Hospital Netley, Netley Abbey, Southampton.*

My scalp began to prickle, my throat tightening.

Dearest, dearest Ruby,

I know you've probably given up on me by now and if that's the case I don't blame you. There were so many times I wanted to write to you to let you know I was still alive but the Germans wouldn't let me. I couldn't remember the address of your offices either so I had to send this to the hospital. I hope it's reached you OK and not fallen into enemy (your pa's or grandma's) hands!!

I know it must be a shock, finding out I'm alive after all this time. It's a shock to me too to be honest – there were so many times I thought I wasn't going to make it. I want to tell you about them all but the guy typing this letter for me will probably die of boredom if I don't hurry up.

As you'll see from the address I'm at the American military hospital in Southampton. Don't worry, I'm OK, it's just my hands aren't so good right now and it hurts to hold a pen for too long, which is why I'm dictating this.

If this letter gets to you do you think you can make it down here? I'd give anything to see you again.

All my love,

Sam xxxxx

My breath caught in my throat in a sob. I scanned the letter again, my lips moving soundlessly as I reread Sam's words.

I was shaking. It couldn't be true. It *couldn't*. Someone was playing a cruel joke on me.

Then I noticed something at the bottom of the page: *PTO*, written in laborious, crooked capitals. I turned it over and, on the back, saw a clumsy but recognisable drawing of a girl's face – mine – and next to it, a stitchwort flower.

I clutched the letter, trying to remember how to breathe. Tears were rolling down my cheeks and dripping off my chin. Toffee came bounding up and whined softly, concerned. I picked the little dog up, burying my face in his wiry fur. Seeming to sense I needed comfort, he let me hold him instead of trying to wriggle away.

'Oh, Sam,' I whispered. '*Sam.*'

33

RUBY

10th May

Come on, come ON, I thought as the train puffed and clanked its way towards Southampton, the final leg of my journey. It had taken all day, and getting back to Bartonford would take me all day tomorrow, leaving me with only a few hours to see Sam. Not for the first time, I found myself wishing fervently that I didn't live so far from everywhere. I could have waited until the weekend, but that was too long: besides which, it was a nightmare simply getting to Ilfracombe on a Sunday, never mind travelling halfway along the south coast.

No one knew where I was going or who I was going to see. I'd told Father Vera was back over in England for a few days, in London, and wanted desperately to see me, and I'd given Howler a story about an aunt in Bournemouth who'd been bombed out and was unwell. Thankfully, both had believed me, although by the time I'd finished pleading with Howler my poor old non-existent aunt was virtually at death's door.

I'd told Alfie I was going to see Vera too, sickened by guilt at lying to him.

But I had to see Sam. I *had* to.

The letter was in my pocket. I took it out and read it again, for what must have been the hundredth time; I had to keep looking at it to reassure myself it was real. I still had no idea how I'd held it together when I'd returned to the cottage two evenings ago and Father had met me at the door, a rare smile on his face. 'I've just had Alfie Blythe here,' he'd said. 'He's asked if I'll let you marry him – I said yes, of course, and I will write a letter giving my permission.'

I'd stared stupidly at him; Alfie had gone completely out of my head. Father was still smiling. 'I'm glad, Ruby. He's a nice chap and it means I'll still have you close by.' Patting me on the arm – the closest he ever got to a hug – he'd stood back to let me past, not seeming to notice my dazed expression.

'Humbug, dearie?' The woman in the seat opposite thrust a disreputable-looking paper bag at me, tearing me away from my thoughts. All day, at the most inconvenient moments, she'd been trying to chat to me about this or that, or offer me food. I knew she meant well – she was fat, kind and motherly, the sort I always seemed to attract when I was travelling alone. I shook my head and gave her a tight little smile, mentally thanking whoever was above that at least it wasn't a fish paste sandwich on Victory bread this time. 'No, thank you.'

The woman reached into the bag's sticky depths and extracted a striped humbug, popping it into her mouth. 'Watching your figure, eh?' she said with a conspiratorial wink. 'Well, when you get to my age, dearie, it won't bother you so much! I've had these since Easter time. Makin' them last, see?' She sighed. 'The war might be over but there's still no end to the rationing yet, is there?'

I nodded and gave her another smile, wishing I smoked or had brought my knitting so I had something to do. Instead, I leaned back, gazing out of the window. Sam wasn't expecting me – there hadn't been time to write to him. I'd just hopped on the train, hoping for the best. Excitement, nerves and a fresh surge of guilt swirled inside me. What sort of person was I turning into? Two days ago, I'd agreed to marry Alfie. I should have come clean – told him straight away that I couldn't do it because I was already engaged to someone else and had just found out he was still alive – but I hadn't. I'd avoided him, pretending to be busy. What a coward I was! I hated myself for it. And yet the thought of seeing Sam again eclipsed all that; eclipsed everything.

At last – long last – we reached Southampton. Even though I'd seen photographs of it in the newspaper, the reality of the bomb damage was a dreadful shock. It must have been terrible, listening to Jerry drone over night after night for years on end, wondering if your house would still be standing in the morning. As for those awful rockets they'd dropped on London – Doodlebugs, they'd called them, a name that seemed inappropriately jolly to me – I couldn't begin to imagine how frightening that must have been. Oh, well. It was all over now.

'Goodbye, dearie,' the woman said as the train pulled into the station and I got up, brushing smuts off my skirt and lifting my overnight bag down from the rack. I didn't actually know where I was going to stay tonight; I hadn't thought that far ahead. Perhaps someone at the hospital would be able to help me find somewhere.

I waited to help the woman off the train with her things, then bid her goodbye too. I could have waited for another train to take me to Netley station, which was almost next door to the hospital, but it had started to rain so I hailed a taxi cab instead. All I wanted to do was get there. 'Going to see your sweetheart, are you, love?' the driver said when we arrived, pulling up in front of a vast brick building that looked a quarter of a mile wide, at least.

The way he was looking me up and down irritated me. 'Actually, I'm a newspaper reporter,' I said frostily. I paid him with the exact change, grabbed my bag, got out and slammed the door hard, gratified to see the annoyance on his face as he drove away.

The entrance hall of the hospital was cavernous. I looked around for someone to ask about Sam, but couldn't see anyone. Eventually I caught the arm of a white-coated doctor walking past. 'Can I help you, ma'am?' he said in an American accent, sounding slightly annoyed. I showed him Sam's letter and explained why I was there. 'Ah, yes, Private Archer,' he said, and a jolt went through me. He was here – really here.

'Well, it isn't strictly visiting hours—' the doctor began.

'*Please*,' I begged him. 'I've come all the way from Devon.'

'I'll see what I can do,' he said. 'Wait here.' He walked off.

I waited for what felt like hours, until eventually a brisk, efficient nurse, also American, arrived to take me down to his ward, which was at the end of what seemed like miles of corridors. The building had rows of tall windows, none of which actually seemed to let in any light. The floors were scuffed, the paintwork cracked, and underneath the tang of disinfectant, which reminded me of Barton Hall, there was a strong smell of mildew. I barely noticed any of it; my heart was thudding and I felt slightly sick with nerves and excitement. Doubts were crowding my mind, too. What if the doctors had got it wrong? What if it was a case of mistaken identity, and it wasn't Sam after all?

As we entered the ward, I felt as if my heart was trying to climb into my mouth. I couldn't see him anywhere.

'Down here.' The nurse led me to a bed at the end of the ward, screened with curtains, and stuck her head around them. 'Private Archer, you have a visitor,' she said. She nodded at me, and left.

Sam was propped up against his pillows, his eyes closed. At the sight of him, my heart gave another great lurch. He looked older, thinner, more tired wearing a pair of blue and white striped pyjamas unbuttoned at the neck. His hands, resting on top of the covers, had thick bandages wrapped around the palms, leaving his fingers free. As I stepped around the curtains, his eyelids fluttered open.

I was shaking. 'Hullo, Sam,' I managed to say.

He sat up with a start. '*Ruby?* Oh my God, is it really you?'

I flew to him; his arms went around me; then we were kissing, and I was crying, and when I finally pulled away I saw there were tears rolling down his face too.

'I thought you were dead.' My voice was trembling. 'Vera got a letter from Stanley. He said you were captured by the Germans at a farm. He said he heard you get shot—'

He shook his head. 'Not me. They shot the farmer and his family, and their dogs, but they took me and Freddie Gardner to one of their camps. Oh, Christ, I'm so sorry about our wedding. I couldn't get to Ilfracombe. They closed the camp and they wouldn't let anyone out – I couldn't even get a message to you—'

'It doesn't matter. It doesn't matter at all.' I sat down on the edge of the bed, gently taking one of his bandaged hands in mine.

His fingers squeezed mine. 'I thought I was never gonna see you again. God, Ruby—'

I saw shivers go through him. I stroked his arm. 'It's OK. You're safe now.'

Gradually, his trembling began to subside.

'Tell me what happened if you want to. But only if you want to.'

He took a deep breath, and then he told me: about landing on the beach in France; about being captured, and being sent to a prisoner of war camp in Germany; about his attempt to escape, and working in a soap factory. He and his friend Davy had put cement powder in one of the mixers instead of pumice to try and sabotage it, but something had gone wrong and the factory had burned down, and they were put in prison in the middle of Dresden. For some reason the name of the city was familiar, but I couldn't work out why. 'We were due to be executed,' Sam said, 'but then the bombing raid happened.'

Shock jolted through me. Now I knew why I'd recognised the name: I'd seen a story in Father's paper about it. In mid-February, the allies had coordinated a massive bombing raid on the city, causing a firestorm that had cost thousands of people their lives. 'You were there?'

'Right in the goddamn middle of it.'

He was trembling again.

'Don't talk about it.' My heart was pounding, my throat tight.

'No, I want to. I need to tell someone. I—'

He took in a deep, shuddering breath.

'The bombs blasted a hole in the prison wall. Davy – the guy I was in there with – he was killed, but I managed to get out. I wandered the streets for a while. Everything was burning. It was like being in the middle of hell.

'At one point I thought I'd had it – a building at the end of the street I was on collapsed and I got trapped. But then more rubble fell on top of the stuff that was burning and put the flames out. I don't recall how I got out of the city. I just walked, at night mostly, and rested during the day. It was easier to stay hidden that way. I kept expecting to be picked up and arrested again, but I saw almost no one. Most of the towns and villages I came to were ruins. Eventually I ended up crossing the border back into France. By then I was sick – really sick – I was running a fever. My hands had gotten burned during the firebombing and they were infected.

'I found my way to this farmhouse somehow – it looked a bit like the one I was hiding out in before I was captured, but it can't have been, because that got burned down. There was still a family living there who were part of the French Resistance, like the ones who helped me and Stanley after we got to France. They managed to get in touch with the Brits and well, here I am. For now, anyway.'

I looked at him, at the familiar lines of the face I loved so much and had been sure I would never see again. I still couldn't believe he was here – that he was *real*.

'Stanley's all right, you know,' I told him. 'He was found by the British. They brought him here, and now he's back in America with Vera. They're both working at the *Washington Post*.'

Sam's face sagged with relief. 'Really?'

'Really.'

'Oh, thank God.' He managed to smile. 'Hey – how long do we have? Are you staying in Southampton overnight?'

I shrugged. 'I don't know. I was in such a rush to see you that I came down here without making any arrangements. Father and A... er, Grandmother think I'm visiting Vera in London – they don't know she's over in America – and Howler thinks I'm visiting an invalid aunt in Bournemouth. I was going to look for a room somewhere.'

My stomach twisted as I thought of Alfie again, waiting for me back in Bartonford, oblivious and trusting.

Sam threw back the covers and swung his legs out of bed. 'You wanna get out of here for a while?'

'Is that allowed? Are you well enough?'

'Pass me those clothes.' He nodded at a shirt, trousers and jacket, slung over the back of a chair beside the bed; I hadn't even noticed it was there. I turned my back on him while he dressed.

'Can you help me with these buttons?'

I looked round again, and felt a jolt. His shirt was hanging open, exposing his jutting ribs, hips and collarbone.

The smile he gave me was a shadow of its former self too. 'Believe me, I look a hell of a lot better than I did a coupla months ago.'

As we left the hospital, creeping furtively like a pair of naughty children, I was expecting a nurse or doctor to try and stop us, but no one did. 'They drive jeeps down here sometimes,' Sam said as we made our way down the long corridor with the rows of windows that didn't let in enough light.

I raised an eyebrow. 'That would explain the marks on the floor, then.'

Then we were outside in the fresh air and lightly misting rain. Sam turned his face up to it, breathing in deeply. 'Where to?'

I linked my arm through his. 'I have no idea. Let's just walk, if you can manage it.'

'Sure. Nothing wrong with my legs.'

We began to walk. 'What happened to your hands?' I asked Sam. At the same time he said, 'So, how's life in Devon been since I left?'

We both laughed. 'You first,' he said.

So I told him about Grandmother, and how awful she still was, what was happening at the *Herald*, and all the stories and gossip circulating around Bartonford. Everything except being engaged to Alfie. Every time I looked round and saw Sam beside me, I wanted to pinch myself because I was convinced this was all some wonderful dream; I was scared that if I mentioned Alfie, Sam would be upset or angry, and it would spoil everything. I'd tell him later, I decided. And of course, I would break things off with Alfie as soon as I got back to Bartonford – I'd go and see him the moment I stepped off the train, before I went home. If I'd had even the slightest inkling Sam was still alive, I'd never have said yes to Alfie in the first place.

We passed a parade of shops, and Sam said, 'Wait here.'

He ducked into a jeweller's. I stood outside, feeling oddly self-conscious and wondering what on earth he was up to. He reappeared about ten minutes later, holding a small velvet box.

I opened it. Nestled inside was a simple silver ring with a single ruby set into it.

He grinned. 'Told you I'd get you a ring, didn't I?'

I was half afraid he'd go down on one knee like Alfie had,

but he just slid it onto my finger. I held out my hand, admiring it. 'It's beautiful,' I said in a shaky voice. 'The most beautiful thing I've ever owned.'

'Aw, no. I had to send some more money home for Ma but when I get the rest of my pay I'll get you a nicer one – gold, with a diamond. If you still wanna get married, that is.'

My heart soared; my stomach sank. Oh, God, how had my life become so complicated?

'Ruby?' Sam was frowning now. 'You do want to, don't you?'

'Yes – yes – more than anything!' I said. He flung his arms around me and we kissed.

Tell him, I thought. *You HAVE to.*

I took a deep breath, the words on the tip of my tongue. Then I noticed how quiet he was. Now it was my turn to frown. 'Sam? What is it?' Had he guessed, somehow? No – that was ridiculous – impossible.

He took a deep breath too. 'A sergeant came to see me yesterday. From the US army.'

'Oh – are you being transferred to another hospital? Well, don't worry – I'll come and see you. I'll find a way.'

'No.' He shook his head. 'I'm being discharged.'

'Discharged?'

'Yeah. My hands—' He held them up, waggling his fingers where they poked out above the bandages. 'They're healing OK, but I won't ever be able to fire a gun again. There's too much scar tissue. I leave for Portsmouth on Monday.'

'No! *No!* That's not fair!'

'I know. I know.'

'This bloody war.' My voice was trembling; tears sprung into my eyes.

'Yeah, but if it wasn't for the war we'd've never met each other at all.' Clumsily, he wiped my face with the backs of his bandaged hands. I could tell he was trying to sound matter-of-fact, but underneath it I could sense his turmoil; it matched mine. I'd had *one day* with him – not even that. And now he was being taken away from me again.

'It won't be forever. Only a little while. I *have* to go back and find Meggie and Ma, make sure they're OK. But I'll come back for you, I promise.'

I pressed my face against his shoulder. 'I suppose we'll just have to make the most of each other while we're here, then.'

I decided then not to mention Alfie after all. Sam didn't need to know – not yet. Not when I was going to end the engagement to Alfie as soon as I got back to Bartonford anyway. I'd tell him later, once we were back together again.

Walking down to the seafront, we passed a little boarding house, a sign saying *VACANCIES* by the front gate, and I remembered that I didn't have anywhere to stay tonight yet. 'Sam – I ought to book a room,' I said.

He looked at me, and I felt that old, familiar spark pass between us. Heat flared in my belly and my face as I remembered those afternoons in the lodge, holding each other, kissing, our hands slipping under one another's clothes. Who knew when I might see him again?

I swallowed. 'Can you – can you stay too?'

'I guess so. If that's what you want?'

With an enormous effort, loathing myself for it, I finally pushed all thoughts of Alfie away. 'Yes. Definitely. If you won't get into trouble?'

'I'll already be in trouble for going AWOL. And I'm done

with the army anyway.' He held up his hands again. 'I'm no use to them like this.'

I could hear from his tone what he was thinking: *No use to anybody*. I gave his arm a squeeze.

The boarding house was a shabby sort of place, but the nets at the windows were clean and there were pots brimming with late spring pansies either side of the front door. As we walked up the path, I twisted the ring on my finger, a rapid pulse beating in my throat, and tightened my grip on the handle of my overnight bag. 'You're really sure?' Sam said softly. 'Because if it's not, just say. It's fine.'

I nodded, and he rang the bell.

34

SAM

Inside the house, the bell clanged. Ruby was fiddling with the ring. *Mrs Ruby Archer*, I thought, and something inside me jumped. Being here with her felt both wonderful, and utterly surreal. I still couldn't get used to being back here in England instead of in the camp or the prison; to the fact that the war was over, and I was safe. I dreamed about the bombing in Dresden every night, waking up shouting, not knowing where I was. When it was really bad, the doctors had to give me a sleeping draught. And even during the day, the memories of everything that had happened since that terrible morning on the beaches hovered at the edges of my mind like shadowy storm clouds, always threatening, never quite going away. I wasn't the same Sam who had arrived in Devon for training almost two years ago. He had disappeared the moment we landed on Omaha and the snipers began firing at us.

The door opened and the hotel's owner, a sharp-faced woman with neat grey hair, ushered us inside. I caught her looking Ruby over with a keen expression as I signed the register, using my surname for both of us, but when she saw the ring, she relaxed a little. 'I'm sorry you couldn't have had better weather for your honeymoon,' she said as she turned to pluck a key from the hook behind the desk.

'We don't mind, do we, darling?' Ruby turned to me with a smile that looked slightly forced, and my stomach flipped again.

The boarding house was smaller than I thought it would be. The owner, who told us her name was Mrs Leeming, took us up two winding flights of stairs and along a narrow corridor to our room. 'Supper will be served at half past seven in the dining room,' she said before she closed the door. I looked around, and felt a rush of relief. The landing might have been poky but the room was spacious with white walls and a bright rug on the floor, and although the curtains and bedspread were faded, they had a cheerful floral print on them. A wide bay window overlooked the sea, with a chair either side so you could sit and gaze at the view, and there was a stove and a kettle for making tea.

'Oh, it's lovely,' Ruby said, flinging herself down on the bed. 'There's so much *space*. And no Grandmother!' Laughing, she lay back, spreading her arms out. I watched her, smiling, but there was a heavy feeling inside me as, once again, I remembered the sergeant coming to see me yesterday to tell me I was being discharged. Goddammit, it wasn't *fair*.

We whiled away the hour until dinner, on the deserted beach. As we walked along the shoreline arm in arm, watching the waves roll in, I felt at peace for the first time in as long as I could remember.

The supper back at the hotel was nothing special – haddock and potatoes, and a sponge pudding – but it was a whole lot better than the crap they'd given us in Germany at the camp and the prison, and pretty good compared to the food at the hospital, too. I was too nervous to eat much anyhow. Afterwards, we went up to our room. It was getting dark, so I drew the curtains and lit the lamp.

'I'm going to take a bath,' Ruby said.

'OK.'

When she was gone, I remembered I didn't have any pyjamas, only the clothes I was wearing. I took off my shoes, socks, jacket and pants and got into bed in my underwear and shirt. The door opened and Ruby came back in. She was wearing a robe over a long nightgown, her damp hair in two loose plaits. She turned and locked the door with a nervous-sounding laugh. 'We don't want Mrs Leeming coming in, do we? Can you imagine?'

I found myself laughing too. 'Oh, God, no.' I folded back the counterpane beside me. After a moment's hesitation, she crossed the room.

'Do you mind if we put the lamp out?' she said.

'Sure.' I turned it down, plunging the room into darkness. I heard her take off her robe and felt the bed move, the covers rustling as she climbed in beside me.

'Sam?'

'Yeah?'

'Have you ever – I mean – have you—'

I shook my head before realising she couldn't see me. 'No,' I said. My voice sounded strange, not like my own.

She was quiet for a moment. All I could hear was the blood roaring in my ears. Every muscle in my body was a tightly wound spring. How was I supposed to tell her I had no idea what I was doing? What if I messed this up? What if she hated it?

'You don't have to,' I said. 'Not if you don't want to. I don't mind. We can just – just lie here or something.'

'No, I want to.' Her ferocity took me by surprise. 'I want to more than anything.'

I felt her turn over, her breath tickling against my face. We kissed, gently. 'You're really sure?' I asked.

Gently, she took my hand and placed my unbandaged fingers on her breast. I stifled a moan; I hadn't realised she'd taken off her nightgown too. I felt her heart beating inside her chest, rapid as a bird's; her skin was warm and soft, and in that moment, I knew I wanted her more than anything.

'I'm sure,' she said, kissing me again, and started to unbutton my shirt.

35

RUBY

Making love to Sam wasn't anything like I had imagined it would be. It was clumsy, awkward – uncomfortable too, although Sam tried to be gentle – and over almost as quickly as it had begun.

Afterwards, Sam rolled back over to his side of the bed and fell almost immediately into a heavy sleep. I lay awake, gazing up at the ceiling in the pitch darkness. I felt disappointed, and for some reason a little lonely, although he was right there beside me. I slid out of bed, taking care not to wake him. Picking up my dressing gown from the floor, I wrapped it around me and felt my way across to the door.

When I returned from the bathroom, Sam was still asleep. I lay down beside him, listening to his deep, regular breathing. What would it be like once he'd gone again? I couldn't imagine it – I didn't want to. It would be even worse this time, knowing he was alive but that I couldn't be with him. Meanwhile, I had to break things off with Alfie; oh, how I was dreading that!

Beside me, Sam twitched and groaned, making soft whimpering sounds like a wounded animal. 'Meggie,' he murmured. 'Meggie – no!'

I leaned over and lit the lamp. Sam's eyes were half open; he was thrashing at the air, as if trying to hit something or push someone away. 'No!' he shouted, half sitting up. '*No!*'

As he continued to shout I heard footsteps on the landing outside our room. There was a tap on the door. 'Is everything all right in there?' I heard Mrs Leeming say.

'Fine!' I called. I put a hand gently on Sam's shoulder. 'Sam, Sam, wake up. It's OK. You're not in Germany anymore. You're here with me, Ruby, in Southampton.'

Using the same low, soothing voice I used to call Father back when he was dreaming of Belgium, I repeated myself, imagining Mrs Leeming standing outside the door, her ear pressed against it, wondering what was going on.

Gradually, Sam relaxed into my arms. 'It's OK,' I said. 'It's OK.'

His eyes fluttered open. 'Where – where am I?'

'The hotel in Southampton. You were having a bad dream.'

In the low light from the lamp, his face was pinched with fear; his eyes still held that faraway look I knew so well.

'I thought I was in Dresden. In the fire.'

'You're not. That's all over now.' I put my arms around him and kissed his cheek. 'Nothing bad can happen to you here.'

'There was a kid,' he said, in a halting voice. 'I tried to save her, but I couldn't – that's how I burned my hands. She reminded me of Meggie. Now, whenever I remember her, it's Meggie's face I see.'

He began to cry, not the silent tears he'd shed when I first saw him on the ward but jagged, ugly sobs, wrenching from deep inside him. I held him. I didn't know what else to do.

When he'd calmed down, we made love again. This time, it was different. As we moved with each other I felt as if I was being pieced back together, not into the girl I used to be but somebody completely new: a woman who could do anything, go anywhere, be anyone she wanted.

Afterwards, lying in each other's arms, he murmured, 'I wish I didn't have to leave you.'

I felt a sudden pain in my throat. 'So don't.'

'I have to.'

'I know – your mother and sister. I know. I wish you were here for a few more days, though. At least we'd have time to get married before you went. I could forge another letter from Father – or even find a way to pretend I'm twenty-one—'

'I wish we could too. But I have a plan,' he said. 'I'm gonna find a job, get a place to live. Then I'll send for you, and we can have our wedding. It'll only be a little while. And if we wait until October you won't need to fake anything – you can marry me with a clear conscience.'

'D'you promise?' I said. 'Because I don't know how much longer I can bear it at the cottage. Goodness knows when Grandmother will be leaving – no one knows when the army will let people go back to Tyneham even though she and Father have both written to ask – and I—'

I clamped my mouth shut just in time to stop the words slipping out, going hot and cold all over at how close I had come to saying: *I won't be marrying Alfie now, so I won't be moving out of the cottage to live with him. I'm stuck there.*

Sam didn't notice anything amiss. 'I promise,' he said.

I rested my head against his shoulder and closed my eyes. This time, when he fell asleep, he didn't have any nightmares.

When I woke up again, it was morning, and sunlight was streaming into the room. I turned over, reaching for Sam, and saw the other side of the bed was empty. Panic scattered through me. Had he left already?

Then I heard the chink of crockery. Sam was coming over to the bed, a tray balanced awkwardly on his bandaged hands. 'I made tea,' he said. 'Hope I got it right.'

I took a cup and sipped it. 'It'll do, I suppose,' I said, suppressing a smile.

He made a face, and nudged me.

'Watch out! I'll spill it, and then Mrs Leeming really *will* have something to complain about!'

He tried to tickle me instead. I put my cup down and wriggled away, laughing. '*Stop* it!'

'Make me,' he said with a mischievous grin. I was relieved to see it after last night, when he'd sobbed in my arms.

'All right then, you asked for it!' I began tickling him back, poking him in the ribs, until, breathless with laughter himself, he held his hands up.

'OK, OK, I give in!' he gasped. 'Truce.'

I smiled triumphantly, and picked up my tea again. 'I should think so too.'

He relaxed against me, leaning his head on my shoulder. 'I love you, Ruby.'

'I love you, Sam.' Suddenly, I had a lump in my throat.

As we drank our tea, I looked at the silver ring. The ruby winked in a stripe of sunlight that fell across the bed where Sam had opened the curtains slightly. I'd have to take it off before I got home; if Grandmother saw it, she'd be furious. As for Alfie... My stomach twisted again, even though I knew it was the only thing I could do.

'No time for breakfast,' Sam said at last, putting down his empty cup. 'I have to go. Find out how much trouble I'm in for going AWOL.'

I got out of bed and dressed quickly. 'I'll walk back with you. My train isn't for a couple of hours.'

We made our way back through Southampton to the hospital in silence. I clung tightly to Sam's arm, wondering how long it would be until I saw him again. Outside the hospital gates, I turned to face him. 'You'll write to me, won't you?'

'Of course I will. Every day. Just try and stop me.'

'But send the letters to the *Herald* – here, I'll give you the address – don't forget it this time.'

I had my reporter's notebook in my bag. I scribbled down the address of the *Herald* offices, tore out the page and handed it to him.

He kissed me. 'Look after yourself, OK?' His voice was hoarse. 'We'll be together again before you know it. Don't forget how much I love you.'

I nodded. 'Don't you forget how much I love *you*, either,' I said.

He closed his eyes, leaning his forehead against mine, and I breathed in his familiar smell – soap, tobacco and cinnamon gum – trying to fix the memory of him in my mind. He kissed me again. Then he was gone, walking back up the drive towards the hospital. I watched him until he was out of sight, a tearing pain in my chest.

I spent the next two hours aimlessly wandering the streets of Southampton, lost and dazed, still feeling Sam's last kiss on my lips. How could our time together be over so quickly? We'd only just found one another again.

By mid-morning, I was on my way back to Devon, alone again except for my thoughts, weighed down by our parting, and the knowledge that, now, I had to find a way to tell Alfie – poor, loyal Alfie – I couldn't marry him after all.

36

RUBY

12th May

'What did I do?' Alfie said as we sat on the bench in the town gardens – the same bench I'd found him on last year, when Maud Tinney had chucked him. His face was very white except for two spots of colour high up on his cheekbones. He looked as ghastly as I felt. I'd called for him as soon as I arrived home from Southampton.

As the town hall clock chimed six – at last, the churches and clocks could sound again – I gazed helplessly at him. 'Alfie, I'm sorry.'

'We've known each other for years and years. No one understands us like we understand each other, do they? Sometimes I feel as if I can hear what you're thinking before you even say it. We have a connection, Ruby! You know we do.'

I fought back a sudden, hideous and unexplainable urge to laugh.

'Alfie, you're a very dear friend,' I began, my head in

turmoil as I searched for the right way to say it. *But there's someone else...*

'And you're very dear to me. Ruby, *please*.' He grabbed my hands. 'Don't do this. We'll be happy – I know we will – we'll have two children – a boy and a girl – and when Father retires I'll take over the running of the works – I'll have a good salary. We can go on holiday to Cornwall. I can buy a little car!'

'I can't,' I said, my voice cracking. 'I'm sorry, but I can't. There's someone else.'

'Who is he?' Alfie said.

My heart contracted painfully inside my chest; I slid my gaze away from his wild, desperate one, unable to look at him.

'Who. Is. He?' Alfie ground out from between gritted teeth.

'I'm sorry,' I said again, wretched with misery and guilt. 'I thought he was dead. If I'd known he wasn't, I would never have—' I stopped, realising how that sounded. 'I mean, I wouldn't have let you—' No, that wasn't right either. Oh, God, what could I say that didn't sound completely dreadful? When I looked up at Alfie I saw, to my horror, that he had tears in his eyes.

'Alfie, don't. I'm sorry. I never meant to hurt you. Please don't think you're second best because you're *not*. It wasn't like that at all.'

I reached out to take his hand. He pulled away and stood, squaring his shoulders. 'Is it one of those Americans?' He spat out the last word as if it was poisoning him.

I nodded.

'Hah! I should have known – I suppose you met him up at the camp?' He swiped angrily at his eyes with the heel of one hand, his jaw clenched.

'He's nice, Alfie – kind – you'd like him,' I said stupidly, desperately.

'Don't, Ruby.' His voice was so cold it took my breath away. 'I should be grateful you told me before I wasted money on a ring, I suppose.'

I thought of Sam's ring, threaded onto a chain around my neck and hidden under my blouse, and felt another swirl of self-loathing and guilt.

'Come on,' Alfie said. 'I had better walk you home.'

At dinner that night, I steeled myself, and took a deep breath. Father and Grandmother would know soon enough anyway – better that they heard it from me.

'Alfie and I have broken off our engagement,' I said.

That was enough even to make Father look up from his notes. 'Why?' he said. 'What on earth happened?'

Grandmother just looked at me, her eyes narrow and watchful.

You're twenty years old, I reminded myself. *And in a few months' time you'll be old enough to marry without Father's permission.*

Another deep breath. 'I'm engaged to someone else.'

You could have cut the air with a knife. Father's mouth dropped open; all the colour drained from Grandmother's face and she dropped her fork onto her plate with a clatter.

'*What?*' she said.

'I was engaged to him before Alfie asked me, but I thought he'd been killed. Then I found out he wasn't.' I swallowed. *In for a penny, in for a pound*, as they said. 'I – I haven't been down in London. I've been in Southampton, visiting him. He's in the military hospital there.'

'Southampton?' Father said. 'But that's – that's the *American* military hospital.'

'Yes.'

'You're engaged to an *American*?' Grandmother said. 'How? *When?*'

I looked her in the eye, trying to sum up a confidence I didn't feel. 'His name is Sam Archer. He's one of the soldiers who came here to train for D-Day. You met him at that WVS party – he was the soldier I danced with. He's being discharged – he's returning to America to see his family – but once he's got a job and somewhere to live he's going to send for me and we're going to get married.'

Silence.

'No,' Father said, standing up so suddenly the legs of his chair shrieked against the floor. 'You will not marry this man, Ruby. I forbid it.'

His voice was shaking. I stared at him.

'You may marry anyone else you wish – anyone at all – with my blessing,' he continued. 'But not *him*. Not an American.'

'What on earth do you have against the Americans?' I cried. 'Sam's a good man – he's honest, kind – I love him, and he loves me!'

'I don't care!' Father thundered, with more passion than I'd ever seen in all the years of my life. 'I will not have my daughter marrying an American and going over there – I will *not!*'

I faced him across the table, my heart racing. 'But *why*? I'm not a child anymore, Father. If you're going to forbid me to do something, then tell me the reasons behind it!'

Another tense silence.

Grandmother sniffed. 'She might as well know, Cecil,' she said. 'It's past time.'

Father's chest heaved. 'I – I can't. I can't talk about her,' he said, as I looked from him to Grandmother and back again, wondering what on earth she meant.

'It's your mother, Ruby,' Grandmother said. 'She's still alive. Well, as far as we know, anyway.'

I went cold all over, then hot. 'Wh – what?'

'She left when you were a baby, to go to America with another man. She was *bored*, apparently – life wasn't exciting enough for her. She was offered a part in a play over there and despite your father begging her not to go, she went – and left you behind. Of course, we didn't find out about *him* until she wrote to your father to say she wasn't coming back. But there was an American actor at the theatre in Exeter where she'd been working – it can only have been him.'

Grandmother's tone was victorious, almost as if she was enjoying herself.

'So – so where is she?' My skin was tingling, my head spinning with this revelation. I felt as if I was going to be sick.

'We've no idea. No one's heard from her since then,' Grandmother said.

I looked at Father again.

'Why didn't you tell me?' I cried. 'Why did you let me think she was dead?!'

He didn't answer. Emotions swirled through me. My mother was alive. She was out there somewhere. But why had she left me behind? Had she ever tried to contact me? I wanted to be furious with her, but at the same time I felt oddly excited – what if it was possible for me to find her one day?

I decided to change tack. I needed to know more; perhaps if I could get Father to come around to the idea of me marrying Sam, he might talk to me about my mother. 'Father, *please*,' I said. 'This isn't the same, not at *all*. I'm not running away – this is still home. But I love Sam and I want to spend the rest of my life with him.'

He still didn't speak; wouldn't even look at me.

'*Father.*'

He turned away from me and left the room. A few moments later, I heard his study door thump closed.

'Well, I hope you're happy,' Grandmother said.

I wanted to shout at her – something terrible to wipe that smug, self-satisfied look off her face. I wanted to ask her why she and Father had lied to me about my mother for so long – had let me think she was *dead*, for God's sake.

But I couldn't think of a single thing to say.

37

SAM

June

'S on. *Son.* You gettin' off here, or what?'
     A hand landed on my shoulder and I jolted awake
with a shout. I'd been lost in a half-waking nightmare about
the Nazi camp burning to the ground; there were people
trapped inside the tents – hundreds, thousands of them – and
somehow, for some reason, Ma and Meggie were among
them. I was trying to fight my way in there to save them but
kept getting beaten back by the flames.

Slowly, my head cleared, and I realised where I was:
sprawled across the seat at the back of a Greyhound bus, the
driver standing over me with a frown on his face.

'Steady now, son, I ain't gonna hurt you,' he said. He
saw the Purple Heart and Bronze Star pinned to the lapel,
and the kitbag I'd been using as a pillow and added, more
gently, 'We're at Coltonsburg.'

I looked out the window and, in the afternoon sunshine,

saw the familiar buildings of the bus station: a place that, at one point, I'd thought I'd never see again.

I thanked the driver and got off the bus. It chugged away, leaving me standing there with my bag at my feet. Although I'd been dozing on and off for the last few hours, I still felt exhausted, and not quite able to believe that, after all these weeks, I was finally here.

Parting from Ruby again had made being yelled at by the sergeant for going AWOL from the hospital a breeze. I couldn't believe we'd found each other only to be torn apart again. There was nothing I could do about it, though. By the following evening I'd been at sea on a US Navy destroyer filled with sick and injured troops. At the beginning of June, we reached New York, where I was given a medical, and that was it. I was no longer a private in the 116th Infantry Regiment – just ordinary Sam Archer, civilian.

I'd telegraphed Ma before we left England, via Mr Addison, but there had been no way to get a reply at sea, and there had been nothing waiting when we arrived in New York. I'd telegraphed her again anyway, and sent a message to Ruby at the *Herald*, too, to let her know I was safe.

As I thought about Ma, I felt a wave of apprehension. I'd been away more than two years: had she and Meggie given up on me? Forgotten me? What if Kirk had—

I pushed that thought away. I was pretty good at not thinking about things I didn't want to think about these days, at least when I was awake.

I thought I'd have to walk all the way back to Kirk's farm, but I managed to hitch a ride most of the way with a Bible salesman. While we drove, he yammered on at me about God and whatnot. I was so wound up and nervous I felt like asking him where God had been on Omaha Beach that day, or in the prisoner of war camp, or Dresden, but he was twice my size and I needed the ride. I was pretty damn relieved when he dropped me off at the top of the track that led down to the farm, though.

At first, I thought the place had been abandoned. The porch on the main house had all but fallen off, and some of the windows were boarded over. There were weeds everywhere just like there always had been, and Kirk's truck sat in the middle of the yard, its tyres flat and balding.

Shit, I thought, letting the kitbag slowly slide from my shoulder. *Where have they gone? What am I gonna do now?*

Then I heard footsteps running from behind the house. Meggie. When she saw me she stopped dead, staring at me with wide eyes. She'd grown like the weeds in the yard since I last saw her. Her hair was longer, tangled, her dress too short, revealing her bruised knees, and her face was smudged with dirt. I waited for her to squeal, 'Sam!' and fling herself at me, but she just carried on staring.

'Hey, Meggie-Meg,' I said at last, my voice hoarse. 'It's good to see you.'

'Where have you *been*?' She sounded angry; her sunny, innocent little-kid look had gone. 'Pa said you ran away – I cried and cried when you didn't come back.'

'Aw, no. I didn't run away. I've been in France and England, in the army, fighting Hitler. Didn't Ma tell you?' I showed her my medals, and her eyes got very round. She shook her head. 'Ma said you went away, but she wouldn't say where,' she repeated. I realised Ma must have kept the truth from her so she didn't let it slip to Kirk where I was.

Then she noticed the scars on my hands. 'Are you hurt?'

'It's OK. They look a lot worse than they are.' Truth was, the scars were starting to pain me. I wanted to get inside and sit down, and wrap a cool, damp washcloth around them.

'Where's Ma?' I asked.

What I really meant was, *Where's Kirk?*

She ran up the porch steps, bellowing, 'Ma! *Ma!*' Instinctively, I winced, expecting Kirk to burst out and yell at her for making so much noise. Then I realised that if Meggie was shouting like that, he probably wasn't around. I followed, more slowly.

I dropped my bag and stuck my head in through the screen door. The house was darker than I remembered; smaller, too. It didn't smell too good either, like the drains were stopped up. I heard voices approaching, and then Ma came out on the porch. Her dress was even more worn than Meggie's and there was a fading bruise under one eye. I didn't ask how she'd got it. Some things never changed, I guessed.

'Sammy,' she said in a soft voice. For a moment, I hung back. Then Ma stepped forwards and hugged me. She held me for a long time, like I was a little kid again, when it was just us and she was comforting me when I was sick or I'd had a nightmare.

She let me go. 'Look at you!' She was smiling, but there were tears in her eyes. 'You're all grown up!'

Ma, you have no idea, I wanted to say. I shrugged. 'I guess.'

'Oh, Sammy, I was *so* worried.'

'Where's Kirk?' I asked, glancing through the doorway again, wondering if he was about to appear.

'I don't know. He went out somewhere this morning.'

I felt myself relax, just a little. 'Didn't you get my other letters? And the rest of the money I sent you? I know it's been a while. I couldn't send anything when I was in the camp, or write. They wouldn't let me, but—'

'I… yes.'

Something in her tone made me look more closely at her.

'Ma? You did get it, didn't you? A while ago you said Mr Addison was letting you keep it at the store.'

She closed her eyes. 'I'm sorry, Sam,' she whispered.

'Why? What for? What happened?'

'Kirk found out. He said if I didn't let him have it, he'd report you to the army for being underage and have you court-martialled and put in jail.'

Anger washed through me in a blinding wave as I thought about all that money I'd saved so carefully; how I'd gone without so I could send a check back home every week.

I turned, scanning the yard. 'Where is he? Where is that bastard?'

'Sammy, don't. It doesn't matter—'

'It *does* matter! That money was for you and Meggie, to put food on the table and clothes on your backs!'

'We're OK. There's plenty to eat—'

I snorted. 'Don't lie to me, Ma. Look at you. Look at the state of this place. Meggie looks like she ain't had a decent meal in weeks. Anyhow, it doesn't matter. I've got plenty more money. I'm getting you and Meggie outta here. Today.'

Ma stared at me. So did Meggie, her arm curled around one of the porch posts.

'Go pack some things, Ma,' I urged her. 'We can leave before he gets back – get a bus to Washington.'

'Washington?' She sounded dazed, as if she couldn't quite believe what she was hearing.

'Yeah. I'm gonna look for work there. I'm engaged, Ma, to an English girl. Her name's Ruby. You'd love her. She—'

'Well, well, ain't this nice?' a voice sneered behind us. 'A real family reunion.'

Ma jumped like a startled rabbit. I turned and my heart sank as I saw Kirk sauntering across the yard, a cigarette dangling from his lower lip.

'So, you came back at last, boy. Thought you'd gotten yourself killed.' He eyed my medals. 'Where'd you steal those from, huh?'

'They're mine. I earned them fair and square.'

He snorted.

'Kirk,' Ma said softly. He acted as if he hadn't even heard her.

I gazed at him for a moment, wondering why the hell I'd ever been scared of this pitiful, ugly piece of shit. 'Where's my money?' I said.

'What money?'

'Don't you fucking *what money* me. The money you stole from me. The money I sent home for Ma.'

'I've no idea what you're on about,' he drawled.

'You bastard.'

'Kirk. Sammy—' Ma pleaded behind us.

'You keep outta this,' Kirk told her, his head whipping round.

'Go back inside, Ma,' I called to her. 'Take Meggie with you.'

'Kirk, please—' Ma said.

'Get back in the house, you stupid bitch!' Kirk roared. Ma gave a little gasp of fear, and, scooping up Meggie, retreated inside.

Kirk and I faced each other like a couple of territorial dogs.
'I want it back,' I said.

He grinned. 'Well I ain't got it no more. What you gonna
do 'bout *that*, huh?'

I launched myself at him with a roar.

We grappled, throwing punches, ducking and wrestling
our way across the yard. I landed a hard blow on the side
of his chin; Kirk staggered back, but he'd had more than his
fair share of barroom brawls and almost immediately he was
back on his feet. Before I'd had time to react he'd punched me
in the stomach and, as I doubled over, his other fist caught
me in the mouth.

I felt my lips smash against my teeth, tasted blood, its
coppery stink filling my nostrils, and suddenly I was no longer
in the farmyard but back on the beach in France, mortars and
bullets whizzing past me, hearing men scream as they died. It
was no longer Kirk standing in front of me but a Nazi officer
with a swastika on his arm – the one who used to smile as he
tore up my letters to Ruby. I grabbed his throat, squeezing,
squeezing, until his face turned purple and he was making
choked wheezing sounds.

Suddenly, the noises stopped and the officer was a dead
weight under my fingers.

When my vision cleared I was back in the farmyard. Kirk
was slumped at my feet, face pulpy, eyes swollen shut, blood
trickling from one ear.

I could still hear screaming.

It was Ma. She fell to her knees in the dirt beside us. 'Kirk!'
she sobbed, as Meggie hung back by the porch steps, her eyes
huge.

Ma looked up at me. 'You killed him! You *killed* him!'

'No. *No.*' I looked round at Meggie. 'Meg – go back in the house!'

But she stayed where she was, gazing at me with pure terror on her face. It was a look I'd only ever seen her wear around Kirk.

'Ma.' I put a hand on her shoulder. She slapped it away and shook Kirk, sobbing. 'Baby, wake up. *Wake up*,' she wailed.

Kirk's eyelids fluttered, but he didn't move.

Meggie began to wail too. 'Pa! *Pa!*'

I took a step towards her. '*You get away from her!*' Ma screamed. '*Get away from her right now before I call the sheriff!*'

Realisation hit me like a sniper's bullet. *She ain't going to leave him, even if he dies. She ain't going to let Meggie leave either. Everything you've done – everything you've been through – it was all for nothing. She's only ever cared about him.*

Bile rushed up into my throat. I ran to the corner of the yard and vomited, collapsing to my knees in the mess, my legs no longer able to hold me.

38

RUBY

July

It was high summer. Above Barton Hall, the sky was filled once more with the screams of the swooping swifts; the roses were blooming, saturating the air with their heavy scent as the weather alternated between sunshine and thunderstorms. Despite the fighting still going on in Asia, the atmosphere in town was one of celebration, flags and bunting fluttering from the buildings and across the streets. But at the little cottage at the edge of the grounds, it felt as if life had plunged permanently into winter.

Grandmother, who was still with us – there had still been no word from the British Army about when Tyneham's residents might be able to return – was smug and sharp-tongued; Father barely acknowledged my existence. Our Monopoly nights were a thing of the past, and he no longer asked me to help type up his notes. I felt like a ghost in my own home.

Unsurprisingly, Alfie wouldn't speak to me at all. I couldn't avoid him because he still brought the post to the *Herald* offices every day, but he would hand me the pile of envelopes in silence, turn and walk straight back out again. His father was furious too, snubbing me if I passed him in the street, and although Mrs Blythe was a little more understanding I could tell she was disappointed. Perhaps I deserved it. I should never have agreed to marry Alfie in the first place. But how was I supposed to know Sam was still alive?

Sam. I clung to the memory of his promise to send for me – the one thread of hope I still had left. But even that began to fade as I waited and waited for him to write, telling me he'd found a job and somewhere to live. Every day, when Alfie brought the post, I prayed that this time, one of the letters would be from Sam. But aside from a cable to say he'd arrived in New York back in June, I'd not heard from him.

I didn't feel well at the moment either. It was nothing I could put my finger on, just a general feeling of not-rightness. I was tired all the time, no matter how early I went to bed, and the smell of food had started to turn my stomach, especially in the evenings. I tried to hide it, but Grandmother noticed of course. 'The war might be over, but that's no reason to go wasting good food,' she snapped one night as I pushed a pile of cabbage around on my plate, unable to stomach eating it. 'We're still being rationed, in case you hadn't realised.'

The following evening I was cycling up the hospital drive after work when a sudden, fierce wave of nausea gripped me. I broke out into a cold sweat. I leapt off my bike, flinging it to the ground, and broke into a run, but I knew I wasn't going to make it back to the cottage in time. I darted behind a hedge where I vomited into a flower bed, the contents of my stomach coming up in a hot, disgusting rush. Thankfully, there was no one around.

I felt a little better afterwards, but only briefly. As soon as I got back to the cottage my stomach began churning again. I dropped my bike again and ran for the outhouse. As I huddled over the toilet bowl, retching, I thought miserably of Sam. Oh, why, why, *why* didn't he write?

'What on earth's wrong with you?' Grandmother snapped when I told her I didn't want any dinner.

'I've been sick,' I said shakily. 'I think something I've eaten hasn't agreed with me.'

'Well, you needn't go blaming my cooking,' Grandmother said sourly. '*We're* all right.'

Feeling washed out and dizzy, I took myself up to bed, where I fell into an exhausted slumber.

The next morning, I still felt rotten, and couldn't even face drinking a cup of tea. I made it through the day on aspirin and sips of water, and called in at the doctor's surgery on the way home.

Doctor Williams had been our family doctor ever since taking over his father's practice ten years ago. Although old Doctor Williams had always had something of a fierce reputation, his son was a kind-faced, bespectacled man in his mid-thirties with long, piano player's fingers and a mass of light brown hair, which he wore swept back off his forehead. He had been called up at the start of the war and had returned from the army just a few months ago. Now, like so many others, there were lines etched in his forehead that hadn't been there before.

'Good afternoon, Ruby. How can I help?' he said as I sat down in front of his desk, smiling kindly at me.

I smiled back rather wanly. 'I was awfully sick last night. I think I must have eaten something I shouldn't, and I still feel dreadful.'

'Hop up on the table and let's have a look at you.'

Feeling like a small child, I let him examine me. He prodded my stomach gently. 'Does it hurt anywhere?'

I shook my head.

'Hm. Can't be your appendix, because you had that out when you were a nipper.' He frowned. 'Any other symptoms? How long has this been going on?'

I tried to think back. 'I'm not sure. I've been feeling off colour for a while, but last night was the first time I was actually sick.'

He frowned again. 'You're engaged to that Blythe lad, aren't you?'

A fresh jolt of guilt went through me. 'I was, but... it didn't work out. We broke up in May.'

'Hm. Excuse me if this is rather an indelicate question, but I must ask... Before then, did either of you take any – ahem – precautions?'

'Precautions?' Now it was my turn to frown. Then, faintly, an alarm bell began to ring in the back of my mind. A freezing cold wave of horror crashed over me and I sat up abruptly.

Because we hadn't, had we? That night in the boarding house in Southampton, the thought hadn't even entered my head.

'When did you last menstruate?'

'I – I don't know. I – I've never been all that regular – not like some women—' Meanwhile, in my head, I was frantically counting back. How long *had* it been?

The lines in Doctor Williams' forehead deepened. 'Ruby, I'm very much afraid to tell you that you're pregnant.'

'No,' I said faintly. 'I can't be. I *can't*.'

'I'm afraid you are. The lack of periods – the sickness – it all adds up. In every other way you're the picture of health.'

'It could just be worry, couldn't it? I have been under rather a lot of strain lately.'

'I'm sorry, but I really don't think that's it. There's a test I'll do to make sure, but if I were a betting man...'

'Oh, *God*.' I pressed my hands against my eyes, as if by shutting him out I could make him go away – could make *all* of this go away.

'I'll prescribe you something to help with the sickness.' Doctor Williams patted me clumsily on the shoulder. 'Chin up. Women have babies all the time – nothing to it!'

But when I opened my eyes again his expression was grim.

I cycled slowly home, too shocked even to cry. I was having a baby. *Sam's* baby. And there was no way of letting him know.

Perhaps it's a punishment, I thought. *For lying to everyone – for going out with Alfie when my heart belonged to Sam – for hurting Alfie like that. Oh, Vera, I wish you were here! You'd know what to do!*

My mind was whirling. What was I going to tell everyone? How would Father and Grandmother react to *this* bombshell? I could conceal the pregnancy for a little while, but eventually people would start to notice.

But the answers didn't come; I had no idea what to do.

39

RUBY

August

I'm having a baby. Sam's baby. Every time the thought popped into my head, I felt a wave of terror mixed with a fierce rush of elation.

So far, I'd kept it to myself. Doctor Williams had given me something that stopped me being sick, and Grandmother had believed me when I blamed my tiredness on work, although my ARP shifts had come to an end, something I was very relieved about, as I wasn't sure I'd have been able to cope otherwise. As the weeks passed, I wore baggy jumpers to hide my slowly expanding waistline, and loosened my skirt by fastening it with a safety pin. And Father made things easier by continuing to pretend I didn't exist.

Of course, it would only be a matter of time before I *had* to tell them; I knew that. But first, I needed a plan. I had to find somewhere else to live, perhaps one of the rooms in the middle of town that Vera used to rent. We were already on top of each other here; even if Father did come round, I couldn't imagine trying to stay here with a baby. And I would have to pray that Howler would let me keep my job – I'd need every penny I could earn.

But perhaps staying in Bartonford was a mistake. Perhaps I should write to Vera for help – ask her if I could come to America to stay with her and Stanley for a while. If only I wasn't so tired all the time! It felt as if my brains had been scrambled; I drifted around in a panicked haze, unable to settle on a decision about anything.

The only thing I'd managed to do was write to Sam, but there had been no reply. Lately, there'd been a little voice in my head that kept nagging at me: *What if you never hear from him again? What if that night in Southampton was all he wanted, and now he's got it he's forgotten about you?* It was getting harder and harder to ignore.

I'd never felt so alone in my life – not even when I'd thought Sam was dead. Only the thought of the baby – of that tiny life, growing inside me, my last connection to Sam – kept me going.

'There's a letter for you on the mantelpiece in the parlour,' Grandmother said in her usual icy tone one evening, when I arrived home from work. I was so exhausted I could have gone straight to bed and slept the night through, but her words swept my tiredness away. *Please let it be from Sam, PLEASE*, I pleaded as I rushed in there.

But the handwriting on the envelope, although familiar, wasn't Sam's. The letter had a London postmark. I turned it over, frowning, to look at the return address. My heart did a quick double-thud when I saw the name: *Mrs S. Novak.*

I took it upstairs to read in the relative privacy of the bedroom I still had to share with Grandmother.

Ruby darling, Vera's letter, which was dated a few days ago, began. *I'm so sorry I haven't written for such a long time. It's unforgivable of me – you must think I've forgotten all about you! But so much has happened and there simply wasn't time to sit down and pen you a letter until now.*

As you might have guessed from the postmark, I am no longer in America. Stanley and I couldn't find a decent place to live and there were problems with his family (goodness me, how someone like Stanley can have a mother like that, I don't know!), so when a job came up with Reuters in London, he applied for it and here we are! The fare back to England cost us almost all our savings so for now we have rooms in Bloomsbury – it's on the poky side but we can't complain, especially when we think of all those poor people bombed out of their homes who still have nowhere to go.

I'm working for a local newspaper, the Bloomsbury Chronicle, *and once we've managed to save up a bit again, we want to start looking for a little house somewhere. Luckily, this part of London doesn't seem to have been as badly damaged as some of the others, so overall it's really quite pleasant here – we feel awfully lucky.*

Gosh, doesn't it seem funny to think the war is over? We thought it would never end, didn't we? Of course in some ways it feels as if nothing has changed – we still need coupons for everything and can I get a new pair of stockings anywhere?? But if I never have to hear an air raid siren again as long as I live, I will die a happy woman!

I hope you'll reply, darling, and that we're still chums. I would love you to come and visit us!

All my love,
Vera xx
P.S. *Stanley sends his love too. You should see the cabbages he's growing in the back garden of our boarding house! They're twice the size of anything Bartonford Town Council managed to grow in the town gardens – they'd be green with envy.*

I clutched the letter, feeling relief wash over me. Snatching up a piece of paper, I scribbled a reply.

Dear Vera,
Thank you so much for writing. I'm not angry – don't be a goose! I'm not surprised you didn't have time.

I took a deep breath, wondering what to say next. Should I try to make polite conversation? Mention the weather, tell Vera what I'd had for dinner, what the latest gossip from the *Herald* offices was?

No, I had to get straight to the point. I took a deep breath and carried on writing.

Vera, I need your help. I'm in a bit of a fix. I am having a baby – Sam's baby. Yes, Sam is alive! I'm guessing you don't know, otherwise you'd have said in your letter, but he was rescued in Germany after being in a camp and a prison, and brought back to England, to a hospital in Southampton. He wrote to me from there – of course, I went straight down there to see him! We spent the night together and, well, I'm sure you can guess what happened after that.
No one knows yet. Sam was sent back to America

before I found out, and I haven't heard from him since he got there. I've written but there's been no reply and I don't know how to get hold of him or even where he is.

I wonder if I could come and stay with you for a week or two whilst I work out what on earth I'm going to do. Things are unbearable here – Father and Grandmother are both furious with me for getting engaged to Sam (for reasons I'll tell you all about when I see you – finally their hatred of the Americans makes sense!) and I dread to think how they'll react when they find out about this.

If you could help me I would be so grateful. I don't know who else to turn to. I will pay my way while I'm with you, and I won't be a nuisance, I promise – as soon as I've found a place of my own I will come back to Devon and get out of your hair.

Love,

Ruby xx

After a moment's thought, I scrawled a P.S.:

Please reply to me at the Herald *offices, not here!*

I posted the letter the following morning. Days of awful suspense followed, until the following Friday when Alfie brought the post to the *Herald* offices. Nestled among the envelopes containing the small ads and obituaries there was a telegram, addressed to me.

Yes of course. Wonderful news about Sam – we had no idea! Come as soon as you can. Say if money needed. All my love, Vera

*

Another week later, and it was all arranged. I'd asked Howler for a holiday – I was owed it and more – and that Friday afternoon, I left work early, claiming a headache. Really, it was because I knew Grandmother was out that afternoon at a meeting of the Bartonford WI, and I would be able to pack my things in peace. In my handbag were return train tickets to London which Vera had sent me; I was leaving first thing tomorrow.

The suitcase I'd taken to Southampton was under my bed. I pulled it out, remembering that day and that night I'd spent with Sam. Only three months ago – it felt like years. I longed to feel Sam's arms around me again; his lips on mine. Where was he? Why, *why* didn't he write?

I began folding clothes into the suitcase, and sighed, wondering how much longer my things would fit, and how I'd manage to get new clothes when everything was still rationed with no end in sight. Perhaps Vera would be able to help with that, too. I undid my cardigan and turned sideways, looking at my reflection on the long mirror on the wardrobe door. I was beginning to show already, just slightly; my breasts were bigger too. I smoothed my hands over my stomach. *Oh, Sam, I wish you were here.*

From the bedroom doorway, I heard a sharp intake of breath.

I whirled round and saw Grandmother standing there, wearing her coat and clutching her handbag, a hat balanced on her curls. She was staring at me, her mouth open in a wide O. She tried to speak, but no sound came out.

I drew my cardigan around myself again, jutting out my chin. 'Yes, Grandmother?' I said, trying to sound defiant, although my heart was beating a rapid tattoo inside my chest.

'You – you—' she stuttered, still gaping at me. For a moment, my head whirled as I tried to come up with an excuse. Then I thought, *Why should I?* Before long, I'd be showing properly and it would be impossible to hide it.

'It's Sam's, in case you were wondering,' I said. 'But don't worry, I'm going away for a couple of weeks while I sort things out. I was going to write and tell you and Father about the baby when I got there, but well, you know now, I suppose.'

Grandmother turned and hurried from the room. It was the fastest I'd ever seen her move. Moments later, I heard the front door of the cottage thud shut below me. *Where's she going?* I thought, and then, *Oh, who cares?* I finished packing and went slowly downstairs, where I poured myself a glass of water and sat down at the table.

Ten minutes later, Grandmother returned, with Father in tow. He was wearing his white coat, his spectacles slightly askew and had a notebook tucked into his pocket.

'Look at her, Cecil!' Grandmother said. 'There – that's the thanks she gives you! Everything you did for her, and she lets that *American* get her pregnant.' She sniffed and turned to me. 'Where is your Sam, anyway?' Her voice dripped with sarcasm. 'Still going to send for you, is he? I don't think so! A fine mess you've got yourself into now!'

Father didn't speak. He wouldn't even look at me.

'But it will all be all right,' she continued, her voice softening suddenly. 'I know people who can help. I can have it all arranged by the end of the week. There's a place in Plymouth – it's very nice, quiet and clean. You can go there and they will take care of everything. When you come back we can tell people you were ill, and went away for a rest cure. No one need ever know there was a baby at all.'

I stared at her, going cold all over as I took in what she was saying.

'No,' I said at last. It felt like a tremendous effort to get the words out. 'Absolutely not. I am not giving my baby away.'

Grandmother's voice sharpened again. 'Do you want everyone to talk, like they did with Jennie Pearson? I doubt they'll let you keep your job at the paper, and then what will you do? Because if you think we'll let you continue living here, you can think again!'

'I've already told you – I'm going away for a couple of weeks. I'll sort something out, and then you won't have to worry about me.'

'They won't want you. No one will – not once they realise what's going on!' Grandmother's tone was shrill now, her face twisted and ugly. 'Cecil, help me! There must be something you can do – perhaps we can lock her up in the hospital while I arrange things.'

'Lock me up?' I choked. 'Are you *mad*?' I turned to Father. 'Father! Make her stop! This is preposterous! I'm a grown adult, not a child! It will all be all right – you'll see!'

Finally, Father looked up and met my eyes briefly, before sliding his gaze away again.

'Ruby should do whatever she thinks is best,' he said coldly, carefully, to Grandmother, taking off his spectacles and polishing them on a corner of his coat. His face was utterly expressionless. 'She has made her bed – now she must lie in it. But if she insists on marrying that man I will have nothing to do with her anymore, or the baby.'

'*Cecil!*' Grandmother shrieked. 'You can't mean that! We have to *do* something! People will work it out. They'll talk –

it'll be like Ellen all over again. Remember how ashamed you were, the lies we had to tell so no one found out what had really happened! If we send Ruby away and have the baby adopted we won't have to deal with any of that nonsense.'

I just stared at them, letting Father's words sink in. And in that moment, I made my decision: after I boarded that train for London tomorrow – whether Sam sent for me or not – I wouldn't be coming back to Bartonford. The man standing in front of me wasn't my father anymore; he was a stranger. He'd become one the day he told me my mother was still alive and he'd lied to me about her my entire life.

It was funny, because in a way, this was what I'd wanted – *longed* for – for years now: to be independent; to be free of the guilt and obligation that had kept me tied to Bartonford, to Father, to this dreary little cottage for so long. So why did the thought of leaving it all behind feel like such an awful wrench?

I was careful not to let any of this show on my face, though. I kept my face calm, determined that I wouldn't let either Father or Grandmother know how I really felt. I'd save my tears for tomorrow. The thought of anyone trying to take my baby – *Sam's* baby – away from me filled me with a fierce, desperate sort of anger.

'Very well, Father,' I said. I wasn't worried about Grandmother; I knew her threats were empty ones. I was taller and bigger than her, and without Father to help her there was no way on earth she'd be able to force me to do anything. When neither of them spoke, I turned and went calmly back upstairs to finish packing my suitcase, feeling strangely relieved – at least the decision was made now.

Oh, Sam, I thought. *I wish you'd written to me. I wish I knew where you were so I could let you know what's happening.*

But I couldn't. It was as if he'd disappeared off the face of the earth.

40

SAM

June–August

'Wait here, OK?' I told Meggie. 'Don't talk to any strangers. If anyone asks, your big brother has a job here and you're waiting for him to finish work so he can take you to the candy store.'

Meggie nodded, chewing a few strands of hair. I eyed her critically, trying to see her as a stranger would, or a cop: a little girl in a shabby dress with dusty knees. There hadn't been any time to get spare clothes for her and I hadn't had a chance to buy her any yet.

I hadn't killed Kirk after all; by the time I'd finished puking my guts up, he'd started to come round, making weird groaning, wheezing sounds in his throat. Although he could hardly stand, Ma had helped him up and gotten him inside somehow. They seemed to have forgotten about Meggie – she'd been left out on the porch, sobbing. When I'd gone over to her and put my arms around her, she'd stiffened. My stomach had jolted. 'Meggie-Meg, it's OK. I'd never hurt you, never,' I said. 'You hear? I was only trying to protect myself from Kirk. Otherwise he'd've hurt *me*.'

Sniffling, she'd relaxed against me, slowly.

'You wanna get outta here?' I'd asked her.

She'd nodded.

I'd crouched down, holding her by the tops of the arms so I could look her in the face. 'I mean *really* get outta here, Meggie. I've got a friend who might be able to help us, but if you come with me, you'll never see this place again.'

'That's OK,' she'd said. 'I don't wanna stay here anyway. Kirk comes into my room at night sometimes. He scares me.'

'What does he do?' I'd said sharply.

'He just sits there and stares at me.'

I'd clenched my jaw and my fists, taking in deep breaths. I knew I had to get myself under control, otherwise I'd go inside and finish what I'd started.

'Right,' I'd said when my heart had stopped racing. I'd picked up my bag, which had still been sitting where I'd dropped it on the porch, and taken her hand. 'Let's go.'

'Where are we going?' she'd said.

'Washington, like I said. I've got a pal there who might be able to help me get some work.'

I'd thought then, briefly, about sneaking inside to get some things for her, then decided against it. We'd just have to manage until we got to the city. As we'd crossed the yard every muscle in my body had been tense, ready to break into a run; I'd been expecting Kirk to burst back out of the house any second, maybe with his rifle aimed at my head. But he hadn't. We'd gone out onto the road, which was sun-baked and dusty, and started to walk while I'd listened out for cars.

One had turned up eventually and we'd managed to hitch a ride for the first fifteen miles or so.

After that it had been a mixture of walking and hitching. I'd bought us a dinner of hotdogs and soda from a little store in some backcountry town even smaller than Coltonsburg, and we'd spent that night in a farmer's field. The next day had been the same. The morning after that, we'd arrived in Washington, and now, three days later, we were here at the *Washington Post*. It stood on 14th and E streets NW, a tall building with a grand stone facade, carved figures along the roofline and a funny-looking little circular window at the top.

I took a deep breath, shouldered my bag and climbed the steps. When I got to the top, I tugged at my collar to straighten it, checked my shoes were clean, and went inside.

The smartly dressed woman at the front desk eyed my medals and the scars on my hands as I approached. From somewhere inside the vast building, I could hear the clatter of typewriters; the air smelled of ink and cigarette smoke.

Nervously, I cleared my throat. 'Excuse me, ma'am, but is there a journalist who works here called Stanley Novak?'

She frowned. 'Who did you say?'

'Stanley Novak. He was a pal of mine in the army.'

'Wait here.' She pushed her chair back with the air of someone being greatly inconvenienced, and disappeared through a doorway behind the reception desk, her heels clicking efficiently against the tiled floor.

Five minutes later, she returned. 'I'm sorry, he's not here anymore.'

I felt my heart sink into my boots. 'What? I mean – are you sure?'

'That's what they said.'

'Do you know where he's gone?'

The woman sighed, and went back through the doorway.

'He's in London, England,' she said when she came back. 'He went there with his wife.'

London. I closed my eyes, pinching the bridge of my nose.

'Here. He left a forwarding address.'

I opened my eyes and saw she was holding out a piece of paper with something written on it. I tried to smile at her, wondering what goddamn use a forwarding address was to me if Stanley was all the way over in England again. 'Thanks.' I went back outside, stuffing the paper into my inside jacket pocket where I promptly forgot about it.

To my relief, Meggie was still waiting for me at the bottom of the steps. *Now what?* I thought. I felt grimy; my head ached and I was starving hungry. As surreptitiously as I could, I took my wallet from my inside jacket pocket and counted what I had left. There wasn't much; I'd been counting on Stanley for a place to stay until I got a job and started earning enough to find a room for Meggie and me. Well, that wasn't gonna happen now. 'C'mon,' I said to Meggie. 'Let's go get some breakfast.'

'Was your friend there?' she asked as we walked back down the street.

'No, he's in England now.'

'England? That's a long way away. How will he help us if he's there?'

'I don't know, honey. I'll think of something.'

We found a diner, and went in and sat down in a corner booth. I told Meggie she could order whatever she liked, aware that this might be our last decent meal for a while. As I drank my coffee and ate my pancakes I tried to work out what we were gonna do.

I spent all that day traipsing around the city, asking at every store, every restaurant, every bar, *anywhere* I thought looked promising if they were hiring. But the answer was always the same. Whoever I spoke to would look me up and down, take in my scarred hands and shake their head slowly, apologetically. 'Sorry, son, but we've got all the help we need.' It seemed that every soldier returning from the war had had the same idea – and they'd all gotten there before me.

As the day went on, I began to be gripped by panic. Kirk had taken all the money I'd saved. The bills in my wallet might last another few days if I was lucky, and careful, but after that, the only income I had was my army pension, and that would barely cover food. If I didn't get a job, I couldn't get a place for us to live. And if I didn't have a place to live, I couldn't send for Ruby.

Later that afternoon, Meggie and I stopped in a park to rest. As I sat down on a bench to take the weight off my aching feet, a great wave of weariness crashed over me. For a moment I wondered if bringing Meggie with me had been a dumb idea, but then I remembered what she'd told me about Kirk coming in her room at night. No, getting her to leave had been the right thing. At least that bastard couldn't hurt her now. But where were we gonna go? What were we gonna do?

Head north, I thought. *There's gotta be work out there somewhere.*

'Sam, what are we doing now?' Meggie asked. She looked as tired as I felt, and there was a querulous note in her voice.

'How do you like the sound of an adventure, Meggie-Meg? Just me and you,' I said, with a cheerfulness I didn't feel.

'An adventure?'

'Yeah. It'll be fun!'

'OK...' She chewed her lower lip, looking doubtful. As soon as I looked away from her, I felt the smile drop off my face. Thank God it was still summer. If we were lucky I'd find work and somewhere to crash before the weather changed.

Before the stores closed for the day I spent the last of my money on a change of clothes for Meggie, a toothbrush each and a couple of blankets, stuffing everything in my bag. There wasn't enough left over for food; we'd manage, somehow. We spent that night in another, smaller park, where I slept fitfully, plagued by the usual nightmares about being lost in a fiery inferno.

The next morning, we hit the road.

But there was no work anywhere. Sometimes I'd strike lucky and pick up odd jobs mowing yards or painting fences, earning enough to buy us a decent meal that night. Occasionally a kind stranger would take pity on us and give us food. Other days I'd have to resort to stealing from gas stations or rummaging through trash cans. When I couldn't find any way of earning money we'd hitch or walk, heading slowly but steadily northwards. We slept in barns and fields and outbuildings and under bridges.

Meggie never complained, but she grew thin and tired-looking, deep shadows under her eyes, and her clothes were shabbier than ever, holes wearing in the bottoms of her shoes. I knew I didn't look much better. I'd thought about writing to Ruby, too, to tell her what was happening, but every time I tried I got stuck. I didn't want to worry her, and putting my situation down on paper in stark black and white felt too much like admitting how bad things really were. *Another week and you'll be back on your feet*, I kept telling myself. *Write to her then.*

But finally, in mid-August, I was forced to admit defeat.

It had been a bad day. I'd gone from door to door, begging for work, and been turned away at every house, every store. Now we were holed up in a tumbledown shack at the edge of an abandoned lot, waiting for night to fall. Meggie was already asleep. We'd had nothing to eat. *No one wants you*, I told myself. *You're washed up, done.* I looked at Meggie. She'd been crying on and off all day from hunger and exhaustion; there were tear tracks through the dirt on her face, and her eyelashes were still damp.

You should take her to the sheriff tomorrow, a little voice in my head said suddenly. *Tell them you can't take care of her. They'll look after her – find her a nice family somewhere. She'll have new clothes to wear, a roof over her head, plenty of food…*

For a few, brief moments, all I felt was an overwhelming sense of relief. Then the doubts came crashing in. What if it didn't work out that way? What if she ended up in a home, or they sent her to someone like Kirk? What if they sent her *back* to Kirk? I couldn't abandon her like that. I just *couldn't*.

I began searching through my pockets in the vain hope I might have overlooked a dollar bill somewhere; even a few coins would be better than nothing. There was nothing except for a crumpled piece of paper, deep in the inside pocket of my jacket. I smoothed it out and looked at the name and address written on it in neat, sloping script. *S. NOVAK, c/o*

The Bloomsbury Chronicle, 45 Leonard Square, Bloomsbury, London, ENGLAND. My stomach lurched.

I'd forgotten all about that woman at the *Washington Post* giving me Stanley's address. I read it again, and again, a plan beginning to form in my head. It was crazy – desperate. It probably wouldn't work. But just like when I'd joined the army – and man, that felt like a lifetime ago now – what choice did I have?

Carefully, I folded the piece of paper up again and returned it to my inside pocket. Then I settled back against my pack, suddenly wide awake, to wait for morning to come.

41

RUBY

Early September

*D*ear Father,
  I hope you are well and that the weather has been good where you are. It's been a little dull here in London so far, but at least it's dry.
  I am still staying with Vera and Stanley and have been very busy doing some work for the newspaper they write for. It still feels strange to be living in a city, and I don't think I will ever get used to seeing the ruins of all the bombed-out buildings. How terribly people here must have suffered! I wonder if they will ever be able to rebuild it all. And yet everyone seems so cheerful.
  I feel fairly well at the moment and the baby is healthy...

I laid down my pen and sighed, gazing out of the open window of my room. It was at the back of Vera and Stanley's little flat, and from where I sat at my small writing table I could see the building's tree-shaded gardens below me, lush and green with the last of the summer's growth. It was the middle of the afternoon; someone was having a bonfire somewhere, and the breeze that blew in smelt faintly autumnal, stirring a sense of nostalgia inside me. Strange to think that this time six years ago I'd been walking on the beach when Alfie and Annie Blythe had come to tell me war had been declared. *Six years!* How things had changed since that day. It seemed impossibly long ago – a whole other lifetime. What would the Ruby back then think if she'd known where she would end up now?

This was the third letter I'd written to Father since arriving in London. The first two had gone unanswered. I'd tried telling myself that Grandmother had intercepted them, but deep down, I knew that wasn't true. I was sending them directly to the hospital. How would she be able to get her hands on them before he did? She was sly, unpleasant, and she'd never liked me, but that felt like a stretch, even for her.

There was still a tiny part of me, buried deep, which hoped for a reconciliation – that was why I kept writing, I suppose. The thought of mine and Sam's baby growing up without a grandfather made me feel achingly sad, even though I couldn't get Father's final words to me out of my head.

As for Sam, I wanted to write to him, too, desperately, but how could I when I didn't even know where he was? Instead, I'd been spending almost every penny I earned through the little bits of newspaper work Vera sent my way on stamps, paper and envelopes, writing endless letters to the US army, the American Red Cross and any other organisation I could think of to ask if they knew of Sam's whereabouts. So far, I'd had no reply from them either. Stanley and Vera tried to comfort me by pointing out that there was an enormous number of American soldiers being demobbed now the war had ended in Europe, and that they were sure I'd hear something from someone soon.

'It could take a year or more for everyone to get home, I reckon,' Stanley said. He had tried to help too, getting in touch with old colleagues of his at the *Washington Post*, but he'd had no luck either. Sam seemed to have vanished off the face of the earth. But I had to find him. I *had to*. I loved him. I needed him. And our baby needed him too.

It felt as if an age had passed since I arrived in London, even though it had only been a month or so. I'd been in such a state of shock that the enormity of what had happened back in Bartonford only began to sink in once I was safely at Vera and Stanley's flat. When we'd got there Vera, who'd met me at the station and managed to commandeer a taxi to drive us back to Leonard Square, had taken my suitcase and jacket, told me to take off my shoes, sat me down on her sofa and made me a cup of tea. I'd been exhausted from a sleepless night, the long journey and, of course, the baby.

'Oh, Ruby,' she'd said with a dreadful expression of sympathy, and that was what undid me – I'd burst out crying and couldn't stop, jagged wails tearing out of me.

Not surprisingly, Vera had been alarmed. 'Darling, what's wrong?' she'd said. 'Is it Sam? Have you heard from him? Has something happened? Oh, goodness, do stop – you'll make yourself ill.'

'It's Father,' I'd sobbed when I'd finally been able to speak. 'Grandmother realised I was pregnant and I had to come clean to them about Sam, and now he's kicked me out.'

'*What?*' A thunderous scowl had flashed across her face.

'I don't know what to do – I can't go back to Bartonford but I've got nowhere else to go-o-o—'

'Oh, don't be ridiculous, you can stay here as long as you want, even after the baby's born if you need to. So put that worry out of your head right now.'

'But won't Stanley mind?'

'Of course not! Why ever would he?! Now, take a sip of tea, blow your nose, calm down, and start at the beginning. Why on earth has that father of yours kicked you out for having a baby with the man you're *engaged* to, for goodness' sake? It's hardly Jennie Pearson all over again, is it!'

So, once I'd got myself under control, I'd told her everything, including the revelation about my mother running away with an American.

'Goodness,' she'd said. 'Well, I suppose it all makes sense now, why your father and grandmother hated the Americans so much... I always wondered if there was more to it. But do they honestly believe Sam's like that? Stanley wouldn't be here if it wasn't for him!'

'I just can't believe he lied to me like that!' I'd sniffled. 'All those years, my mother's been *alive*, and he let me think she was dead!'

'Do you think you'll try to find her?'

'I don't know. I don't even know where *my* American is, do I?'

'Hasn't he written to you yet?'

Shaking my head, I'd collapsed back against the sofa cushions, my exhaustion suddenly overwhelming me. Dear, dear Vera. She looked exactly the same – as immaculate and stylish as always – and suddenly I'd wanted to cry again, this time because she was being so kind, and I'd missed her so much.

She'd wrapped me in a motherly hug, then wiped the tears

off my face with a hanky as if I were a small child. 'You look all in,' she'd said. 'Finish your tea and then I'm sending you for a lie-down. We'll find Sam, and you can decide what you want to do about your mother, but first, *rest*, and no arguments.'

Now, sighing again, I crumpled the letter to father up in my fist. As I turned to drop it into the little wastepaper basket beside my writing table, I felt the baby stir inside me, a faint, mothlike fluttering. I pressed my left hand against the slight swell of my stomach and felt it again beneath my fingers. The light coming in through the window caught the ruby in my silver ring – I wore it on my finger again now – and made it wink.

Oh, Sam, I thought for the millionth time. *Where are you?* The thought of not having him here when the baby arrived terrified me. Oh, I wasn't worried about what people would think – I could buy a wedding band, and lie and say the father had been killed in the war so people would think I was respectable – but I knew what it was like to grow up without a parent. I didn't want that for our child, too. And it didn't seem fair, somehow, that after Sam and I had been through so much, we'd been torn apart again and that he might never get to meet his own son or daughter.

I clenched my hands into fists. *Please, God, let him be OK. Let him still be alive. Let him write to me. PLEASE.*

I pushed my chair back and went through into the little kitchen next door to get a glass of water. What I'd said in my discarded letter to Father was true: the baby was healthy, and I felt well again now – the sickness and exhaustion of the first few months had more or less passed – but I was still plagued by a deep weariness that seemed to have seeped into my bones and set like concrete. Despite Vera and Stanley's insistence that I could live with them for as long as I wanted, and Vera promising me that after the baby was born they'd get me a proper job at the newspaper, the whole situation felt impossible, endless. Without Sam, I simply didn't know what I was going to do.

I took a glass down from the cupboard, wondering who I should write to next – the American Red Cross again? They were probably sick of hearing from me by now. I'd just turned on the tap when I heard feet pounding up the stairs outside the flat. The door burst open and then Vera was calling me: 'Ruby! Ruby, where are you?!'

'In here!' I called back. She came flying into the kitchen. She was breathing hard, her hair in disarray, her shoes were dusty and there was a hole – an actual hole – in one of her stockings. She looked as if she'd run all the way here from the newspaper office half a mile away. I stared at her, taking in her wide eyes and the hectic colour of her face under her foundation and powder. 'What's wrong?'

She waved something at me – a rectangle of white paper. 'It's Sam,' she gasped.

A wave of freezing cold went through me. My ears started to ring and black spots began to dance in front of my eyes, just like they had that day Stanley's letter arrived at the Herald offices and I thought Sam had been killed.

'Oh, *hell*,' I heard Vera say. Next thing I knew, I was sitting in a chair with my head between my knees, while the black spots and noise in my ears slowly cleared.

'I'm so sorry – I'm such a goose! What a fright I must have given you!' Vera filled me the glass of water I'd not got round to pouring yet. 'Sit up – slowly – and drink this. Everything's all right!'

Taking the water, I looked up at her and saw she was grinning from ear to ear. 'You – you mean Sam's all right?' I said.

'Yes! Read this!' She thrust the piece of paper into my hand. I looked at it and saw it was a cable, with the address of a telegraph office in Philadelphia, USA, at the top.

Stanley, it said. *Making my way to New York with Meggie. Need to get to England. No money for passage. Hate to beg but if you can help please reply to this straight away & if you're in touch with Ruby please tell I love her & sorry for not writing. Sam.*

A sound that wasn't quite a sob, wasn't quite a laugh escaped me. I clapped a hand to my mouth, letting go of the cable, which fluttered to the floor.

'Stanley's already replied,' Vera said, talking fast. 'He's booking passage on a ship for Sam and his sister and is wiring him some money as we speak. When they arrive in England we'll sort out paperwork, get them to London, whatever it takes. Stanley's got all sorts of useful contacts who can help out. So don't worry about a thing, OK? And for goodness' sake, Ruby, *breathe*. Think about the baby!'

'Why didn't he write to me?' I said, my voice sounding high and strange. 'What's he been *doing*?'

'Well, you'll be able to ask him yourself in a few weeks' time, won't you? Oh, goodness, I can't leave you like this. Stay where you are while I nip downstairs to the office and tell them I won't be coming back in this afternoon. Then I'll get us both a nip of brandy. I'm sure the doctor would tell me off but I don't think a tiny bit will hurt you, under the circumstances.'

I nodded, and swallowed. 'Has Stanley told him about the baby?'

'No – do you want me to ask him to?'

'I think it would be a good idea, don't you?'

'Righto. I'll go and phone now,' she said. 'And I mean it – don't move a *muscle*,' she added warningly over her shoulder as she went out. I watched the door close behind her, and leaned down awkwardly to scoop the cable up off the linoleum. Then I sat staring at it, my eyes hot with tears, an incredulous smile slowly breaking across my face.

42

SAM

October

I stepped off the train at King's Cross Station and stared around me in a daze. We were here. *Really here.* The air was thick with smoke and soot; the clamour of voices, the tannoy, the shriek of train whistles, the thump and clank of pistons and the hissing of steam echoed up into the curved roof high above me, leaving me feeling completely disorientated. I couldn't remember the last time I'd slept properly, or eaten a square meal. There'd been a delay getting into Liverpool and it had been a rush to get on the London train – there'd been no time to think about anything else.

'Sam! Yoo-hoo!'

I turned and saw Vera and Stanley hurrying towards me, Stanley walking with a slight limp. My heart flipped over. 'Where's Ruby? She OK?'

'She's fine,' Vera said. 'A little tired today, that's all, so we left her at home to rest.'

Stanley snorted. 'Forced her to, more like. She would've walked here in her bare feet if we'd let her.'

Vera took hold of my hands. 'Oh, Sam, she's going to be so glad to see you! We all are!'

Stanley, who had a hat balanced at a jaunty angle on his head, smiled and stepped forwards to embrace me, slapping my back. 'Hey, buddy. So damn relieved you made it. Until Ruby wrote and told us about you being in Southampton, we thought you hadn't.'

I remembered the last time I saw him, lying in the straw at that farm in France with his leg all shot up. Sixteen months ago. It felt as if a lifetime had passed since then. 'I thought you were a goner too,' I said. 'Guess we both got lucky, huh?'

He shook his head. 'You're telling me. So where's that sister of yours? You lose her somewhere?'

I looked round. 'Meggie? Where did you go?' I spotted her a short distance away, leaning over to look into a crate full of hens. 'Get over here!'

She danced across to us. 'There's birds in there, Sam!' When she saw Vera and Stanley she hung back, suddenly shy. I wiped a smut off her face with my sleeve, and gave her a little push forwards. 'Say hi to my friends – Vera and Stanley,' I said.

'Hello, darling.' Vera crouched down and held out her hands. 'Welcome to England. We're awfully glad you're here! And don't you look grown up? How old are you now? Ten?'

'I'm nine and a half,' Meggie said. She gave her a smile, still shy, but allowed Vera to hug her. She was wearing a green cotton frock, old but clean, which I'd bought from a thrift store in New York with the money Stanley had sent me. It had paid for the suit I was wearing too. We both needed a haircut pretty badly, though.

'C'mon.' Stanley clapped me on the arm. 'You look done in.'

He had a car parked outside, dark blue with gleaming chrome trim. 'Beauty, isn't she? It's an Austin Twelve.'

'Yes, and it drives like a bilious donkey, so hold on tight,' Vera warned as Meggie and I slid into the back seat. I was so tired, I didn't care if the thing shook itself to bits underneath us. I leaned back against the seat and closed my eyes. I was too wired, too excited to sleep, but maybe I could rest for a while...

'Sam, we're here.' Vera leaned over from the front seat, gently touching my arm, and I jolted awake again. I didn't even remember falling asleep; I guess it was everything finally catching up with me, and the relief of not needing to watch Meggie like a hawk for a while. The car had stopped on a pleasant-looking street; we were parked outside a row of tall buildings with narrow windows overlooking a tree-lined square. They all had window boxes brimming with flowers, and everything looked cheerful and clean, almost as if there hadn't been a war at all.

My heart began to thud. Somewhere up there, Ruby was waiting for me. And she was having a baby – *our* baby. I hadn't quite been able to believe it at first when the second cable came through from Stanley to the Philadelphia telegraph office. I'd had to read it four times before it sank in. And after that, I hadn't been able to stop worrying. Was she OK? Healthy? Was she getting enough to eat? Why was she in London with Vera and Stanley instead of back home in Devon? Stanley hadn't gone into detail about that; he'd just said: *Ruby's fine and staying with us for the foreseeable; will explain everything when you get here.*

'I hope you're up to climbing a few stairs,' Vera said as Meggie and I got out of the car. 'We're on the top floor.' She indicated the building we were parked directly outside, which was painted white.

'Yeah. I'm fine.' I'd've found my way to Ruby even if she'd been on the moon: a few flights of stairs were nothing.

Was I imagining it, or had that been a face at the window just now, looking down at us? My heart was thumping harder than ever as the four of us made our way up to Vera and Stanley's apartment, and it wasn't from exertion.

As we reached the top floor, a door flew open, and there she was. Her hair was curled, and she wore a green cardigan and a pretty floral frock, which swelled over her stomach. I stared at her, and she stared back. Then she flung herself into my arms, laughing and crying all at the same time. 'Sam. *Sam.*'

I clung to her, scared that she wasn't real – that if I let her go, she might disappear again. I couldn't take that – not again. 'Hey,' I said into her hair.

'Do you two want a bit of privacy?' Vera said. 'Meggie, why don't you come and help me make some tea?' My little sister was staring at me and Ruby, her eyes wide and slightly puzzled.

'Meggie, this is Ruby,' I said. 'You remember me telling you about her?'

'Hullo, Meggie.' Ruby held out her hands. 'It's so lovely to meet you, darling.'

'Are you gonna be my new sister?' Meggie asked, peering up at Ruby with her hair half falling over her face.

'Yes, if you'd like me to be.'

A tentative smile spread across Meggie's face. 'I never had a sister before.'

'Well, that makes two of us. *And* you're going to be an auntie!' Gently, Ruby took one of Meggie's hands and laid it on her stomach. 'There – can you feel the baby kicking?'

Meggie's eyes got even wider. 'When is it going to be born?'

'Next year, in February, all being well.'

Meggie's smile was almost splitting her face in two now. I couldn't stop grinning either.

'Come on,' Vera said to Meggie. 'Let's go and make that tea. You can help me choose which cups to use. If that's all right with you, Sam?'

'Sure,' I said.

'Can we go down to the square?' Ruby said once they'd gone into the kitchen. 'It's such a beautiful day, and I've been cooped up all morning – I think I might go mad if I have to stay inside any longer.'

'What about all those stairs?' Overhearing her, Vera came to the kitchen doorway and frowned at her in a motherly sort of way.

'I'm pregnant, not an invalid.'

Stanley grinned, and Vera rolled her eyes at me over Ruby's head. 'Well, that's me told.'

Still holding hands, Ruby and I went back downstairs. I felt a little nervous at leaving Meggie behind, and had to tell myself not to be so dumb. It was because of everything we'd been through, I guess, and all that time I'd spent in England and Europe wondering if I'd ever see her again. Truth was, it was probably Vera I needed to worry about – once Meggie got over being shy she'd start driving her half mad with questions.

Outside, there was no one about; Ruby and I sat down on a bench at the side of the square. When we kissed, it felt like coming home.

'Oh, gosh, you've got lipstick all over your face,' she said when we'd finished, swiping at me with a handkerchief.

'I don't care.' I was still smiling so wide my jaw was starting to hurt. 'Oh my God, Ruby, am I dreaming? 'Cause if I am, I don't ever want to wake up.'

'If you are, then so am I.' She still hadn't let go of my hands. She looked at the still-livid scars across my palms, tracing them gently with a fingertip, and I noticed she was wearing the ruby ring I'd given her in Southampton. 'Do they still hurt?'

'Not anymore, except if I'm real tired. Anyway, never mind that. What happened to you? Stanley wrote to me – he said you'd had to leave Devon.'

Her smile faded. 'Yes. After I found out about the baby, Vera wrote to me to say she and Stanley were back in England, so I arranged to come to London for a couple of weeks, just to get a bit of breathing space, but then Father and Grandmother discovered that I was pregnant and, well, it didn't exactly go down well.'

When she told me about what had happened with her mother, and her father kicking her out, I stared at her in astonishment. How could her ma have left her like that? And how could her pa have turned his back on her? How could you do that to your own flesh and blood and feel OK about it?

Then I thought about Ma, and how she'd chosen Kirk over me, her own son. 'I guess you can't always rely on people, can you, even if they're your parents,' I said. 'Are you gonna do anything about your ma? Try and find her?'

She pressed her lips together. 'At first, I wasn't sure I wanted to. After the shock wore off, I was so angry – I couldn't fathom why she'd just leave like that and not try to get in touch – not even write a letter! But as time went on I thought about our baby, and what it would be like if I had to leave and wasn't able to get in touch for some reason. And that made me wonder if perhaps she did try, but Father and Grandmother threw away the letters or something. I wouldn't put it past them! And of course, with them not speaking to me any more, there's no way to find out. Stanley's been making enquiries – he has lots of connections thanks to working for that newspaper in Washington – and he thinks he might have found an address.'

'But that's marvellous!' I said. 'Have you written to her yet?'

She pressed her lips together again. 'I'm writing her a letter now. Perhaps you can read it for me – help me work out what to say.'

'I'll do whatever I can to help,' I said.

'What about you?' she asked. 'Why didn't you write to me? I was so *worried*!'

I took a deep breath. Then I told her everything that had happened since I set foot back on American soil.

'I'm sorry,' I said. 'I kept telling myself it would all work out, you know? That I'd get a job and a place for us to live and then I could write to you and you'd come over and it would all be OK. But things just kept getting more and more screwed up, and I didn't know how to tell you. I felt like such a goddamn failure.'

'I hope you really hurt your stepfather,' she said savagely. 'What a – a *bastard*.'

She leaned her head on my shoulder, and we sat there for a while, like we used to at the lodge.

'There's something else I need to tell you,' she said at last, sitting up again. 'Oh dear – I do hope you won't be angry. I should have told you in Southampton, but I didn't want to spoil our time together when we only had one night.'

I looked round at her and saw she was frowning, biting her lip. 'What is it?'

'When – when I thought you were dead, Alfie Blythe asked me to marry him. And I – I said yes. I broke it off as soon as I got back from seeing you – I would have broken it off before if I'd had time, but all I could think about after your letter arrived was getting down to Southampton. I shouldn't have done it but at the time I thought I was never going to see you again, and Alfie was so keen – I couldn't bear the thought of spending the rest of my life alone, looking after Father till he died, and—'

'Hey, hey.' I squeezed her hand gently, cutting off her frantic stream of words mid-flow. 'Don't worry. I get it. It's fine.'

'You're not – you're not cross?'

'Why would I be? If anything *had* happened to me I'd hate to think of you without anyone at all. That would have been crazy. This Alfie – he treated you right?'

'Yes. He was a perfect gentleman. It hurt him badly when I told him I couldn't marry him after all – I still feel jolly guilty about that. But oh, Sam, I didn't love him. It would have been wrong to marry him even if you *were* dead, I think. So it all worked out for the best.'

I squeezed her hand again. Christ, how close we'd come to losing one another.

Suddenly, she jumped. 'Oh!'

'What's wrong?'

She laughed. 'Nothing. The baby's moving again. Here.'

She placed my hand on her bump. I felt a faint fluttering

under my palm. My heart leapt. 'Holy smokes.' Up until that point, it hadn't quite sunk in that I was gonna be a father, but now it hit me properly for the first time.

Christ.

'Are you all right?' Ruby asked, frowning slightly when she felt me stiffen.

'Yeah.' I let out a shaky breath. 'It's just—'

'What?' she said gently.

I let out another breath. 'I hope I can be the kind of father this kid deserves. That is, better than Kirk.'

'Oh, Sam, of course you will be. Look at what you've done for Meggie. You're *nothing* like him, and you never will be.'

'I goddamn hope not.'

'I *know* not.' Her expression was alight with conviction, and in that moment I loved her more than ever. *I promise I'll do the best I can, for both of you,* I told her inside my head. *And I'll keep doing it until the day I die.*

'If it's a girl, I want to call her Ellen Rose,' Ruby said. 'That was my mother's name.'

'Sure.' I thought for a moment. 'And if it's a boy, can we call it James David? Jimmy for short, maybe?'

'Of course. Is Jimmy—'

'I dunno,' I said. 'I haven't been able to find out what happened to him. And, well, you know about Davy.'

'This damn war's taken so much from everyone,' Ruby said pensively, pressing her lips together.

'Not everyone. It didn't take you. Or me. Or Meggie or Stanley or Vera.'

'No, I suppose not.' She gently squeezed my hand. 'I've been writing to the Red Cross, trying to find out where you were – perhaps we can ask them about Jimmy?'

'Definitely,' I said.

Her smile returned, a dimple appearing in her cheek. 'So, are we still going to get married? Because you owe me a wedding, Sam Archer.'

'You bet we will! I'll need to find some work first, though, so I can buy you a proper ring and all.'

'Oh, Stanley's sorted all that out already. He's got a job lined up for you at his office if you... Oops!' She put her hand to her mouth. 'I think he wanted to tell you about that himself. Don't let on that you know, will you?'

'I won't say a thing.'

I leaned in for another kiss. Then there was a shout from across the square. 'Sam! Ruby! The tea's ready!'

Meggie was hanging out of one of the top-floor windows, waving at us.

I laughed. 'We'd better go in. Once she starts yelling she never stops. She'll be driving Vera and Stanley nuts.'

I stood and helped Ruby to her feet. With our fingers entwined, we walked back across the street.

THE END

ACKNOWLEDGEMENTS

Although writing can be a solitary occupation, a book is never written in isolation. In no particular order, I want to say some enormous thank yous to:

My wonderful agent, Ella Kahn. You've stuck with me and pushed me to become a better writer than I ever thought I could be. It was you who saw the potential in Sam and Ruby when they were just a subplot, and said they deserved their own book. I'm so thrilled we managed to make it happen!

The brilliant team at Head of Zeus, especially Hannah, Helena and Martina for your enthusiasm and razor-sharp insight, and the design team for the stunning cover. I couldn't think of a better home for this story.

My fabulous writer friends, who've been on this journey with me from the beginning, in particular Kerry Drewery, Elsie Chapman, Sheena Wilkinson, Rachel Ward, Eve Ainsworth and all the ladies in my writers' group – you've provided inspiration, feedback and virtual hugs just when they were most needed. And Becca Mascull, for helping my find my feet as I began the fascinating but sometimes overwhelming task of researching this novel.

My family for never saying "don't give up the day job" (even when I did!); Pat, who's the best mother-in-law anyone could wish for, and Graham, of course. I wish you could be here to read this – I know you'd be smiling.

Duncan, for your unending love and support which goes right back to when I first told you I wanted to try and give this writing thing a go; Gunner, for keeping the writing sofa warm, and Auburn for stepping into her brother's paws when he had to leave us.

My readers – I'm grateful to each and every one of you for your support, and I hope you will love Ruby and Sam as much as I do.

And finally, all the brave women and men from all over the world who made unimaginable sacrifices during World War 2, and who inspired me to tell this story in the first place.

ABOUT THE AUTHOR

EMMA PASS grew up in Surrey and has been making up stories for as long as she can remember. She wrote her first novel – a sequel to Jurassic Park – when she was thirteen, in maths lessons with her notebook hidden under her work.

She previously worked as a library assistant and has published two novels for young adults and a non-fiction creative writing e-guide. In 2020 she was commissioned to create a poetry-film for the Derwent Valley Mills World Heritage Site. She is now a full-time writer, creative writing teacher, editor and mentor. She has ME and, at the age of 40, was diagnosed as being on the autistic spectrum.

Emma lives in Derbyshire with her artist husband and a very naughty retired racing greyhound called Auburn. When she's not writing she loves to read and knit (often at the same time).